―――――――――★―――――――――

He had taken hold of her wrist. She tried to pull away, but he tightened his fingers so that she could not get free. His strength seemed formidable.

"What's the matter, Mr. Lutterworth?" Emma asked, and then silently cursed herself for the unmistakable panic in her voice.

She forced herself to look directly at him and then wished she had not. There was a gleam in his eyes; it seemed to her to carry both acknowledgment of her fear and pleasure in it.

―――――――――★―――――――――

"Cooper constructs an engaging puzzle..."
—*Publishers Weekly*

Previously published Worldwide Mystery titles by
NATASHA COOPER

ROTTEN APPLES
THE DROWNING POOL

SOUR GRAPES

NATASHA COOPER

WORLDWIDE.

TORONTO • NEW YORK • LONDON
AMSTERDAM • PARIS • SYDNEY • HAMBURG
STOCKHOLM • ATHENS • TOKYO • MILAN
MADRID • WARSAW • BUDAPEST • AUCKLAND

For Jane Conway-Gordon

SOUR GRAPES

A Worldwide Mystery/August 1999

First published by St. Martin's Press, Incorporated.

ISBN 0-373-26319-8

Printed in U.S.A.

Author's Note

There is as yet no University of St Albans. That is a figment of the author's imagination, as are all the characters in this novel.

Acknowledgments

The idea for this novel came to me during an inspiring talk on lie-detection given by Dr Gisli Gudjonsson. His *Psychology of Interrogations, Confessions and Testimony* (published by John Wiley & Sons) subsequently proved to be extremely useful. Naturally, he bears no responsibility for anything I have written here.

Many other people have given me advice and help while I was writing the book. They include Jan Barnett, Mary Carter, Joanna Frank, Gerald Johnson, Jennifer Kavanagh, Clare Ledingham, Tony Mottram, James Turner and Richard Wright.

Natasha Cooper,
London, November 1996

ONE

'ARE YOU DEAF? They fitted me up. I told yer. They nicked the tyre lever from me garridge and left it by the body with 'er blood all over it. 'Course it's got my fingerprints on it. 'Smine. But I never done it, see. I hated the bitch, but I never killed 'er.'

Emma switched off the tape recorder, relieved to be able to silence the resentful, accusatory voice at last, and pushed the matching polygraph chart to one side. As it slithered over the edge of her desk it took a pile of others with it and knocked over a box of paperclips, spilling the contents across the mud-coloured carpet. She put her head in her hands and tried to remember what enthusiasm felt like.

Nearly twenty-five, she was working for a postgraduate degree in criminology at the newly established University of St Albans and hoping to make a career in lie-detection. At that moment it seemed a mad idea, and ludicrously over-ambitious too.

The man to whose voice she had just been listening was serving a life sentence for the murder of his mother-in-law. By the time Emma had gone to him in search of material for her thesis, he had been in prison for five years. Seeing the fury in his eyes, hearing it in his voice, feeling it as he leaned towards her each time he accused her of stupidity or deliberate misunderstanding, she had found it easy to imagine him bludgeoning someone to death.

At the same time she had sensed in him a vulnerability that had upset her. His obvious need for reassurance had made her feel brutally exploitative as she questioned him about the killing in order to record the changes in his heart rate and breathing whenever he switched from truth to lies or back again. She had left his prison disliking herself and wishing that she had never heard of lie-detection.

She was the youngest of three children born into a family that had lived in the same part of Gloucestershire for generations. Her parents would have denied any suggestion that they were rich, but they lived in a large and beautiful old house her father had inherited, and they had always had enough money to pay for the things they considered important, which Emma had come to believe was a pretty good definition of wealth. All their friends came from similar backgrounds to their own, and they treated most outsiders as either dangerous or contemptible.

Emma had not been a particularly happy child, but she had not questioned any of her family's assumptions until her late teens, when she had moved to a semi-independent life in London. There she had begun to allow herself to admit not only that she loathed the hypocrisy and snobbishness of their world but also that she might be happier outside it. Later she had become convinced that she had only to escape in order to find everything she wanted. Her confidence had proved to be unjustified.

The work she was trying to do in St Albans was hard, but she had been prepared for that. What she had not expected was the hostility she kept meeting from the other postgraduates. Lots of the people she had encountered when she was doing her first degree at London University had laughed at her accent, her clothes, her assumptions, and the few things she had told them about her life at home, but they had been relatively kind in their amusement. It had been easy to like them.

Her fellow criminologists were quite different. They seemed to believe that she was fair game for whatever malicious or mocking impulses they might feel, and they felt a great many. Emma had long ago modified her accent, flung her velvet hairbands in the bin, and never talked to anyone about the life she had lived in Gloucestershire, but it was becoming very clear that she had not yet done nearly enough to placate her colleagues.

Some were police officers, others psychologists or social workers; one was a solicitor. Most of them were older than Emma and, unlike her, they had had formal dealings with criminals or their victims before they even arrived at the university. They could talk to each other with the ease brought by shared experience, and most of them seemed to enjoy showing the one outsider among them just how ignorant they thought she was.

It all seemed horribly reminiscent of the way her mother's friends had behaved when a newly rich couple had bought a house in the neighbourhood. They had committed a whole series of solecisms that still seemed trivial to Emma and yet had unleashed torrents of contemptuous malice from everyone else. They had endured it for less than a year and then sold the house, taking an enormous loss, and moved back to London. One of the very few things of which Emma remained certain was that she was not going to follow their example, however tempting it might seem.

There were not many other women taking her course and she had been surprised to discover that they were quite as aggressive as the men. One of the most difficult was a police officer called Janet Ranton. Right at the beginning of their first week, she had looked Emma up and down and asked what on earth could make someone like her think of taking up criminology.

Surprised by that first example of unprovoked hostility, Emma had decided to make the insult bearable by turning it into a joke, which was her usual defensive strategy. Imagining herself wearing one of the hairbands and her long-discarded pearl earrings, she had retrieved her inherited drawl and swallowed vowels and murmured, 'Well, cooking

d'rectors' lunches had got fearf'lly boring, and I couldn't
stand another seas'n in Klosters, so I had to think of something else to do. Crim'nol'gy seemed like a t'rrific gas,
acshly.'

Instead of laughing, as Emma had expected, Janet Ranton
had taken the answer at face value and become even more
disdainful. Later, when Emma had read a closely reasoned
analysis of various interrogation techniques to a select group
in her supervisor's room, she had had the satisfaction of
watching Janet's pityingly superior expression change to
one of stupefaction.

Sighing at the memory of her short-lived triumph, Emma
bent down to retrieve the polygraph charts and collect the
scattered paperclips. As she sat up again, she decided that
her gloom came from nothing but ludicrous self-pity. She
reminded herself of the one excellent friend she had made
in St Albans, vigorously slapped the papers into neat piles
on her desk and decided to give up work for the evening.

Washing the dust and carpet fluff from her fingers, she
stared into the mirror that hung over the basin. The fluores-
cent light was harsh and drained away most of the colour
in her cheeks, but it did nothing to disguise the girlish blue-
ness of her eyes or the fairness of her hair. In spite of everything she had done since she had left home properly, she
still looked almost exactly as she had in the days when she
was trying to believe that happiness lay in obedience to her
family's shibboleths. She bared her teeth at her reflection in
the mirror and reached for the bottle she had bought in
Boots some days earlier.

BY THE TIME she had finished, her thick short hair was black
and she thought she looked much better and infinitely
tougher. She tried out various expressions and was glad to
see that even her smile looked less gently acquiescent than
usual.

Not until she had cleaned the basin and thrown away the black-streaked towel did she begin to imagine the taunts her new look might arouse from her colleagues and to practise suitably throwaway responses. None of them seemed as convincing as she would have liked and she let herself think a little wistfully of the one person who could be relied upon to be encouraging about what she had done. Emma decided to tell her about it at once.

Dear Willow,

I've just dyed my hair. Are you pleased? Do be. I rather need someone to please about something at the moment.

I thought of red, but, unlike lucky old you, I haven't the right sort of face for that and so I've gone black; well, dark-brown really. I almost look French, I think, and even a bit actressy. Quite different anyway.

You asked how the thesis is going and I must admit (to you and you alone) that I can't seem to get anywhere very useful with my lie-detecting. Several of the people I've been interviewing in prison do seem to be innocent of what they've been banged up for, but that's as far as I've got. I can't see any pattern in the things they said to the police or the reasons why they said them, and I'm sure that's what I need to do. Otherwise I'll just be regurgitating their cases without coming to any kind of conclusion.

Some of them (like a woman in Holloway for killing her four-year-old child) are 'pleasers', who seem to have confessed in order to placate angry authority (which, as you can imagine, I can understand all too easily!); others seem not only seriously dim but positively babby (I'm sure you'll appreciate my careful avoidance of jargon here!), not really able to distinguish reality from fantasy; and yet others seem to have confessed because that was the only way to stop a hostile interrogation they could no longer bear. Then there are a few who seem to have felt such strong guilt about themselves generally that they came to believe they must be guilty of the crime they were accused of as well as all the rest.

It all fits with the published material, which is a good thing, I suppose. At least it suggests I'm on the right lines, but I need to find something new. I can't just rehash other people's work. Oh, Willow, what am I going to do? I sometimes think that if I have to go to one more prison and talk to one more furious, miserable, possibly violent inmate, I'll crack up. There are times when I get back here and find I have to fling off all my clothes, scrub myself under the shower and wash every single thing I was wearing.

That's that. Sorry to be so dull and moany. How are you? And Tom and Lucinda? Whenever I get really low, I think of you all in the Mews and feel MUCH better. I hope the book's going all right. Will you give them both my love—and my respects to Mrs Rusham? I wouldn't dare send her anything more than that!

Lots of love,
Emma

PS Don't worry about any of that. I was just getting the moaning off my chest because I know you're a safe and sympathetic listener and won't take any of it too seriously. After all, it's none of it at all important, and I wouldn't even post this letter except that I can't bear the idea of lying to anyone I care about. All the above is what I wanted to say to you and so I've said it. I've given up pretending about anything. At least, I hope I have. Most things anyway. But please, please, dearest Willow, don't think that I expect you to read any of it!

Emma read through the deliberately casual, slangy letter, noticing the plethora of childish exclamation marks, and smiled at Willow's probable reaction. Putting a small asterisk at the end of the postscript and another before the salutation, she added: 'You'd better read the PS first. It's the only sensible bit of all this stuff. Love, Em.'

WILLOW KING opened the letter after breakfast two days later. Her husband, Superintendent Tom Worth, was away in Strasbourg, attending a conference on Euro-policing and international terrorism; Mrs Rusham, her nanny-cum-housekeeper, had taken two-year-old Lucinda out to the park; and Willow herself was supposed to be getting down to work on her latest novel.

It had stopped moving for her and seemed duller than anything else she had ever written, almost duller than anything else she had ever read. She had not sunk quite so low as to believe it worse than her nearest rival's new book, but she was clinging on to that last scrap of dignity with difficulty.

Having reread Emma's letter and considered the misery in which it must have been written, Willow decided that she would have to do something to help. If it had not been for her, Emma might never have thought of taking up criminology and would probably have been a great deal happier.

Willow poured herself another cup of coffee and carried it upstairs to her bedroom. There, sitting on the edge of her bed, she dialled Emma's number, glad that as a postgraduate she was allowed the simple luxury of her own telephone.

'Emma Gnatche.'

'Hello, Em. It's Willow here. I got your letter. I...'

'I felt awful about sending it. I *am* sorry.'

'Don't be. It was fine. But you sound as though you need to get away from that place for a bit. How about coming to spend the weekend with Lucinda and me?'

'Wouldn't I be in the way?'

'Far from it. Tom's away Europolling, and we'd love some company. Come on Friday evening and spend the weekend with us.'

'I must say that sounds like my idea of heaven.'

'I'm being selfish,' Willow went on, 'because it would be wonderful for me if you could give me a hand with Lucinda on Mrs Rusham's day off. She's quite an appealing little bundle in her own way—Lucinda, I mean—but she takes a lot of effort. You'd be a real help.'

'It sounds wonderful,' said Emma with a deep sigh, 'but it would be a bit pathetic of me to run away.'

'Nonsense. While you're here, I thought I might be able to give you a hand with the thesis.'

'But I…' Emma began and then stopped.

'What I thought we ought to do is get hold of Jane Cleverholme,' Willow went on as though hardly aware of the interruption. 'The *Daily Mercury*'s bound to have run lots of juicy stories about injustice after false confessions, and, as editor, Jane must have access to all the facts behind the stories. A false confession is what you're looking for, isn't it?'

'Probably, although…' Once again Emma found it impossible to complete her objection.

'There you are then,' said Willow briskly. 'If you had a really dramatic case that no other lie-detector has written up, it surely wouldn't matter too much if your conclusions turn out to be the same as other people's.'

'Maybe not,' said Emma. After a moment, she added, 'I'm not sure.'

'I am. Why don't I ring Jane and see if she'll come for dinner while you're here?'

'Well, if you really don't mind,' said Emma, not wanting to be ungrateful. After a moment she added more brightly,

'Actually, I think it's a brilliant idea. I can't imagine why I never thought of talking to Jane myself.'

'She may not have any better cases than the ones you've already looked into,' said Willow, as though she thought she had to armour Emma against possible disappointment, 'but I'd have thought it was worth a try.'

'Yes. No, I mean. Actually, I'm not sure what I do mean, but even the thought of a new way of tackling it all is great. And the prospect of seeing you is even better. It is sweet of you to be so sympathetic.'

'I've been glum myself in the past,' said Willow, lightly skating over her own current difficulties. 'So shall I see you on Friday in time for dinner?'

'Yes, you will. And Willow?'

'Yes?'

'Thank you.'

TWO

EMMA RANG THE BELL of the Worths' Belgravia mews
house at ten past six the following Friday evening. Mrs
Rusham opened the door and said with all her usual formality, 'Good evening, Ms Gnatche.'

'Hello,' said Emma, impressed that her radically changed
appearance had been accepted without either a comment or
any obvious surprise.

'Mrs Worth is upstairs giving Lucinda her bath. She suggested you might like to leave your luggage to me and go
up to join them.'

'Oh, thank you, Mrs Rusham. But there's no need for you
to do anything with my bag. There's hardly anything in it
and I'll deal with it later. How are you?'

'Well, thank you.'

'I am glad.'

Before Emma could say anything else, the housekeeper
had shut the front door, murmured something about completing her preparations for dinner, and returned to the
kitchen. Emma obediently went upstairs to find Willow on
her knees beside the bath, assisting her two-year-old daughter to drive a flotilla of boats up and down the length of
water. There was also an incongruous dinosaur, which Lucinda seemed to prefer to the real boats, and an old, cracked,
plastic mug, which she liked even more.

As Emma looked round the door, Lucinda filled the mug
with water and flung the whole lot over the side of the bath,
shrieking with giggles. The mug caught Willow's shoulder
and emptied its contents all over her loose yellow cashmere
jersey.

'See if you can keep the water *in* the bath, Lucinda,' said Willow calmly before reaching for a large towel from the heated rail and mopping first her clothes and then the floor. She looked up at the sound of Emma's laughter and smiled.

'What a moment for you to arrive! How are you? You look wonderful with the black hair.'

'Do you think so? You are kind. I'm not at all bad, in spite of that shocking letter I wrote. Not now I'm here, anyway. It's lovely to see you both. Hello, Lucinda.'

The child greeted her with a doubtful look and then a series of vigorous kicks, which sent yet more water surging over the edge of the bath and did not seem to worry Willow at all. Emma had always known that her friend would be an efficient mother, and a well-informed one, but she had never expected to see such ease or tolerance in her.

Emma had been eighteen when they had first met, and she had found Willow frightening as well as dazzlingly impressive. In those days Willow had been a part-time civil servant, writing her pseudonymous—and extraordinarily profitable—romantic novels between Thursday and Monday every week. The two parts of her life had been kept quite separate and at first Emma had known nothing of the civil service half.

The woman to whom she had been introduced was 'Cressida Woodruffe', the author of a series of novels Emma had enjoyed for years. It had amazed her to discover that anyone as sophisticated and successful as 'Cressida' should have had time and affection to spare for someone as young and inexperienced as she had been, and she had revelled in their friendship.

Even then, before she had known anything of the real woman or lost her residual fear, Emma had seen in Willow something she had always longed to achieve for herself. It had not been the success or riches, the beautiful flat, or any of the luxuries she enjoyed: it had been Willow's freedom to live exactly as she chose without having to take crap from anyone. In those days Emma would never have thought of using such a word, but later on she had decided that it summed up Willow's determined independence better than any other.

Since then Willow had admitted to her secret double identity, left the civil service, changed her writing style, married Tom Worth and, at the age of forty-four, given birth to Lucinda. As Emma had begun to grow up and Willow to learn to trust other people, they had found they still liked each other and shared a surprising number of tastes and ideas. Willow had even told Emma a little of what her life had been like before she had started writing and what had driven her to attempt such a dramatic change.

Understanding how much imagination and courage it must have taken, Emma had often thought that the almost perfect relationship Willow seemed to have achieved with Tom was a suitable reward. Altogether her example had convinced Emma that with enough vision, grit and honesty every human being could build a life in which he or she could be happy. She still hoped that she was going to manage it for herself, but she was not always convinced that her grittiness would be enough to see her through.

'Lucinda's looking good,' she said as Willow leaned forward to scoop the child out of the bath.

She immediately started wailing. Willow ignored the sound, wrapped her tightly in another warm towel and sat down with her facing Emma.

'She is, although she can't resist getting as much of the bath on the floor as she possibly can. I think she must take after her father in that respect. He's a shocker when it comes to sloshing water on to the floor.'

'He can't be that bad,' said Emma, laughing as she stepped carefully around a large puddle. Poised to sit down on the only dry part of the edge of the bath, she added, 'Shall I clear up?'

'No, don't worry. Mrs Rusham takes it as an insult if I do any of the things she considers part of her job, and she took on post-bath blotting from day one.'

'She is amazing.'

'Isn't she? And it's such a boon that she and Lucinda love each other, which means I can leave them to it in the day and work with a clear conscience.'

'How is the work?'

'A little like your thesis,' said Willow, screwing up her pale, bony face and pushing some of her hair out of her eyes. 'I've got stuck and I can't see my way at all. Hence my sympathy for your state.'

'Isn't it awful?' said Emma, immediately feeling less of a failure. If even Willow had similar problems, perhaps they were perfectly normal after all.

'Yes. But it always passes, so long as one keeps on working. That's the only secret. By the way, Jane *is* coming to dinner tonight and she thinks she has details of just the case you need in her files. Look, could you take Lucinda for a second while I fetch her pyjamas? I always keep them in her room out of the wet for as long as possible.'

Emma received the damp and wriggling bundle and sat down in Willow's chair. She was pleased that Lucinda did not protest and she dropped a kiss on the child's sopping head, noticing how envious she felt of yet another aspect of Willow's life.

'D'you mind that she isn't red-headed like you?' she asked as Willow returned with an astonishingly vibrant red-and-green tartan bundle in her hand.

'No. I'm thankful. I think she looks a bit like Tom, don't you?'

'I'm not sure.' Emma turned Lucinda and stood her up.

'With his broken nose and that big square chin it's hard to say. I suppose her eyes are a little like his. Why?'

'I keep trying to work it out. She certainly doesn't look anything like any of my relations.'

'Perhaps the next one will.'

'Emma,' said Willow. 'Come on. I'm forty-six.'

'So? You can't have an only child, can you?'

'I was one.'

'I know. That's what I mean. You weren't happy, were you?'

'No. But...' Willow hesitated and then deliberately lightened her voice: 'Nor were you; and you're one of three. At least there'll be no one for Lucinda to bully—or be bullied by.'

'Touché. I'm sorry. That was a silly thing to say and tactless. I suppose I'm a bit distracted. Look, shall I go away and offer to help Mrs R lay the table for dinner as penance?'

'She'll have done that already and you don't need to do penance anyway. Come and listen to Lucinda's story—unless that would bore you?'

Emma merely shook her head, glad to have been forgiven, and struck by how much Willow had changed. When they had first started to see something of each other, Willow had resisted anything that smacked of criticism from anyone. Emma could not remember having received a direct rebuke herself, but she had witnessed several, and there had been moments of cold withdrawal during which she had become aware that she, too, had transgressed.

Led by Lucinda, who kept deviating from the direct route to investigate something interesting on the way, they progressed slowly to her bedroom to explore the further adventures of Ant and Bee. When the book was finished and Lucinda's foot-high illuminated penguin had been switched on and all her necessary toys arranged at the foot of her cot,

Willow turned off the overhead light and followed Emma out of the room.

'I must get out of this wet sweater,' she said quietly. 'Jane won't be here for half an hour or more; would you like a bath?'

Emma almost laughed. Willow had always taken enormous pleasure in baths herself, and she assumed that everyone else shared her trust in hot water as a cure for all life's ills. Her bathrooms had always been havens of warmth and comfort, colourful with pictures and books and well stocked with fruit or Mrs Rusham's luxurious home-made biscuits in case she felt hungry while she washed.

'I'd love to sluice off the journey's grubbiness,' said Emma, still smiling, 'if you're sure there's enough hot water and you don't mind.'

'I'm quite sure,' said Willow, not having noticed Emma's amusement. She opened another white-panelled door. 'Here's your room. I'll see you downstairs when you're ready. There's no hurry. Jane always likes her drink on Friday evenings and so even if she gets here before you're ready it won't matter. Take your time and relax. Oh, good. Mrs Rusham has brought up your bag.'

'She shouldn't have bothered. I could have done it. Are you dressing up for Jane?'

'No. I told her to come as she was. Be comfortable.'

'OK.'

Willow went away and Emma took out the few clothes she had brought with her and hung up most of them. She ran herself a deep hot bath in the adjoining bathroom and added some scented foam from one of the expensive-looking bottles Willow kept for her guests. Lying in the water, amused by the series of witty feminist cartoons that had been hung above the bottles since her last visit, Emma tried to do as Willow had advised, and relax.

The small but infinitely comfortable house felt wonderful

after the bleakness of St Albans. Even in her gloom Emma
could appreciate the irony of that since she had spent so
much time and energy trying to escape from the almost
equally luxurious surroundings of her family's house. But
there was freedom in Willow's mews, which there had never
been in Gloucestershire.

The sensation of imprisonment Emma had felt there had
not come only from the rigid mealtimes and the unwritten
rules that made everyone lie about the things that really
mattered, smile when they felt like howling, eat everything
that was put in front of them, however disgusting it might
be, and pretend to like people they loathed simply because
they came from the right sort of background. There had been
her half-brother's bullying, too.

His own mother had abandoned him when he was just
three, and, although Emma's mother had been careful to
make no difference between him and her two daughters, it
was hardly surprising that he should have resented them. If
he had been equally cruel to her elder sister, Emma might
have been able to forgive him and accept the excuses her
mother always made for him. But he had behaved as though
he adored Sarah, reserving all his spite for Emma, the baby
of the family.

Looking back and thinking of some of the things he had
said and done to her, she wondered why they had not taught
her to stand up to the much less violent bullying she endured
at St Albans. After a moment it occurred to her that Anthony's efforts might have sensitised rather than toughened
her, so that each new attack added to the effects left by the
last and made her even less able to resist.

Emma sank lower under the water and closed her eyes,
ignoring the sounds of Mrs Rusham coming upstairs to clear
up the other bathroom, various telephone calls and even the
ringing of the front doorbell. It was wonderful to know that

she was not responsible for anything at all and could just let go for a while.

Later, dressed in faded jeans and, as a sop to Jane's well-known flamboyant taste, a long scarlet shirt and shorter blue-and-green brocaded waistcoat, Emma went downstairs to find Willow saying goodnight to Mrs Rusham. When she had left the house, Willow whisked Emma into the drawing room, where a plate of crab tartlets and a bottle of white wine in a cooler stood as testimony to the housekeeper's familiar efficiency.

'Jane rang to say she'll be a bit late,' said Willow, pouring wine into two of the three waiting glasses. 'There was some crisis with somebody's lawyers, but she should be here in about half an hour.'

'Thanks,' said Emma, accepting the wine and a tartlet. 'Wow! That tastes amazing. What's she put in with the crab?'

'Nutmeg and cream, I think. Now, tell me.'

'Tell you what?'

'Everything. Anything. Your supervisor, the polygraphs, the prisons, this mysterious Jag who's been appearing in your letters. Whatever you feel like.'

'He's not that mysterious,' said Emma, settling back into one of the feather-stuffed chairs and stretching out her feet to lay them on a square pouffe and smiling as she thought of him. 'He's a New Zealander, a postgraduate psycholinguist working on "private language as threat", six foot five, very straightforward, very nice. We're becoming friends and I like him. Quite a lot actually. I think. That's about it.'

'How did you meet?' asked Willow, refraining from asking any of the questions to which she really wanted answers in the interests of allowing Emma the sort of privacy she herself would have demanded as a right.

'At an undergraduate lecture on ambiguity. We both thought it looked interesting, went along, saw that we were years older than everyone else there and got talking. Oh, and his real name's Jack, but he's been Jag since babyhood.'

'But he's not a criminologist?'

'No, unfortunately. It would be nice to have someone as easy as him to share my work with instead of the high-achieving, sneering bunch I have got.'

'What about the work itself?' asked Willow hopefully. 'Isn't that interesting enough to make up for the people and the sneers?'

'Yes,' said Emma at once, adding more honestly a moment later, 'Well, I suppose so, in a way.'

As Emma began to talk about some of the ideas she had been discussing with her supervisor, Willow felt reassured. Behind the depression that had been so clear in Emma's letters was obviously a keen interest in the work she was doing, and it did not sound as though she had manufactured it to copy—or please—Willow. Encouraged, she decided that Emma would probably get over her gloom quite soon; and if she did not worry so much about what the other graduates thought of her she might find that she minded their teasing less. If she stopped giving them the reaction they wanted, they would presumably get bored and lay off her.

The two of them were deep into a discussion about offender profiling, and whether it could make investigators miss important facts that did not happen to fit in with the profile, when the doorbell rang. Willow was so interested in what Emma was saying that she began to wish she had not invited anyone else to join them. But it was much too late for that and she told Emma to help herself to more wine while she went to let Jane Cleverholme in to the house.

THREE

'I NEARLY didn't recognise you, Emma,' said Jane the moment Willow brought her into the drawing room. 'Love the hair. It's a huge improvement.'

'Do you think so?' said Emma, standing up to greet her properly. There were some habits she did not know she had and was not even trying to change.

The two of them were different from each other in almost every possible way except their liking for Willow, but they managed to get on reasonably well when they met. Jane, who was a year or two older than Willow, had worked on tabloid newspapers ever since leaving her East London grammar school in the mid-1960s.

When Willow had first encountered her, Jane had been a gossip columnist on the *Daily Mercury*, successful in work though not in love, tough-talking, colourfully dressed and funny. Since then she had progressed through various parts of the paper until she had been appointed editor of the whole thing just over two years earlier. She had no idea how long the owners were planning to keep her, and the mixture of power and insecurity had given a new harshness to some of her opinions—and, so Willow had heard, to some of her dealings with her staff.

It had definitely not helped in her search for love, which was as dramatic as ever and quite as fruitless. Willow had come to the conclusion that Jane sabotaged every relationship that threatened to become at all serious, but she was not sure why or even whether Jane was aware of what she was doing.

'Yes, I definitely like it,' she was saying to Emma in

apparently sincere admiration. 'You look a lot less sweet, which must be a good thing.'

'That's exactly what I thought,' said Emma, laughing in real pleasure. 'I'm getting used to it, although at the beginning I wasn't sure I'd be able to live up to it.'

'I think it suits you a lot,' said Willow, pouring Jane a glass of wine and offering her the half-finished plate of tartlets. 'Have one of these before Em and I scoff the lot.'

Jane took one, shaking her head. 'You do yourself well, don't you, Willow? Living in the lap of luxury like this, while we hard-working, impoverished peasants—'

'You may work hard,' said Willow with some of her old asperity, 'but as for impoverished! Quite apart from your enormous salary, you haven't paid for a meal of your own or a holiday or a theatre ticket for years.'

'It's not the same somehow,' said Jane, acknowledging Willow's dig with a wild grimace, 'as having Mrs Rusham attend to your every whim. It's not fair.'

'Come on, Jane,' said Emma at her most coaxing. 'You must admit that Willow's earned it all with some phenomenally hard work.'

'I'd have to be tortured before I'd admit it's anything more than wholly undeserved good luck. But, since she shares most of it with the rest of us, I suppose I can put up with it.'

'You're all charm and generosity tonight, Jane,' said Willow. 'Were the lawyers particularly tiresome?'

'Aren't they always? But don't get me started on them now. My temper's short enough as it is. Let's talk about Emma's thesis. At least that won't make me angry. What exactly are you after, Emma? A miscarriage of justice or a false confession?'

'Both would be best,' she said, ashamed of dumping her problems on someone as busy as Jane. 'In a way Willow's right when she says it'll have to be a case no one else has written up. But that's not actually the most crucial thing.'

'So what is?' Jane was beginning to look more interested.

'Whether I can work out the reasons why whoever it is did confess. You know, whether it was his psychology, what the police did to him…whatever, and then use that to come to some kind of conclusion for the whole thesis. D'you see what I mean?'

'Yes. And once you've decided on the case,' said Jane, thinking how young Emma's apologetic earnestness made her seem, 'how are you going to set about finding the reasons?'

'Well, first I'd need to talk to whoever it is and do a polygraph test. Then I'd read up whatever I could find about the crime itself and the evidence the police had before they arrested him. And I'd try—but it might be difficult—to get them to talk to me and say what they did and said to make him confess… All that sort of thing.'

Knowing that her voice sounded much less confident and knowledgeable than she would have liked, Emma stopped smiling and tried to add a little of Mrs Rusham's briskness to her delivery. 'Have you got any suitable cases in your files, Jane? Willow said you'd be bringing some notes with you tonight.'

'I know. I told her I would, but then I thought I'd better find out a bit more about exactly what you wanted. You see, there is one particular man I thought you might consider, but I didn't bring the file because I wasn't sure he'd do for you, although…'

As Jane stopped talking, Emma decided that she need not have worried so much about her own lack of confidence. For once Jane seemed to share it. The wicked glint in her brown eyes had gone completely and she seemed to be almost pleading with Emma as she added, 'I must say it would be a help if you did think he was worth looking into.'

'Why?' asked Willow before Emma said it. 'Have you been having legal problems with this one as well?'

Emma made herself wait until Willow was satisfied.

'No. Nothing like that,' said Jane. 'But in a way…I suppose you could say I've been having moral problems with it. Well, something like that.'

Surprised, Emma glanced at Willow and saw that she was equally taken aback.

'There's a man called Andrew Lutterworth,' Jane went on oblivious to their reaction, 'who's doing four years for causing death by dangerous driving. Two deaths in fact. He's about to become eligible for parole. His wife talked to me recently and…' She stopped talking so that she could drink, but she showed none of her usual pleasure in the wine and seemed hardly to have tasted it before she swallowed and put down her glass.

Willow and Emma looked at each other again. Neither of them had ever seen Jane quite so tentative.

'You probably remember,' she went on, 'the campaign we've been running on and off for years now about people who kill while driving and get off with a fine or a piddling little sentence?'

'Yes,' said Willow, 'but four years isn't exactly piddling for a driving offence, especially if it was his first.'

'It seems quite piddling to me,' said Emma. 'Two people died.'

'Yes, I know, but it's not as though he was accused of murdering them—or even of manslaughter. If the crime was bad driving, four years does seem quite a lot. The effects of what happened were terrible, but that's not the point. In this country punishment isn't supposed to be a means of avenging the victims.'

'Well, it should be,' said Jane, sounding almost harsh. Before either of the others could protest, she added more calmly, 'At least in a case like this. It was a particularly bad accident and he behaved outrageously. He ought to have got the maximum possible sentence.'

'Which is what?' asked Emma, anxious to take at least some part in the discussion about the material for her own thesis.

'At the time he was convicted: five years. It's more now, thanks to people like us pushing our outrage on the politicians. Don't look at me like that, Willow. Whatever his intentions might have been, this man drove his car smash into a woman and her baby, and he didn't even bother to call an ambulance. If he had, the mother at least might have lived, although the child was too badly mashed up to have had any chance at all. That was what we majored on in our stories: that she could have been saved if he'd had the decency to think of anyone but himself.'

'So how was he caught and why did he confess?' said Emma, still not sure why Jane thought the case would interest her and determined to find out before Willow thought of something else she wanted to ask or explain. 'He did confess, didn't he?'

'Yes, he did eventually. Not at first. He was caught because he was stupid enough to forget that the car itself would identify him. I suppose, to be fair, he might have been too shocked to think. Anyway, he'd probably have got away with it if he'd driven off at once and had the car panel-beaten back into shape before anyone saw it. It was such a filthy night that there were very few people out and about, and no one's ever found any witnesses to the crash. As it was, he tried to be that little bit too clever and tripped himself up. He abandoned the car at the scene of the accident and claimed that someone had stolen it earlier in the evening from outside his London office.'

'Well, mightn't it have been nicked?' Willow's voice sounded very cool after Jane's impassioned one. 'Cars often are.'

'It's possible, but the police didn't believe him and nor did the jury, even though he went to some trouble to set up the alibi. In fact he managed to report the theft on his mobile, pretending to be still in London, before the police had even discovered the crash in Buckinghamshire. But after he'd been taken in for questioning, he did eventually tell the real story. Then when he'd had time to think about it again, and presumably listened to his lawyers, he changed his plea to not guilty and said he'd been too confused and fuddled to resist the police's bullying. At that point he claimed he had been exhausted from not having had enough sleep for days because of his work and confessed just to get them off his back.'

'It sounds relatively familiar from what you've been telling me, doesn't it, Emma?' said Willow, pouring more wine for them all. 'Confessing to stop the hostile interrogation. Perhaps that, at least, was true.'

Emma nodded. 'Yes, it could have been. What kind of man is he, Jane? Likely to be a victim of bullying?'

'Let's eat while we talk,' said Willow before Jane could answer. 'Otherwise the food'll dry out. Bring the glasses, will you, Em, while I go and fetch it?'

'Yes, of course.' Emma tried not to sound irritated and quickly turned back to look at Jane again: 'So: what kind of man?'

'An accountant in a big firm. Clever, knowledgeable, arrogant. Quite able to cope with bullying by anyone, I'd have thought, even if the police still went in for that sort of thing.'

'Don't they?' asked Emma innocently as she obediently collected the glasses.

Jane smiled. 'Nowadays they go only as far as PACE allows, which isn't very far.'

'I can see your lawyers have got to you,' said Emma, laughing as she thought of some of the things Jane's newspaper had printed in the fairly recent past. 'Have you been sued much recently? I don't remember reading anything about libel for a while.'

'No. We tend to settle these days.' Jane ran both hands through her mop of orange hair and then held the back of her neck as though it was aching. 'As soon as judges are allowed to fix damages, we'll fight again, but not until then. Juries are far too generous with other people's money; it's just not worth it. And with the wretched lottery making them all used to thinking in millions, it's going to get even worse.'

They walked together into Willow's apricot-coloured dining room, where she had lit the six candles that stood clustered together in the middle of the table. Mrs Rusham had put small glass pots of early white jonquils between the silver candlesticks, and laid the three places with what Emma recognised as the best china. She was touched to see how much effort Willow and Mrs Rusham had made for her weekend holiday and all her irritation disappeared in a wave of gratitude.

'Do sit down, both of you,' said Willow as she disappeared through the door that led into the kitchen. She returned with a tray a minute or two later. 'Could you take the plates, Em?'

As Emma distributed them, Willow took two covered dishes off the tray and put them beside Jane's place.

'Help yourself,' she said, 'while I fetch the spuds.'

The 'spuds' turned out to be a gloriously savoury dish of potato slices layered with white onion and garlic cooked in strong veal stock, and the contents of the covered dishes were revealed as venison casserole and a mixture of celeriac, carrot and parsnip cut into thin batons. It was all the most wonderful change from the diet of instant soup and noodles, cottage cheese and perfunctory canteen food to which Emma had become accustomed.

'You said you'd talked to this Lutterworth's wife,' she

said to Jane when they had finished giving the venison the awed attention it deserved. 'Why?'

'She came to see me,' said Jane as her expression turned from satisfaction to something much bleaker. 'I'm not sure how she ever got into the building, let alone up to my floor, but she did. I heard my name and when I looked up there she was, this completely unknown, utterly respectable-looking woman standing in the doorway of my office, telling me that she must have three minutes of my time. I had no idea what she wanted.' Jane slopped some more wine into her glass, but she did not drink. Staring at the flowers and candles in the middle of the table, she went on in a hard, flat voice, 'As soon as she saw she'd got my attention she told me who she was. And then before I could get her thrown out she said that she'd simply come to ask me not to print anything about car crashes and unfair sentences for drivers who kill until after her husband's parole hearing.'

'Wasn't that a trifle cheeky?' said Willow, knowing how much Jane resented any attempt to censor what she put in the paper, or in fact anything she might want to write or say to anyone.

'Oh, sure. To start with I was furious: you know, someone trying to interfere with my editorial independence, but then I started to have…if not exactly doubts, at least second thoughts about what we'd been doing.'

'You?' Willow sounded flabbergasted. 'But why?'

Jane did drink then. A moment later she said, 'She told me that her husband was innocent and that he'd never have been convicted if we hadn't reported his case so angrily and printed such violent denunciations of drivers who kill people. She thought we'd whipped up such hatred that the jurors didn't even bother to think about the evidence. I protested, obviously, but she said they couldn't have; if they had, they'd have seen that there wasn't nearly enough to convict anyone on. Later, after she'd gone, I started to look at some of the background stuff in the files and I saw that in a way she was right: there wasn't actually all that much real evidence that he had been the driver.'

'But she didn't really make you believe he was innocent, did she?' said Willow, frowning. She could not see why the case should have had such a strong effect on Jane.

'Not exactly, but she did shake me. I'm not sure I'd have thought twice about it if she hadn't been so quiet in her protest and so bloody reasonable. If she'd wanted money out of us, I'd have felt happier. But she didn't. She didn't even want a retraction or an apology in the paper. All she wanted was for me to listen to what she said, admit that we might have done her husband an injustice, and lay off our campaign. There was something about her that made her impossible to ignore—or forget, unfortunately.'

'D'you know what it was?' asked Emma, who was thoroughly puzzled by the whole story.

Jane turned her head slowly, almost as though she was reluctant to think too hard about Mrs Lutterworth.

'Not really. She was very dignified, and we don't see a whole lot of dignity at the *Mercury*.'

'I can imagine,' said Willow at her driest.

'But it wasn't just that. She was so rational. I think that must have been what threw me, and now I can't get it out of my head. She'd been writing to me at intervals ever since her husband was convicted and I'd disregarded all the letters on the grounds that she must be a silly little woman who had no idea what he got up to while he was out of sight, but she wasn't like that at all.'

'What was she like?' asked Willow. She collected the empty plates to take out to the kitchen and waited in the doorway to hear Jane's reply. 'Apart from being rational.'

'One of us,' said Jane at last. Then she produced an unconvincing laugh: 'You know, Willow: intelligent, attractive, woman-in-her-own-right, even though she doesn't have a career, and thoroughly grown up. All that sort of thing. I liked her, you see. Perhaps it was that more even than the rationality. Anyway, as I say, she almost convinced me.'

'A cynic like you! I can hardly believe it!' said Emma in an attempt to lighten the atmosphere and take back some of the control Willow kept assuming.

Jane shrugged, not looking at all happy. 'So you see, Emma,' she said eventually, swirling the last of the wine round and round in her glass. 'I'm being selfish. If you could use the case for your thesis and find out whether he did or didn't do it, I'd be in your debt.'

FOUR

EMMA RETURNED to St Albans on Sunday evening, feeling much better than when she had left. In encouraging her to talk about her work, Willow had shown so clearly that she believed it would have real value that she had bolstered Emma's shaky confidence. And the case of Jane's killer-driver seemed quite promising.

Jane had had a large file sent round to Willow's house from the *Daily Mercury*'s offices just before Emma had left to catch her train. Her first quick glance at the file had shown her that it was full of press cuttings and all kinds of supporting documents, but she had not had time to read any of them properly. The knowledge of their presence in her bag was making her positively eager to get back to work. A few days earlier she would not have believed it possible and she was passionately grateful to Willow for that as well as everything else.

Only two other people got off the train ahead of Emma, and she was surprised to see them both flinch as they reached the platform and hurry away into the darkness. When she got to the doorway herself, she looked to her left to see what had bothered them and laughed. Jag was standing there waiting for her, with two huge yellow helmets dangling from his left hand.

He was startling enough to have given anyone a fright, she thought. Huge and dangerous-looking in his leathers, he had longish dark hair and an impressive face with powerful features and straight dark eyebrows almost meeting across his handsome nose.

'How did you know I was going to be on this train?'
Emma asked, stretching up to kiss his cheek.

Jag bent down obligingly so that her lips could touch his
face. It felt harshly scratchy, but then he often did not bother
to shave for a couple of a days at a time. That gave Emma
a terrific kick of satisfaction, as did the noisiness of his big
motorbike and his absolute directness. Having grown up
among people who controlled every aspect of their clothes
and bodies and rarely said what they meant, she found it
refreshing to be with someone like Jag, who appeared to
have no taboos of any kind. She was convinced that she
could never embarrass him, whatever she did, and could
hardly believe how liberating that felt.

'I didn't,' he said, 'but I thought it was worth the gamble
when you didn't answer your phone after the last one. How
was the weekend?'

'Great, actually, even though Tom was away. I've told
you about him, haven't I?'

'Just once or twice,' said Jag, looking much less alarming
as he started to laugh. 'But not as often as this Willow of
yours. Did she cheer you up? It looks like it. Here, take
this.'

He held out one of the helmets. Emma obediently buckled
it over her black hair as they walked out into the car park
and then with some difficulty swung her leg over the pillion
of Jag's enormous motorcycle, glad that she was wearing
her jeans. Jag strapped her small squashy bag on to the back,
efficiently straddled the bike, bounced himself into a comfortable position and roared off towards the campus and
Emma's room.

With her leg muscles still quivering and the engine noise
reverberating in her brain, she asked him if he would like
to come up for coffee.

'Great,' he said with all his usual simplicity, turning away
to lock up the bike.

He followed her up the narrow outside staircase to her corridor on the second floor of the red-brick building, pausing to allow her to collect her mail from the pigeonholes at the top of the stairs. When she had unlocked the door to her room, he stood just inside, shaking out his black curls and kicking one great boot against the other. Thinking that the noise of the rattling buckles was almost enough for a small percussion band, Emma dumped her letters on the desk and went to fill the kettle.

'Although I don't drink coffee at night,' he said, still clanking. 'Have you got anything I might like in that English chillybin of yours?'

Emma, her hand on the kettle lead, stood absolutely still.

''What's the matter?' he asked.

She turned to face him, trying to decide how to play it, and saw that he was looking at her in blank surprise.

'Is that some kind of Antipodean come-on?' she asked at last, trying to sound lightly teasing, and was disconcerted when he began to laugh. He came right into the room, shutting the door behind him.

'No, Sunshine,' he said when he had got his amusement under control, 'it was not. I was asking if you had any cold drinks. A chillybin is a fridge where I come from. *Have* you got anything I might like in yours?'

'Lots', she said at once. 'Oh, Jag, I'm so sorry. That was silly of me and…and ludicrously vain.'

'No reason I can see why you shouldn't think I'm after your body,' he said as she found him a glass and a quarter-litre bottle of French beer from the local supermarket. 'I imagine most men are. But that's not how we proposition women in the Antipodes, you know.'

'I'm glad to hear it,' said Emma, half relieved that she had not shown how much she would welcome a proposition and half wishing that she was sure enough to make the first move herself. Since she was not, she cleared the sofa so that he could sit down and politely asked how his weekend had been.

'Fine.' He settled himself on the sofa and started to drink straight from the bottle. 'I got a lot of work done, but I missed you. What did you get up to in London?'

'Talked mainly. Oh, and ate and drank a lot, and helped Willow with her baby.' Emma paused and then added casually, 'She did say that the next time I go I must take you with me.'

'She knows about me?'

'A little.'

'Great.' Jag watched her across the room, unsmiling. After a moment, he added, 'What does she know?'

'That we're friends, that you're immensely tall and come from the other side of the world.' Emma laughed suddenly, impatient with her own doubts. 'I could see exactly what else she wanted to ask, but I didn't see why I should indulge her curiosity.'

'Quite right. She's got no right to question you about your friends.'

Frustrated that Jag did not seem to have picked up that hint either, Emma asked herself how long it would be before she had grown out of the last of the rules she had been taught and learned how to say exactly what she wanted. It seemed absurd to go on giving Jag signals he did not even notice.

After all, she said to herself, what on earth would it matter if she told him she found him madly attractive and wanted more than almost anything else to go to bed with him?

The answer to that question was easy enough: she might not be able to bear it if he turned her down.

Apparently unaware of any of the doubts or frustrations in Emma's mind, Jag poured the last of the beer down his throat and put the little bottle on the floor beside the untouched glass.

'I ought to get back. Are you going to Wright's lecture tomorrow?'

'I hadn't planned to. Should I?'

'Well it is on lying.'

'Oh, great!' Emma tried to concentrate on thoughts of work instead of the increasingly vivid image she had of the two of them making love. 'Jag, thank you. I haven't been paying proper attention to anything for weeks and I'd have missed it if you hadn't noticed. And thank you for meeting me tonight, too. That was way beyond the call of friendship.'

'I wanted to see you,' he said, casually blowing her a kiss. He looked even larger than usual as he stood up, taking up most of the spare space in her small, cluttered room. 'I'll catch you at the lecture tomorrow.'

'Sure. And I'll restock the chillybin with bigger bottles of something more macho before your next visit.'

He laughed at that and came back from the door to kiss her properly, holding her by the shoulders with enough firmness to make her even more impatient with herself. She held his bristly face between her hands, hoping to encourage him, but he pulled back almost at once.

When he had collected his two helmets and gone, Emma told herself she would do better next time. She washed her face in very cold water, which made her feel more in control of herself, and then picked up the small pile of messages and letters she had taken from the pigeonhole. There was a note from her supervisor, asking her to ring him, another from a woman who worked in the language labs and was helping her to analyse some of her more puzzling polygraph results, and a letter from her mother.

She opened that and was relieved to see that it was a relatively anodyne account of the people she had seen since she last wrote, the books she had read, and her plans for opening her garden in aid of the Macmillan nurses during

the summer. She did include the usual lament that Emma
had not been home for so long and that she was not going
to meet any of the sort of people she could possibly marry
at a university like St Albans. But its tone was fairly easy
to take, and at least there were none of the familiar com-
ments about how disappointed Emma's father would have
been by her odd behaviour and unsuitable friends.

He had died just before she left school and, even though
he had always seemed just as conventional as her mother,
it was one of Emma's most cherished private beliefs that he
would have found a way to approve of what she was trying
to do. She remembered him as being a fundamentally kind
man, if unaware of what she was really like, and he had
occasionally shown signs of being able to believe that people who were different from himself might be almost as
valuable. That was something the rest of the family were
quite unable to accept.

Emma put her mother's letter at the back of her desk to
remind her to answer it quickly and got out Jane's file.

Three hours later she was still reading its contents, having
learned a great deal about Andrew Lutterworth, his car, the
accident, and the woman who had died with her child, but
nothing at all about why his wife should have been certain
that he was innocent.

At no stage in the trial or the preceding investigation had
anyone suggested that the crashed car had not been Lutterworth's. He had used it every day to drive from his home
in Berkshire to work, leaving it in an underground car park
where his firm rented his space for all the senior partners.
It shut every evening at 8.30 so that people wanting to work
later than that had to retrieve their cars by 8.25 and put
them in one of the streets outside the office, where restrictions were lifted at half past six.

Andrew Lutterworth claimed at his trial that that was precisely what he had done. There had been no spaces left

directly outside the front of his office and so he had put the car in a neighbouring side street and run back to the building through the rain. When he had emerged from his room just after 10.30, having finished an urgent piece of work, he looked for the car and could not find it. At first assuming that he had merely mis-remembered the parking space he had found, he had walked all round the possible streets. But there was no sign of the car in any of them. He had returned to the original space, seen that it would have been big enough for his car, checked the local landmarks and decided that he had definitely left it there.

He had then telephoned the local police from his mobile to report the theft. Once they had taken all his details, he had rung his wife to explain what had happened and announce that he would spend the night in their one-bedroomed Barbican flat, hire a car the following day and be with her as soon as he could make it in the evening.

The constable who had answered his original call had made thorough notes, but there had been no officers available to visit the site of the theft or talk to Lutterworth face to face. No one had expressed surprise at that. After all, there was nothing to see, and police stations were no longer staffed lavishly enough for unproductive meetings.

Lutterworth claimed that as soon as he had finished making his telephoned report he had walked to his flat, where he had stripped off his rain-soaked clothes, hung them up in the shower cabinet to drip dry, and had a bath. After that he had made himself a toasted cheese sandwich from supplies kept in the freezer and gone straight to bed, only to be woken some three hours later by police officers accusing him of having been involved in a fatal accident in Buckinghamshire. They asked him to provide them with the clothes he had been wearing that evening and accompany them to the local station to await officers from Buckinghamshire.

Emma looked up from the batch of scribbled notes, wishing that they were easier to read. She thought she could imagine the scene. Lutterworth, by then dressed in pyjamas, sleepy and puzzled (or pretending to be), would have led the police to the bathroom to show them his suit and shoes dripping into the tiled shower cabinet. Seeing the clothes, perhaps wet enough to have had smears of blood and oil rinsed out of them, the police must have felt reasonably confident that they had got their man.

Squinting to refocus her tired eyes, Emma went back to the file. She saw with relief that the next note was typed. It stated that Lutterworth's car had been discovered at the scene of the accident by a motorist coming from the opposite direction a little before eleven o'clock. He had found the bodies and, having no mobile telephone of his own, had run to the nearest house to ask the owner to call the police. He had then returned to the scene. Having realised that there was nothing he could do for either the woman or the child, he had felt the car's bonnet and later told the police that it had been only faintly warm. He had waited, as a good citizen should, until they arrived, when he had given them a precise account of his movements, his name and address.

The police had discovered a half-empty whisky bottle rolling about on the carpet on the passenger side of the crashed car. Although there was a driver's airbag, which had inflated, there was not one on the passenger's side. The window on the passenger's side had been broken and there were faint traces of blood on some of the pieces of glass found within the car near the front passenger seat. It was later discovered that the blood could not be matched to either the dead woman or her baby.

As she read that, Emma skipped through the rest of the file in search of any more reports on the scientific evidence that might include a statement that the blood had come from Andrew Lutterworth. Interestingly there was nothing. She was sure that the *Mercury* would have reported anything that supported their view that Lutterworth was guilty.

She went back to reading the notes and cuttings in chronological order. The forensic scientists had discovered plenty of Lutterworth's fingerprints in the car, which was hardly surprising, and plenty of others, including some smudges that suggested gloved hands had touched the wheel and the doors. That did not seem surprising either. Lots of drivers used gloves on cold days. There were many different hairs and fibres in the car, but none of them seemed to have been of any use to either the prosecution or the defence.

What was more damning for Lutterworth was the fact that none of the car's locks had been forced and, in spite of the crash, the alarm system had been discovered to be in full working order. During his interview he had told the police that neither he nor his wife had ever lost their keys or lent them to anyone, something that she had subsequently confirmed.

Car thieves had become highly skilled at breaking into all sorts of cars, but Emma found it hard to believe that any of them irresponsible and clumsy enough to drive so badly would have been able to break into the car without leaving any sign. Lutterworth's alibi looked quite as shaky to Emma as it must have done to everyone else involved.

The *Mercury* had made much of the fact that the woman he was accused of killing had been a 'good woman'. She was a single mother, it was true, and in other campaigns the paper had railed vociferously against unmarried mothers who thought they could have children they could not afford and bring them up at the taxpayers' expense, but the dead woman might have been a saint for the way the journalists had written about her.

She had been twenty-five, exactly Emma's age, and had lived in the village all her life except for the brief, disastrous time she had spent in London, where she had become preg-

nant. Returning to have her child in the familiar surroundings of the village, she had lived off Social Security only
until the child was old enough to be cared for by a childminder and she had then taken two jobs in order to pay her
way. During the mornings, she had worked in the Post Office, leaving at one o'clock to collect the baby. They had
spent every afternoon together, as the *Mercury* believed a
virtuous mother should, and then at six she had gone to
work as a waitress in an expensive restaurant on the edge
of the village.

It had a good enough reputation to draw people from all
the surrounding towns and villages, but that night, a wet
Monday in February, it had been almost empty. The owner,
conscious of how tired she was looking, had given her permission to go home early and she had left at half past ten.
Having put on her customary wet-weather gear of cagoule,
waterproof trousers and wellingtons, she had walked to the
childminder's house, which was at the opposite end of the
village, collected her sleeping baby in its pram and started
to wheel it towards her own tiny rented cottage.

She was hit from behind at a speed, it was later calcu-
lated, of at least sixty miles per hour. As Jane had said, the
Mercury's journalists were incensed by the fact that she had
not been killed outright and might have lived if the driver
of the car had not fled.

Turning to the account of the trial itself in search of Andrew Lutterworth's defence, Emma was disappointed to see
almost no details except that he had retracted the confession
he had made to the police and claimed that the joyrider who
had stolen his car must have caused the crash. The journalist's mocking disbelief came unmistakably through the short
deceptively simple sentences of his report.

Emma wished that the file had included a description of
Andrew Lutterworth's character. It seemed unlikely to her
that a man who had reached a senior position in a large and

responsible firm of accountants would have run away from
such an accident. If he had drunk half a bottle of whisky,
he might well have wanted to avoid being breathalysed by
the police, but if he had been that drunk he would probably
not have had the wit to invent the story about his car's
having been stolen or the steadiness to report it to the police
without sounding slurred enough to alert them.

It seemed even less likely that he would have been able
to get himself back from the wilds of Buckinghamshire in
time to be arrested at his flat by the City police on behalf
of their provincial colleagues, and just about impossible that
there would have been no trace of the accident on his body
or his clothes, even if he had scrubbed himself in the bath
and run water through the bloodstains in his suit.

The file was disappointingly short of all sorts of information Emma wanted and she had reached for the telephone
to ring Jane before she noticed the time. It was after two
o'clock.

THE FOLLOWING MORNING, Emma threw away the cold coffee dregs in her mug and made some more coffee without
even bothering to rinse the mug. She took it back to bed
with the *Mercury*'s file. For once she did not even notice
the smallness or ugliness of her room, and no thought of
her mother's well-appointed house, where all the furniture
was beautiful and the firm beds were made up with
smoothly laundered linen, crossed her mind as she pushed
her feet past the deep ridges she had made in the polyester
sheet that covered her narrow squidgy mattress.

As soon as it was late enough she rang the *Daily Mercury*'s offices.

'Well,' said Jane when her secretary had connected them.
'What do you think?'

'I think the case has definitely got possibilities,' said
Emma. 'And I'm really grateful that you've given it to me.

But there's a lot more I need to know. Have you got any more stuff in your office?'

'I haven't,' said Jane, 'but it's possible that one of the reporters who worked on the story may have something. If you're definitely going ahead, I could arrange for you to meet him. He'll probably have useful things to tell you even if there's nothing more on paper. Where are you going to start?'

'I'll write to Lutterworth straight away to find out if he'd be prepared to give me an interview and take a polygraph test. That won't give away anything. I've already written to his governor, asking for volunteers for my research, so with luck he'll think I'm just doing a follow-up.'

'Although, if Lutterworth is coming up for parole, he might not want to jeopardise that by talking to you.'

'It depends,' said Emma. 'Quite a lot of the inmates seemed to think it might help, even though I've been extra careful to make sure they know I can't influence what happens, whatever their polygraphs show. We'll have to see. Could you ring me if any of your reporters have got anything more I might be able to use?'

'Sure. Give me the number.'

Emma dictated it and then remembered the lecture Jag had recommended. 'But I'll be out this afternoon from about two till five or even later, and I haven't got an answering machine here yet.'

'OK. I'll try and get back to you before two. Otherwise is there somewhere I can leave a message?''

'Not really. I'll ring you back tomorrow morning if I haven't heard anything. You are kind, Jane. Thank you very much.'

'It was good to see you. I'm sorry I was so preoccupied. If only Jemima Lutterworth…'

'She really got to you, didn't she?'

'Yes, she did. Will you be talking to her?'

'Probably not,' said Emma. 'At least not until I've got somewhere with him. I want to work out what I think about him and his story before I risk being influenced by hers. After all, she can't actually know anything. She's only making assumptions from what she thinks she knows about him. That counts for bugger all. No one can know anything about anyone else. Not for sure.'

'True,' said Jane with a gasping laugh. 'How reassuring! I see I should have come to you for comfort ages ago. But don't forget that they've been married for years; I'd have thought she must have a reasonable idea of what he's like—and what he's capable of. Rats! Someone's signalling at me through the door. I'll have to go, Emma. I'll be in touch.'

The telephone rang almost as soon as Emma had replaced the receiver. Her supervisor was calling to find out whether she had got his note and whether she wanted to discuss her embryonic thesis. She temporised, explaining that she was on the track of some new material that might alter the thrust of what she was going to write.

'That sounds encouraging,' said Professor Bonmotte kindly. 'At least, more encouraging than anything you said to me last time we spoke. Look, why not drop in and tell me about what you've got so far? It would be good to see you in any case.'

'Well, if you think it would be useful. I'm planning to go to Wright's lecture this afternoon. Would you be in after that?'

'Yes. Perfect. Come and have a drink and we can talk. There's no need to go into any great detail about the new direction if you'd rather not.'

As she replaced the receiver, Emma thought that she must have been showing more signs of hopelessness than she had realised and resolved to put up a better front. Bonmotte sounded as though he had been quite worried about her. She switched on her laptop computer, retrieved her standard letter to prison governors and edited it to provide a suitable covering note for her proposition to Andrew Lutterworth.

The letter to him took her longer, but eventually she produced a slightly sycophantic version, which she thought might evoke the response she wanted.

FIVE

BACK IN LONDON the following Wednesday evening, Emma was sitting in a trendy wine bar in Covent Garden with Jane and one of her star crime reporters, Hal Marstall. He was only five or six years older than Emma, but he had the kind of confidence she thought she would never achieve, the kind that allows its enviable possessor to admit to mistakes and ignorance without looking a fool. He also seemed to be funny and he was definitely good-looking, with soft dark hair and a pleasantly self-deprecating smile.

Watching Jane watching him with half-resentful admiration, Emma could not help thinking of an occasion several months earlier when Willow had told her a little about Jane's latest unhappy passion for a man much younger than herself. Emma wondered whether Hal could have been the man.

'I'm off.' Having drained her glass, Jane picked up her heavy, sacklike shoulder bag. 'Things to do, people to see. Give Emma whatever she needs, won't you, Hal? And don't forget she's a mate. Treat her kindly.'

'How could I not?' Hal gave Emma a dazzling smile before turning to Jane. She nodded at him without smiling and then kissed Emma in an unusually elaborate farewell, promising to ring her soon.

Hal swivelled on his stool so that he was still looking after Jane when she reached the stairs and glanced black at them. He waved gracefully and waited until she had gone.

'She's a brilliant editor, you know,' he said as he returned his attention to Emma. 'We all admire her, even though she scares the pants off the lot of us. How do you come to know her? It seems rather unlikely, if you'll forgive my saying so.'

'She's a friend of Willow King, who is an old friend of mine,' said Emma, thinking that no one who could talk so dispassionately about Jane could ever have been more than a colleague.

'No! How interesting.' Hal's dark-grey eyes had sharpened, but his voice was as casual as ever.

'Why?' Emma asked warily. She had noticed his eyes. 'D'you know her too?'

'Unfortunately no. And even more unfortunately Jane has a hands-off policy as far as her friends are concerned, which means that the interesting Mrs Worth is off limits.'

'But why should you mind that?' asked Emma so quickly that the question was out before she realised that a sphinx-like smile would have been a much better response. Unable to produce one to order, she added, 'She must be about the most law-abiding person I know: the last person to interest a crime reporter.'

'Except that she's been involved in several investigations herself, hasn't she?' Emma managed to say nothing at all. 'Someone even said that she met her husband when they were both investigating the same murder,' Hal went on. 'He was sure she had done it and so she felt she had to get to the real killer first. She did it, too, didn't she?'

'I've no idea,' said Emma, lying. If it had not been for that particular case, when a Cabinet minister had been murdered in the middle of Clapham Common, she would never have met Willow herself.

'I think she sounds fascinating,' said Hal. 'I can't tell you how much I envy you being a friend of hers.'

'Thank you,' said Emma, wishing that he were not a tabloid journalist. She liked what little she had seen of him and in almost any other circumstances she would have enjoyed telling him how wonderful Willow was. But in the past several journalists had written snide little pieces about the amateur investigating novelist who was married to a senior officer of the Metropolitan Police, and Emma was not prepared to risk encouraging another of them. She resolved to practise Sphinx-like smiles the next time she was in front of a mirror and to be very careful of everything she said.

'And she writes bestsellers, too, doesn't she?' he went on, sounding full of exactly the kind of admiration that would normally have made Emma happy to prattle on for hours. 'D'you like them?'

'She's a good friend,' said Emma before firmly shutting her mouth.

'How dull!' said Hal, laughing. 'Oh, well, it was worth a try. I suppose if you're not going to help me have a crack at the truth about Cressida Woodruffe/Mrs Worth/Willow King, we'd better get down to whatever it is you want me to do for you.'

'Oh, dear, that makes me sound very grudging and very mean.'

'Well, it shouldn't,' said Hal, not laughing any more. He looked at her with what seemed to be genuine admiration. 'You're obviously a loyal friend. There aren't a lot of those about, I can tell you. Look, before we start, shall I get another bottle of this, or would you rather have something else?'

'Actually, what I'd like most is some water. Sorry to sound like a goody-goody. It's just that with all that wine and the nuts, I'm panting with thirst.'

'OK.' He left her for a surprisingly short time and was back with a litre bottle of Perrier and two tumblers packed with ice cubes. 'Now, what exactly is it you want to know about the shit Lutterworth?'

'Lots of things.' Emma reached into the bottom of her blue-nylon rucksack. 'D'you mind a tape recorder?'

'No. At least, not much. I take it you won't be quoting

me anywhere. I mean this is all off-the-record, background stuff, isn't it?'

'That's right,' said Emma, amused at his slight anxiety. She had noticed before that journalists could become extremely twitchy if they thought they might be the target of the sort of reportage they themselves produced. Having switched on her small cassette recorder, she added, 'If I want to quote anything in the thesis I'll submit it to you and get formal permission. How's that?'

'Great.' Hal's eyes twinkled as he smiled in acknowledgment of her laughter, and she felt much safer than she had when he was asking the questions. She also felt as though she had known him for years.

'First of all, I want to know what sort of a man Lutterworth is. You called him a shit: why?'

'I never met him,' said Hal, 'but from everything I heard and saw I'd have said he was a pretty good shit: selfish, pleased with himself, unable to believe that the world did not exist for his convenience—that sort of thing. I know the police loathed him and I'm pretty sure the jury did, too.'

'But why? What did he do to them?'

'It wasn't anything he did: it was his manner. The tone he took in court got right up everyone's nose. He behaved as though no one in the world had any right to question any of his movements that night or any other. I'm sure that's one of the reasons why they found him guilty.'

'Aha! And you thought he wasn't?'

'Good lord no. I'm sure he was.'

Emma searched his face for signs of doubt. 'Something tells me you're not completely certain.'

'Then it's a lying something. I thought he was guilty as hell during the trial and nothing I've heard since has changed my mind.'

'OK,' she said, before drinking some of the icy water. 'But what about his alibi? I know it's not exactly cast-iron, but haven't you ever thought there might have been something in it?'

'Not for more than about a second,' said Hal, shaking his head so that his soft hair danced around his eyes. He pushed it back impatiently, as though he had no idea how attractive it was. 'There was no one at Hill, Snow, Parkes & Partners who would testify that he'd been working late that night. All the defence offered was his word, and that's not worth much.'

'Although there was nothing in the file Jane produced that suggested there was anyone who could categorically prove that he wasn't there, working away.'

'True enough. And of course technically he didn't have to prove anything. It's always up to the prosecution to do any proving that goes on.'

'Yes, I know that,' said Emma, surprised that Hal thought she might not have been aware of anything so fundamental to the British legal system. She tried not to imagine what else he might be thinking about her capabilities. 'I've been worrying about it. As far as I could see from the file, all the prosecution had to go on was his retracted confession and a whole lot of circumstantial evidence. There wasn't anything incontrovertible that put him in the driving seat at the time of the crash, was there? His counsel must have pointed that out to the jury.'

'Yes, he did, several times,' said Hal drily. 'As did the judge in his summing up. It's perfectly true that everything the forensic scientists found could have had an innocent explanation. The hairs and fibres that belonged to Lutterworth needn't have been left in the car at the time it crashed. Fluff from the driving seat could have stuck to his trousers when he moved it from the car park. And so on. But the jury seemed prepared to believe that they had enough to convict him on.'

'And so they did.'

'Yup. Although it did occur to me at the time that if he'd bothered to make them like him—and Heaven knows it's not usually difficult to make people like one—they might well have let him off.'

'Perhaps,' said Emma, feeling uncomfortable. Ever since Hal had commended her loyalty to Willow and stopped asking questions, she had felt her own instinctive liking for him strengthen. It had not occurred to her until then that he might have been doing and saying things designed to achieve precisely that.

'You said no one could prove whether Lutterworth had gone in and out of the building as he claimed,' she said, struggling to get the interview back on to a professional footing, 'but I thought those sort of businesses always have electronic gates and smart cards and things that record everyone going in and out.'

Hal finished his water and then said, 'Most do. And Hill, Snow, Parkes do now, I gather. But they didn't then. At that stage they had uniformed security guards behind a glass screen, monitoring the arrivals and departures, taking in parcels, that sort of thing. They covered the building twenty-four hours a day in four six-hour shifts. None of the men on duty during the relevant shifts that night could remember seeing Lutterworth go out when he claimed to have gone to move his car, or return soaking wet after he'd done so, or even leave the building for good at whenever it was: twenty to eleven, I think he said.'

'But would they have noticed? Big offices like theirs have people going in and out all the time, even as late as that. I can't believe that any of the security guards had the kind of photographic memory that would have allowed them to state exactly who passed them, even if they'd been asked immediately. And I can't imagine that they were,' said Emma. 'I don't suppose they were questioned at all until at least twenty-four hours later. How likely is it that they'd have been able to produce an absolutely accurate account of who did and who didn't walk past them that night? I mean, it's a huge company.'

'Partnership actually.'

'Is that an important distinction?' she asked in some irritation.

'In some ways,' Hal said, but then he laughed. 'Not as far as this discussion is concerned, I know. I suppose I'm just a bit of a control freak trying to get the upper hand again. D'you mind?'

'Not when you're as honest about it as that,' said Emma truthfully.

'I'm glad,' he said, sounding serious again. 'I'd hate you to…to feel uncomfortable with me, Emma.'

'Me? Good heavens, of course I don't. Where were we? Yes. Lutterworth going in and out without being seen by the security guards.'

'So we were. I can accept that he might be missed once, even twice at a pinch, but all three times?' said Hal. 'Come on, Emma. That's as absurd as suggesting that all the security guards had photographic memories.'

She drank some more water, feeling the prickle of the bubbles on her tongue.

'Unless the two on duty were distracted by something? I've been into offices like that after normal working hours and had to wait for a noticeable amount of time until the guard had finished talking to someone else or put down his *Evening Standard* or answered a telephone or something. Haven't you?'

'I can see you've a wonderful eye for a gap in the evidence,' he said without answering the question.

'Thank you,' she said, wondering why he had resorted to such blatant flattery. It seemed surprisingly clumsy for a man who claimed to find it so easy to make people like him. 'Was there anything else that made you sure he was guilty?'

'Well,' Hal said, watching her with what looked like amusement in his attractive eyes, 'like the police, I find it quite hard to swallow the fact that he would have stood in the pouring rain—and it was bucketing down that night—to telephone them about his stolen car. Wouldn't any normal person have run straight back to his office and rung them from there in the dry? I'm sure he only cooked up that story because he knew he was going to get drenched before he could get himself back to London after the crash.'

'Perhaps. But, on the other hand, perhaps he was the sort of man who wouldn't have minded getting wet?'

'Oh, come on, Emma! Think how uncomfortable it would have been. And think about his clothes, too. He certainly cared about them.'

'How do you know?'

'Well, he had his suits made for him, and he always wore Jermyn Street shirts and Church's shoes. I'd have thought he would have hated having all that messed up by the rain.'

'Right,' said Emma, prepared to take Hal's word for that. 'Then I think there's only one other thing that's really bothering me: there was nothing in the cuttings Jane lent me about his blood-alcohol level when he was arrested that night. The police must have tested him, I imagine.'

'They did.'

'And?'

Hal did not say anything, just sat watching her over the rim of his almost-empty glass. She tried to read the expression in his eyes, but they told her nothing.

'Why didn't you put anything about that in any of your reports?' she said to push him into giving her what she wanted. 'Because there was no trace of alcohol in his blood at all?'

'I said you were good at spotting the gaps,' said Hal eventually. 'As it happens, you're right. But there are people who might say the police would have preferred him to be sober.'

'Why on earth?'

'Because there are people who feel that being drunk is something of an excuse. Killing someone in a car crash when you're stone-cold sober does somehow seem worse.'

'Does it?' Emma was genuinely puzzled. 'How extraordinary! So you think they could have suppressed the breathalyser test result because of that?'

'No, I'm not saying that at all. I've no evidence either way. Anyway, no one even tried to test him for several hours. I can't remember exactly how long it was, but I think it was nearly dawn before they went to his flat to arrest him.'

'Not quite dawn, I think. Three in the morning was what you put in one of your pieces, and half a bottle of whisky can't be metabolised that quickly.'

'Oh, no. No one suggests it could. But there's nothing to say that the bottle in the car was full when Lutterworth started his journey, or that he didn't have help drinking it that night.'

Emma thought once more of the puzzling unmatched blood that had been found on the broken window.

'So, like me, you've been assuming he had a passenger with him,' she said casually. 'D'you think it was a girlfriend of some kind?'

Hal shrugged. 'It seems the obvious answer to a lot of the questions that were never asked. At least, as far as I could gather they weren't. It would also explain why he didn't want his wife to know anything about it, why he claimed the car had been stolen at first, and why he confessed when he thought the police might start asking awkward questions about the passenger.'

Seeing the hope of a promising foundation for her thesis disappearing, Emma silently finished her water and thought about all the implications of what Hal had said. She did not even notice that he had stopped talking.

'Even so,' she said after a while, 'I'm not sure that I can see a man being prepared to go to prison to hide the fact that he was unfaithful to his wife. It's not exactly uncommon, after all. And prison for a man like him must mean the end of his career. Surely he'd rather have admitted to the mistress, even if it did cause trouble at home, and kept his job and what I imagine must have been a pretty hefty profit-share. Unless it was the woman whose position… No, I can't believe that. Although, I suppose it could be a Great Gatsby kind of thing and the mistress was driving, and he was just being chivalrous because he was in love with her.'

'But he wasn't,' said Hal. 'Prepared to go to prison, I mean. I don't know about the state of his heart. That's why he changed his plea to not guilty in court and said the police had bullied him into confessing in the first place. He—or his brief—must have thought he could swing it with the jury and get off.'

'I wonder. Did you ever talk to him directly?'

'I tried,' said Hal with his best charming, regretful smile. 'But you know these auditors: they learn secrecy long before they've even discovered how to add up. He wasn't prepared to say a single word to any journalist. And by the time he'd been convicted I was off on another story. His was interesting enough while it lasted, but it wasn't exactly the crime of the century.'

'Even though the woman and her child died?'

'Even though they died,' Hal agreed.

'Did you ever think to look further into it? You know, to try to find out where he'd bought the whisky or who his mistress might have been so that you could talk to her?'

Hal shook his head and smiled kindly down at her. 'What would have been the point? He'd been convicted. He was doing time. And I had other fish to fry.'

'Yes, I suppose you had,' agreed Emma, trying to match his lighthearted tone.

She wondered a little why Jane had not asked Hal to satisfy her anxiety to know whether there was anything in what Mrs Lutterworth had claimed.

'But it does seem a bit of a waste of your brilliant interviewing technique not to have got to the bottom of the story.'

'It is pretty brilliant, isn't it?' Hal said, his tone making her laugh. 'But there are a lot of calls on it and that story was dead in the water by then. Look, I'm going to have to take myself and my brilliant technique off now. Have I given you enough to be useful? I wouldn't want to short-change any of Jane's friends.'

'I don't suppose I shall ever get quite enough,' said Emma frankly, 'but you've been very helpful. If I think of something else, can I come back to you?'

'I can't think of anything I'd like more,' he said, surprising her again. 'And if I'm in your neck of the woods, I'll get in touch with you or drop in. Jane must know where you live.'

'Yes, she does. Do. It would be good to see you.' As she stood up to shake hands with him, she added, 'Look, before you do go, there is just one more thing.'

'Yes?' he said, still holding her right hand and gazing into her face as though he thought she was wonderful. She withdrew her hand and looked over his shoulder at the milling crowd behind him.

'Jane told me that she thought the police had it in for Lutterworth because he was so arrogant. She seems to think that's why they pushed him so hard to confess. I'm not convinced. I think there must have been more to it.'

'Of course there was,' said Hal. 'It's obvious.'

'Not to me, I'm afraid.'

'The police knew he was guilty.'

'Knew?' repeated Emma in surprise. 'But how could they know? There weren't any witnesses.'

'They didn't need witnesses. They knew he'd done it. You get a nose for guilt in their job. Emma, I'm afraid that if I stay any longer, much as I want to, I'm going to be disastrously late and cause trouble. I really must dash. But do ring me if you need anything. And...'

'Yes?' said Emma, wondering why anyone as confident as Hal Marstall should hesitate to ask anything of anyone.

'If you should happen to find out that Lutterworth didn't do it after all, will you let me in on the story before it breaks? As a quid pro quo? I can't see that it would hurt your thesis.'

'That seems only fair,' she said, intrigued to see that he was not quite as sure of Lutterworth's guilt as he had claimed. 'I've promised to keep Jane fully informed. I'm sure she'll pass anything on to you.'

'OK. Fair enough.' He took her hand again and smiled down into her eyes. 'Emma, I really have enjoyed this evening. Thank you.'

'You've been very kind to me. And I'm so grateful for everything you've given me on Lutterworth. I'll never be rude about journalists again, I promise.'

He laughed and kissed her cheek. When he had gone, she poured the rest of the mineral water into her glass and started to write up notes of her discussion with Hal to remind her of nuances that the taped record might not reveal. As she looked up, trying to work out exactly why she had thought Hal less certain of Lutterworth's guilt than he pretended, she caught the eye of a man standing alone at the bar. He smiled invitingly at her and gestured to the bottle of wine at his side. She shook her head and went back to her notes, remembering how she had once hated sitting alone in any kind of bar or restaurant. It no longer worried her in the least and she was tickled by the sensation of progress that gave her.

When she reread everything she had written about her impressions of Hal and the information he had given her, she decided that the most interesting thing he had said all evening was that the police had in some mysterious way known that Lutterworth was guilty and forced him to confess because of that. For the first time since she had heard about his case, she began to feel some sympathy for him. More than that, she found that she was angry on his behalf, and quite sharply angry at that.

Her interest in lie-detection had been forged by several big criminal trials she had attended with Willow, and it had been honed later when she had talked to some of the barristers involved. She had come to understand that in most cases all the lawyers in court knew a great deal more about the defendant and the witnesses—and probably the crime too—than the jurors were allowed to hear. That had always seemed not only absurd to Emma, but also sinister. It was as though a game was being played out between the opposing lawyers, who were usually well known to each other, for the benefit of the jury, who were strangers to everyone concerned.

The rules of the game allowed a great deal of obfuscation and forbade many of the things that might have brought out the truth that the lawyers already knew. Witnesses could be bullied and confused by clever counsel or made to look shifty when they were merely frightened or ignorant, all in the interests of persuading the jury to choose between the two contradictory stories they were being told.

The fact that it was likely to be the lawyers' dramatic skill that would persuade the jurors, rather than the truth of what they were supposed to be judging, had always worried Emma. Whenever she was feeling at all optimistic about her chances of getting her doctorate, she would let herself hope that one day her work might play a part in stopping one violent criminal being acquitted or one innocent person being sent to prison.

But the strength of her anger at the assumptions the police had made about Lutterworth's guilt suggested that she might have had other reasons, less conscious and perhaps more personal, to be interested in uncovering the truth about people. Uncomfortable with her thoughts, she got up to go, leaving her glass of mineral water half drunk.

The pavements outside the wine bar were sticky with drizzly rain and the air was unpleasantly dank. Emma shivered and buttoned up her jacket. A taxi cruised past with its orange light shining, but she hardly noticed. It had been some time since taxis had figured in her life. She had sold her car in her scramble to accumulate enough money to fund her doctorate and had to control her spending much too carefully to use anything but public transport.

She knew that she ought to go straight to the station and catch the first available train back to St Albans and work, but Jag had said he would be busy and the thought of sitting alone in her little brick room was too depressing to contemplate. As she walked through the drizzle towards the tube station, she managed to convince herself that she positively ought to see Willow while she was in London.

For one thing, it would be only polite to bring Willow up to date with news of what was happening. After all without her, Emma would never have heard of Andrew Lutterworth, her thesis would still be moribund and she herself would definitely be sitting alone in her dismal room waiting for something to happen.

As soon as the door of the Mews opened, Emma knew that she had made a bad mistake. Willow looked extraordinarily tense and as unwelcoming as it was possible to look.

'Hello?' she said vaguely, apparently not even recognis-

ing Emma. 'You'd better come in out of the wet. I'd forgotten you were coming. Sorry. How nice to see you.'

'I don't have to come in,' said Emma at once, taking a
step backwards.

'No, no. Do. So silly of me to forget you were coming.
Lucinda's not very well.' Willow's voice sharpened. 'Come
on in quickly and stop the draught. I must go back to her.'

Emma did as she was told, asking if there were anything
she could do to help.

'No,' said Willow, already halfway to the stairs. 'Go on
into the drawing room and get yourself something to drink.
Today's papers are all there. I'll be down as soon as I can.'

Furious with herself for disobeying the old rules about
not dropping in on anyone without warning, Emma found a
newspaper she had not already seen that morning and sat
down on one of the grey sofas to read it. Half an hour later,
Willow reappeared, still looking harassed.

'Look, is there really nothing I can do?' said Emma at
once. 'Don't you want me to get her some medicine, or fetch
the doctor or something?'

'No, there's nothing. I've given her some Calpol. Her
temperature isn't much up.' Willow rubbed her forehead as
though it was aching. 'I really am sorry. I even forgot to
tell Mrs Rusham to produce supper for two. There's bound
to be some food in the kitchen, though. Let's go and look.'

'I don't need any food,' said Emma quickly. 'And you
didn't have any idea I was coming so—'

'Well, I do need food.' Willow's voice had a distinct snap
in it. 'Sorry. I'm a bit worried. But I'd like something to
eat and you're looking pretty peaky yourself. It would do
you good, too. Come on.'

They found Willow's supper in the fridge, but ignored it
in favour of some fresh bread and half an unpasteurised Brie
that Mrs Rusham had been carefully ripening under a muslin
cover. To Emma's consternation, they ate standing up in the

kitchen. She had never known Willow to eat anywhere but at the dining room table unless she was ill, in which case she had a tray in bed. It looked as though Lucinda's illness might be rather more serious than Willow had admitted.

'That's better,' she said, after her fourth slice of bread and cheese. 'Tea? Coffee?'

'Some tea would be nice,' said Emma, who had struggled to eat two slices without any liquid at all, 'but honestly I ought to get back to St Albans if you really don't need help.'

'No, you'd better not go yet. What was it you came to tell me?'

Emma smiled. 'Nothing special. I was in London, seeing Jane and one of her journalists. I just thought it would be nice to see you and Lucinda again. We had such a lovely weekend. But I don't want to get in your hair.' She looked at the kitchen clock. 'Look, I really ought to go in any case.'

'Oh, right,' said Willow, not quite able to disguise her relief. 'Well, if you're sure?'

'Definitely.'

'I wish I could give you a lift to the station, but with Lucinda ill…'

'I'll be fine. It's an easy journey from here. I hope she'll be better tomorrow. I'm sure she will.'

'Yes. Probably. Sorry to be so unwelcoming.'

'You weren't,' said Emma, kissing her. 'It was sweet of you to feed me. I'll ring in a day or two to see how you both are. Please don't worry too much. Oh, how's Tom?'

'Frustrated. He rang yesterday evening as usual and it all sounds fairly awful in Strasbourg, as though the whole bunch are arguing and scoring points off each other just for the sake of it. The sort of thing Tom's always loathed. He promised to ring again tonight. I'm not sure—. Oh, that's probably him now. I must go and answer it. Take care of yourself, Emma. You're not looking well. Good night.'

All the way to the station, Emma admonished herself for

being so stupid and ill-mannered. It was not until she was
back in her cramped, untidy room, which felt lonelier than
ever, that she admitted how much she had minded Willow's
lack of welcome. There was no reason why she should have
attended to an unwanted visitor and, with a sick child, every
reason why she should not, but still it hurt. Emma knew
quite well that it was all her own fault. If she had not gone
barging in, she would never have been rejected. Rational-
ising it all to herself, she made a mug of tea and forced
herself to sit down and work until she had blocked out all
the distress.

SIX

WILLOW WOKE EARLY the following morning and was out of bed and running along the passage to Lucinda's room almost before she realised what she was doing.

At the sight of her mother, Lucinda beamed and stood up in her cot, waving over the top of the bars and squeaking with pleasure. Willow tested the temperature of her daughter's forehead. Finding it cool, she started to breathe more easily. Having scooped the child out of her cot, Willow kissed her brown curls and took her back to bed.

They lay there side by side, chatting for some time. Willow used words, Lucinda mostly gurgles and grunts, but they both enjoyed it until hunger started to make the child petulant. Experience had taught her mother enough to decode the sudden change in the timbre of her chunterings, and together they went downstairs to get some breakfast.

There was still half an hour before Mrs Rusham was due to arrive and so Willow filled the kettle for coffee while Lucinda sucked juice from a beaker. The coffee Willow made was never as good as her housekeeper's, although they used exactly the same equipment and ingredients, but she drank it anyway and ate a piece of naked toast to keep the worst hunger pangs at bay.

When Mrs Rusham arrived, she tightened her lips at the sight of the very trivial mess in the kitchen and announced that she would deal with Lucinda and make some fresh coffee while Willow dressed. Dismissed, she went back upstairs to have a bath.

It was only then, lying relaxed and comfortable in the hot water, that she remembered Emma's unexpected visit. At the time Willow had merely wished her elsewhere and had not paid much attention to what could have brought her to the Mews, but she began to wonder whether Emma had been upset about something. She had definitely looked more tense than usual.

Annoyed with herself for not having noticed it at the time and asked the right questions, Willow got out of the bath, wrapped a towel around herself, and padded wetly across her bedroom carpet to the telephone that stood beside her bed. She dialled Emma's number, hoping to reach her before she left the comfortless room she had described so vividly for the library or wherever it was she spent her days in St Albans.

There was no answer. Willow sat in unusual indecision, making a damp patch on her duvet. In the old days she would not have let herself worry so much about anyone. For years she had believed that complete self-sufficiency was the most desirable goal she or any other human being could achieve, apart perhaps from hard and successful work, and she had defended hers against threats of all kinds. She had never been much good at admitting mistakes, but her discovery that the state of self-sufficiency was a desert rather than a sanctuary had been so startling that she could hardly avoid acknowledging it to herself, even though she would not have dreamed of confessing it to anyone else, except possibly Tom if she were feeling particularly pleased with him at the time.

Trying to decide how best to make up to Emma for her poor welcome, Willow dressed and scrubbed her teeth until the coffee-flavoured staleness of the night was replaced by an almost burning peppermint taste. Then she went into her writing room to find a postcard, addressed it to Emma and quickly wrote on the other side:

In case I don't get you today, this is just to say how
sorry I am that I was so preoccupied with L's malaise
when you came. She is now fine and so my mind is
my own again. If we haven't spoken by the time you
get this, do ring me and we can fix to talk properly
when you've time. I hope all is well—or well enough.

Love,
Willow.

She stamped the card and gave it to Mrs Rusham to post
when she took Lucinda for the customary mid-morning
stroll in Green Park.

The telephone rang while Willow was drinking Mrs
Rusham's perfect coffee and reading one of the three newspapers that were delivered to the house every day. She
reached behind her for the receiver, stretching her shoulder
uncomfortably.

'Hello, is that you, Willow?' asked Jane's voice, sounding
surprisingly wide awake. 'How did Emma get on with Hal
Marstall? Did she succumb to the famous charm?'

'I didn't even know she was meeting him,' said Willow,
struggling to decode what Jane was saying with such ebul-
lience. 'Who is he, anyway?'

'One of our best crime reporters. I introduced them last
night so that she could pick his brains about the Lutterworth
case. Didn't she tell you?'

'No, but perhaps she was going to. She came round here
last night, but I was in a state about Lucinda and wasn't
very receptive. Bother.'

Jane laughed. '"Bother"! That's a pretty pathetic exple-
tive, even for you. I don't suppose Emma minded. You've
always said that she's a lot tougher than she looks. That's
why I didn't bother to warn her about Hal.'

'Warn her? Warn her about what?'

'Oh, just that he can be very seductive when he wants

something. A lot of people have fallen for it and then been surprised when he's abandoned them. He can be fairly callous.' There was a hardness in Jane's voice that warned Willow to be careful in what she said.

'Perhaps that's what sent Emma round here then. I wondered what it could be. She's shrewd enough to see flattery for what it is.'

'Good. At one moment when I saw him turning on the charm, I thought she looked fairly receptive. It did make me think perhaps I ought to stay on as chaperon, but I had to be somewhere else. I wonder what he thinks Emma could do for him.'

'Presumably the obvious thing,' said Willow crossly. She thought that it sounded as though Jane had been thoroughly irresponsible. 'After all she is immensely attractive.'

'I doubt it. Oh, I admit she's pretty enough, but I suspect he inclines to something rather more sophisticated. No, I imagine he heard that voice of hers and thought it might be worth finding out who she knows and what she could tell him about them. That's just the sort of thing he does: charms people into talking in case they come up with something he might want to use one day. If he weren't such a good investigative journalist I'd—'

'This is all sounding a bit personal, Jane.'

'Yeah, well…I'm as much a sucker as the next woman when it comes to beautiful young men who tell me I'm wonderful for all sorts of reasons that are rather more subtle than the usual.'

'Oh, Jane—' Willow began, but the sympathy in her voice must have been too overt, for Jane quickly interrupted.

'I must go. I've got a hellishly busy morning.'

'I'm sure, but before you go, tell me one thing: did Emma say anything about where she was going next? I can't get hold of her this morning, and I wondered where she was, whether she might have gone after Mrs Lutterworth. It's what I'd be doing.'

'I haven't a clue where she is, but I shouldn't have thought she's done that. She told me she wanted to talk to the man himself before seeing his wife. I can't remember why. I suppose I wasn't listening properly.'

'I must say I think that's a mistake.'

'Thank you very much for the compliment, Willow.'

'Idiot. I didn't mean your not listening, as you very well know. I meant Emma's not wanting to talk to Mrs Lutterworth. After all, if her husband is innocent then she must be one of the hottest suspects.'

'Idiot yourself,' said Jane sharply enough to arouse all Willow's old fury at being criticised.

'Come on, Jane, think!' she said quite sharply. 'She was the only person other than Andrew who had keys to the car. Didn't you say that there was no damage to any of the locks or the alarm system when it was found?'

'Well, yes I suppose I did, although—'

'There you are then,' said Willow, who had had several long briefing telephone calls from Jane about the case after Emma had decided to look into it. 'And you told me that she said she knew her husband was innocent. The only way she could possibly *know* that would be if she'd been there when the car crashed.'

There was a pause.

'Come on, Jane, admit it,' said Willow in a quite different tone. When there was no answer, she added provocatively, 'You know perfectly well that no one calls me an idiot and gets away alive.'

'I suppose I might be prepared to apologise,' said Jane through her teeth, 'and admit that I hadn't thought it through, but I still don't believe it. And I don't think you would if you'd met Jemima Lutterworth and heard her talk. In any case she lives in Berkshire, miles away from both the crash and the place where he'd left the car. Why would she have gone anywhere near it?'

'I can think of several reasons.'

'Such as?'

'Well, the most obvious would be that she felt neglected.' Noticing that Jane was no longer anxious to get off the telephone, Willow assumed that it had been her reluctance to talk about Hal Marstall rather than any particularly urgent piece of work that had been making her agitated.

'Look, Jane, if Andrew Lutterworth made a habit of working as late as you said he did every night, don't you think his wife might have lost her temper and decided to get her own back in some way?'

'By stealing his car? Willow, this is just a novelist's fantasy. I think you ought to meet her before you get yourself any further down such a blind alley. If you'd ever met her, you'd understand why your suggestion is so unlikely.'

'Perhaps I would. But it's amazing what even the most apparently sensible people will do when they're pushed over the edge. I'd have thought a pretty good revenge for a neglected wife would be to take her husband's cherished car—and I suspect he did cherish it; most men seem to—and trash it. I don't suppose she planned to kill anyone, but she might well have meant to write off the car.'

'I think it's pretty far-fetched,' said Jane. 'In any case, the police must have checked her out and dismissed her as a suspect.'

'How can you be so sure? Did anyone ever ask them?'

'I don't know, but she couldn't have done it, Willow. She's just not that sort of woman. Take my word for it.'

Willow laughed. After a moment Jane joined in.

'All right, all right,' Jane said. 'I know you'd never take anyone's word for anything. You're far too stubborn. Go and see her for yourself, and then you can apologise for doubting *my* intelligence.'

'Perhaps I should,' said Willow, thinking what a relief it would be to escape her novel for a while. 'I must say I should be intrigued to find out what she's like. And it could be useful to Emma, too; it might even make up for my poor welcome last night. What excuse could I say? May I say I've come from your paper?'

'Whatever you do, don't try that. I told you: she hates us, and by extension all other journalists, so don't pretend to be from any of our rivals either.'

'Pity. So how d'you think I could get in to talk to her without letting her know what we're up to?'

'I can't imagine.' After a moment Jane seemed to think she might have been a little too unhelpful for she added, 'Although I suppose you might be a student of architecture. You are a bit old for that, of course.'

'Why architecture?' Willow ignored the comment about her age. Jane was two years older, even though she often pretended otherwise.

'The Lutterworths commissioned a house from an exotic young architect in the early eighties. It's said to be magnificent, if you like that sort of thing, and it's figured in lots of mags. Not just the *Architectural Review,* but lots of general glossies as well. I suspect they get quite a lot of students wanting to see it. Willow, I really do have to go now. They're banging on my door.'

'OK, Jane. Thanks. I'll take it from here.'

'And report anything interesting?'

'Sure. 'Bye.'

Feeling the old tingling excitement at the thought of being on someone's trail again, Willow left her sticky novel untouched, kissed her sticky daughter goodbye, and told Mrs Rusham that she would be back for lunch at one o'clock. Taking a taxi to an architectural library she had used once or twice in the past, she looked up the Lutterworths' house and read everything she could find about it and them.

The house looked quite as interesting as Jane had suggested, and Willow thought she would enjoy seeing it for itself, as well as for the chance of interviewing its owner. She paid for photocopies of some of the most detailed articles and took them back in time to have shepherd's pie in the kitchen with Mrs Rusham and Lucinda. When she had put Lucinda in her cot for her afternoon sleep, Willow tried to find the Lutterworths' number. They were ex-directory.

'Not very surprising,' muttered Willow and risked Jane's wrath by ringing her again.

Her secretary said that she would be incommunicado in meetings for the rest of the day and so Willow had to exercise a mixture of charm and authority to get the secretary, whom she did not know and who seemed never to have heard of her, to rifle Jane's Rolodex and hand over the Lutterworths' number. After a great deal of exhausting cajolery from Willow, the secretary gave in and produced the number. By then, Willow was feeling some of the impatient rage she thought she had long outgrown and made a serious effort to relax.

When the Lutterworths' telephone was answered, a cool female voice, which sounded both authoritative and guarded, recited the number.

'Might I speak to Mrs Lutterworth?' said Willow.

'I am not sure that she's in. Who is it who wants her?'

'My name is Woodruffe, Cressida Woodruffe. I'm a writer and I'm doing some research for a novel about an architect. I've been looking up houses that have been commissioned from young architects over the past decade or so and I wondered whether I could speak to Mrs Lutterworth about hers.'

'Oh, yes? And have you found many such houses?' asked the voice. It sounded slightly less cool and considerably more irritable than before.

'Very few, Mrs Lutterworth,' said Willow, taking a minute risk. 'Which is why I should very much like to talk to you.'

'I won't embarrass you by asking how you got my number, but please don't think I'm naïve enough to be taken in by this ploy. Goodbye.'

'Please…' said Willow, but the link between the telephones had been severed. 'Damn.'

She swivelled her chair, switched on her word processor and began to rough out ideas for a novel about an architect. It struck her as she was doing it that she was going to an inordinate amount of trouble for something that was none of her business. Emma would probably prove quite capable of finding out anything she needed to know for her thesis, and she was far too generous to demand any kind of reparation for the poor welcome she had got from Willow the previous evening.

On the other hand, as Willow admitted to herself, she enjoyed investigating crimes just as much as she hated the thought of getting down to serious and frustrating work on her book. She also liked composing synopses. The novels themselves were different. They were hard work and caused innumerable problems as well as a certain amount of anguish, but weaving a brief story around a few, half-sketched characters was one of her greatest pleasures.

When she was satisfied with what she had done she rang her agent, Evangeline Greville, to brief her, and then wrote to Mrs Lutterworth, reiterating her wish to talk about young architects, enclosing the very short outline and giving Eve's telephone number.

There being nothing else she could do, Willow filed the documents and called up her first, pathetic attempt at the work she ought to have been doing all along. She became so absorbed in it that Mrs Rusham had to bang on the door to remind her that it was time for Lucinda's bath at half past six.

THE FOLLOWING MORNING Willow's telephone rang just after eleven. She picked up the receiver, gave her number and heard a familiar cool female voice.

'Ms Woodruffe? This is Jemima Lutterworth. I feel that I ought to apologise for my *brusquerie* yesterday.'

'Not at all. I was quite able to understand why you might have felt disinclined to believe me.'

'Really?'

'Yes. I hadn't made the connection before, but after we spoke I made some enquiries to find out why you might have been so resistant and I discovered why your name had seemed familiar.'

'I see. What a pity! Oh well, I suppose it was inevitable. I've spoken to your agent, who assures me that you genuinely are Cressida Woodruffe, which explains how you got my telephone number, and I wanted to say I was sorry for my bitchy comment about that, too.'

'Not at all,' said Willow suppressing her real surprise. She could not think what the woman could be talking about.

'I was in two minds when I wrote to you all those years ago. I wasn't sure someone like you would ever read fan mail. And even after I got your charming answer, it never struck me that you'd keep my letter for so long. It must be five years or more. I'm really very touched, you know.'

'Oh, I hang on to all the letters I particularly like,' said Willow, which was true. 'Yours was…great.'

'You are kind. As I said then, I've loved all your books. I suppose that's why it seemed so unlikely that you could possibly be ringing me up. D'you still want to see the house?'

'Very much.'

'When would you like to come?'

'Whenever it would suit you. I'm mobile. I have someone

to babysit. I could come straight away or tomorrow or whenever.'

'Then why not come now? I've nothing on today. It
shouldn't take you more than an hour and a half at this time
of day.'

'That's very kind. I'll be with you as soon as I can.'
Willow replaced the receiver, delighted with the amazing
coincidence of having an admirer as her only suspect. She
went to look for the letter Mrs Lutterworth said she had
once written.

The few fan letters Willow had received after her first
novel came out had been so unexpected and such a pleasure
to read that she had kept them all. Since then more people
had written with each book that was published, and she did
not have enough space to keep them all, but those she did
decide she wanted were neatly filed in alphabetical order. It
was the work of only a moment to find out whether she still
had Jemima's. She had. At the top of the single sheet of
paper was printed the address and telephone number she had
spent so long trying to get out of Jane's secretary.

Mrs Lutterworth's letter was very attractive, which explained why Willow must have decided to keep it, and it
asked for nothing except to express her admiration of a
novel she had read and liked. She had seen in the book some
of the things that Willow knew had escaped many of the
other people who had read it, and she had taken the trouble
to mention them. Willow had not kept a copy of her reply,
merely scribbled on the back of the letter, 'answer sent
3.2.90', but she was glad that it had been well received. She
fetched a copy of her latest novel, which was to be published in three weeks' time, signed it and added Jemima's
name and the date.

Mrs Rusham said that she was happy to stay with Lucinda
until Willow returned, even if that was much later than the
usual seven o'clock deadline.

'And if my husband rings, would you say that I'm out but will call him as soon as I get in if he's going to be in the hotel? If not, could you find out when I can ring him back?'

'Yes, of course. I hope you have a good meeting.'

'Thanks. I'm sure I will. I don't know what I'd do without you.'

Mrs Rusham's face relaxed infinitesimally. Willow nodded to her and, as she turned to go, happened to see her housekeeper lean forward to take Lucinda out of her high chair. The smile that Mrs Rusham bestowed on the child was quite different from anything she had ever offered Willow: warm, trusting and amused.

Willow left them together in perfect confidence and drove through the pouring rain towards the M4. The weather cleared as she reached the Wantage exit and she left the motorway to drive towards the Vale of the White Horse. It took her some time to find the Lutterworths' house because the signpost to the nearest village was missing the crucial arm. But she got there in the end and followed a gravelled drive between dense hedges of escalonia, which was just beginning to show the first hint of red in its buds. As she reached the end of the hedges her foot pressed down on the brake pedal before she was even aware that she wanted to stop.

Having seen all the magazine photographs of the house, Willow ought to have been ready for what faced her, and yet the real thing was so startling that she realised she was not prepared at all. Ahead of her was a building which at first sight looked like a child's drawing of a horse, but a child who was not quite sure what windows were or where a door should be. The façade consisted of a white rectangle, exactly half as high as it was wide. There was an enormous window off centre, taking up at least half of the ground floor. It had red shutters, which were partly closed. A thick

stone staircase led up to a heavy green-stained wooden door
just under where the roof should have been visible but was
not. There were two other asymmetrically positioned windows, one of which was of clear glass, the other Bristol blue.
No drainpipes could be seen and no roof.

Willow was astonished—and impressed—that the local
Planning Committee had given the Lutterworths permission
for such an extraordinary building. It was true that it could
not be seen from the road, but even so it was a most unlikely
house to find in the Berkshire countryside.

She edged the car into a suitable space at the side of the
gravel square in front of the house, collected her bag from
the back seat and climbed the vertiginous staircase to the
front door. There was a bell there, green-stained like the
door itself and almost invisible. She rang it.

Jemima Lutterworth proved to be much more conven-
tional-looking than her house when she eventually came to
the door. About five foot six and probably size fourteen, she
was dressed in old jeans, a lavender polo-necked sweater
and a very desirable jacket of soft tweed woven in a mixture
of blues, greys and beiges. She had a pleasant but by no
means startling face and her greying hair was cut in a long
bob with a half-fringe. At the sight of Willow, she held out
her hand, saying, 'Do come in. You've made good time.'

Willow went through the heavy green door into the hall,
which formed a lightwell for the whole house. Roofed in
glass set below the front wall's parapet, it was floored with
pale-grey polished stone, and had matching spiral staircases
at each end, reaching down from the gallery where the two
women stood. Climbing plants twined up the pillars that
supported the gallery and large fruiting trees grew in enormous glazed tubs that were randomly positioned about the
hall. The rainwater that had been collected in gutters at the
recessed edge of the roof was channelled down special
grooves in the walls to fountain down into a series of pools

let into the grey floor. The air felt as dizzyingly fresh as that of a flower shop.

Jemima led the way along the gallery to the further staircase, preceded Willow down it, and opened the door into an almost conventional drawing room, which looked out over the riotous garden beyond it.

'Coffee or a drink or something?'

'I'm fine,' said Willow, 'but please don't let me stop you.'

Jemima shook her head and stood waiting for her guest to begin.

'It is the most extraordinary house,' she said truthfully.

'Yes, I suppose it is. I'm so used to it now that it seems quite normal.'

Willow took a pad and pen out of her bag, leaving the signed book until later.

'Do all the staircases ever get to you?' she asked. 'Some of the people I've talked to about their architects are full of praise for the look of the buildings they've produced but hate the various physical inconveniences.'

Jemima looked surprised. 'Do they? How odd. I mean, we saw all the preliminary sketches and discussed everything with Jacob before he even did the final drawings, let alone wrote the spec. or put the job out to tender. We knew there'd be lots of stairs. Of course we don't use them all the time. When it's just us, we tend to use the back door, which means that most of the time we're on one floor and only go upstairs to bed like everyone else. I let you in at the front because I thought you'd like to see the house as Jacob envisaged it.'

'You were right. And I think it's glorious. What's behind the blue window at the front?'

'Andrew's bathroom.' Jemima did not flinch as she said his name and added casually, 'Jacob always said that it was essential for marital harmony that husbands and wives had separate bathrooms.'

'And bedrooms?'

'Naturally.'

'And is Jacob married? Or was he when he built the house?' asked Willow.

'Not then. I believe he is now, but I don't know whether he shares his bedroom or not.' With a return of coldness Jemima added, 'It would be an impertinence to ask.'

'Of course it would,' agreed Willow quickly.

She thought she could understand why Jane had been so shaken by her encounter with Jemima. As Jane had said, Jemima was obviously intelligent and quite unhysterical. There was a dignity about her that made curiosity seem vulgarly intrusive but there were other things as well: an air of honesty and a vulnerability, both of which made Willow see exactly why Jane had been so contemptuous of the suggestion that Jemima might have been the guilty driver. Looking at her, listening to her, Willow could not believe it either.

'What is it?' Jemima asked. 'You seem worried about something.'

'That's sensitive of you,' said Willow, thankful to be presented with an opening. 'In fact it was your mention of your husband that bothered me. I hadn't been sure whether to say anything or not. I mean, it must be so awful for you waiting for news of the parole board. And I didn't want to make it worse by talking about it if you—'

'How did you know he was coming up for parole?'

'When I was trying to find out why you might have been so unwilling to believe I was who I said I was, I talked to a friend who told me a little about what had happened to your husband.'

'Friend? What friend?'

'She's called Jane Cleverholme.' Willow remembered

Jane's advice to pretend there was no connection between them, but she had decided that a measure of frankness would work better with a woman like Jemima Lutterworth than any kind of lying manipulation.

Jemima twitched at the sound of Jane's name, but she said nothing. Willow waited, hoping that she had not blown her chances of hearing anything interesting.

'I wish...' Jemima began angrily and then stopped and shook her head. 'Do you know her well?'

'Yes, I do. Fairly well at any rate. We've been friends for a long time, and I tend to go to her for information.'

'Did she send you here to spy out the background for whatever story she's planning to run when the parole board decides to let Andrew out?' Jemima demanded, her face taking on a suspicious hardness that made her look quite unlike the pleasant woman who had opened the door.

'I'd hardly have said I knew her if that was what I was doing,' said Willow mildly.

Jemima nodded, but she did not say anything.

'Anyway, why should she want to run a story?' Willow added, hoping to get past the other woman's prejudices. 'It's over now, surely. You husband will be released when it's been decided that he's served an appropriate amount of time. There's nothing any journalist can do with any of that.'

'Then you obviously don't know much about them, however friendly you are with Ms Cleverholme. They'll rake the whole thing up again as soon as he's released, and have those horrible headlines about how he didn't care that he'd killed those people and doesn't deserve to be free when the victims' family is imprisoned in grief forever. As if we—'

'That seems rather unlikely. I mean, he's not a sadistic murderer or a paedophile or anything. He had a car accident. Serious, it's true, but the sort of thing that could happen to almost anyone. A moment's inattention on a dark night on a wet road. It's not like a premeditated killing, after all.'

'But he did *not* have a car accident,' said Jemima, turning fully so that she was standing face to face with Willow. 'Let this be understood *once and for all*. He was convicted of a crime he did *not* commit.'

Willow opened her mouth, but the pent-up flow of words seemed much too powerful for Jemima to control and they continued to pour out.

'Yes, anyone could have an accident; even Andrew, although he is a careful driver now. Far more careful than me. But he could *never* at *any* time run away from people he had injured. I've been married to him for years. I know him. He could *not* have done that any more than I could fly. His car was *stolen* that night, and whoever the joyrider was who took it was the person who must have crashed it and killed those people. Andrew should *never* have been convicted. And *that* is why I'm worried about the parole board.'

Determined to take advantage of Jemima's new and surprising readiness to talk, Willow sat down on the flat green sofa behind her and tried to look encouraging. After a moment Jemima followed her to the sofa.

'I don't quite understand,' said Willow. 'What d'you mean when you say that's why you're worried about the parole board?'

Jemima looked puzzled, as though she could not imagine how anyone could not have followed the argument that was so clear in her own mind.

'Because they don't release anyone they believe has not "come to terms with his crime". If Andrew goes on telling the truth about his innocence, they won't let him out. He's either got to lie and say he was driving that night or stay in prison for his full sentence. It's the cruellest possible situation for anyone to be in.'

'But why…?' Willow broke off and leaned backwards.

'What?'

'I thought you might not want to talk about it.'

'It's almost a relief really.' Jemima smiled and her whole face lit up in a way that Willow would not have expected. 'I know that must sound mad after my attempts to choke you off, but there it is. Now I've started I suppose I'd better go the whole way. What is it you want to know?'

'Why he ever confessed to the accident in the first place.' Willow frowned, exaggerating her sense of confusion to make her questions seem less threatening. 'It seems astonishing in a well-educated professional like your husband.'

Tears started welling in Jemima's grey eyes. Willow was not at all sure what to do. She wanted to make some gesture of comfort, but they were strangers and she had no idea what would be acceptable to Jemima or even bearable.

'I'm sorry,' she said eventually. 'I didn't mean to make it worse for you.'

'You're not. Just give me a minute and I'll be all right.'

Nodding, quite able to understand Jemima's wish to be left alone with her misery, Willow got up to look out at the garden, and waited until she had a signal that it would be safe to turn round again.

She did not get one for nearly five minutes. Then in a strangled voice Jemima suggested making some coffee after all. Willow ignored the amount of caffeine she had already ingested and said she would like some very much. When she offered to help make it, Jemima said, 'No, thanks. I'm not very good at sharing the kitchen. I won't be long.'

Willow went on looking at the garden, which was a curious mixture of exuberant shrubs and climbers and disciplined yew hedges. Knowing how long yew took to grow, she assumed that the Lutterworths had spent a fortune on mature trees and wondered whether the architect had had a hand in the garden design as well as the house. For the first time she began to think about the Lutterworths' money.

Partners in large accountancy practices could earn huge sums, as she knew well, and profits had been particularly high during the 1980s when the house had been built; but even so it seemed likely that either Andrew or Jemima had some private money, too. After all, she must be living on something more than whatever was left of his last cheque from Hill, Snow, Parkes.

The sound of her return made Willow turn away from the big window.

'It looks like a wonderful garden. But it must take a lot of upkeep.'

'A certain amount,' agreed Jemima with most of her composure back in place, 'but I quite enjoy it. I do it myself now, you see. After Andrew was…I got rid of the gardener. I had to really and anyway I needed something regular to do. I'd go dotty without any obligations.'

'What's down there inside those yew hedges? I can't quite see from here.'

'How do you take your coffee?' asked Jemima abruptly.

'Black, please. No sugar.'

Jemima handed her the filled cup and poured out some milky coffee for herself.

'I'll take you round and show you later, if you like,' she said, still not having answered either of Willow's questions.

They both drank and then both started to speak at once.

'You first,' said Willow with a smile, putting her cup and saucer down on a small glass table at her side.

'The inner garden within the hedges is a memorial to our son,' said Jemima in a completely expressionless voice. 'Andrew made it soon after Pipp died.'

'Your son? I'm so sorry. I didn't know.'

'No? Well, I'm not surprised. Very few people do, although it's no secret. I've always thought that the papers weren't interested because it might have spoiled their picture of Andrew as a selfish, drunken monster.'

Jemima sighed and sat with her cup forgotten in her hands, her eyes looking back to something no one else could see. Willow said nothing, and after a moment Jemima began to talk again in a less clipped voice.

'Philip was born fourteen years ago, and…' She bit her bottom lip hard. After a moment she was able to continue. 'He was the loveliest child: clever, and wonderfully intuitive. I suppose he was my best friend in a way.'

Her eyes filled with tears that did not spill over the lids. Willow sat watching her. She did not want to ask any questions that might seem insensitive and tried to think of something that would not sound crass or intrusive. It turned out not to be necessary. After a moment Jemima's eyes dried and began to focus again.

'Then four years ago he had to go into hospital to have his tonsils out. That's all it was: a relatively routine operation. It was successful. He didn't have one of those ghastly haemorrhages one sometimes hears about. He was getting better all the time, almost able to swallow comfortably again, and he was due to come home in two days.'

'What happened?' asked Willow when the silence became unbearable.

Jemima looked at her and the tears welled again, but she managed to control them without either sniffing or mopping her eyes.

'He got necrotising fasciitis.'

Willow, who had read several terrifying articles about the condition a few years earlier, was appalled. The *Daily Mercury* had run a whole series of stories about it, calling it a 'monstrous flesh-eating bug', but Jane had apparently had no idea that Andrew Lutterworth's son had died of it. Willow could not remember whether it was caused by a virus or an antibiotic-resistant bacterium, but she knew that it lurked in hospitals, attacked patients who were already weakened by surgery or illness, and was nearly always fatal.

The thought of any mother watching her child die of it was unbearable.

'He was in the best possible hospital,' said Jemima, sounding almost cold in her effort to keep control of her voice. 'But there was nothing they could do. They amputated first one leg to try to contain the infection and then the other. But there wasn't any hope, you see. I'd always known that, but somehow I couldn't stop thinking it would be different for Pipp. It should have been.'

'I am so sorry,' said Willow, her mind full of her own all-consuming anxiety for Lucinda's minor discomfort and mildly raised temperature. The thought of what her death could mean made it impossible to say anything else.

'You've got children, haven't you?' said Jemima after a while.

Willow nodded. 'Well, one. I'm too old to have any more.'

'Me too,' said Jemima. 'Now.'

'It must have been terrible for you.'

'Yes. I went mad for a while,' she said calmly as though she were discussing the price of petrol. But when she looked at Willow, her eyes gave a hint of the full horror of what had happened to her. 'And, you see, that's why I feel so guilty.'

After a moment Willow thought it would be safe—and not too rude—to say again that she did not understand.

'No?' said Jemima, looking as though her head was aching. 'No, I suppose you couldn't. I'll try to explain. Although if…I may not get it out without crying. I haven't much practice in talking about this to anyone and even now…'

'Don't worry about crying,' said Willow, beginning to feel unpleasantly conscious that she was receiving confidences under false pretences. The fact that Jemima had decided to trust her because of her novels and the short, polite letter she had once written made her deceit seem even worse. Reminding herself of why she had come, Willow hardened her heart. 'Since my daughter, Lucinda, was born a couple of years ago I've done more crying than in the whole of the rest of my life,' she said. 'It doesn't shock me any longer, or even seem particularly weak.'

Jemima managed a small smile.

'Good. Well, you see, I wasn't much help to Andrew after Philip died. It took us both so differently. We couldn't talk to each other at all then. I thought his...the way he tackled it seemed so morbid. I wanted to remember Pipp as he was, running and laughing and chasing his friends up and down the staircases. I wanted to remember the happy healthy child I'd loved. Andrew couldn't forget the dying one or what was happening to him—his body and, perhaps, his soul—afterwards. He kept reading bits of Frazer's *Golden Bough* and telling me about all the old funerary customs. It was too horrible. I felt as though I could never get away from death and...and rottingness, and I wouldn't talk to him any more. I couldn't.'

'I'm not surprised,' said Willow gently.

'But because I wouldn't talk, Andrew started to come home later and later every day, and then afterwards I found out where he'd been.'

Willow thought it better not to say yet again that she did not understand. She waited, feeling the other woman's anguish, and quite unable to do anything about it.

'He'd been at the hospital,' Jemima said eventually. She sounded despairing. 'It seems he'd got it into his head that Pipp was lonely—had been lonely as he was dying all those horrible days—and that the only reparation he could make for that was to do something for all the other children who were dying alone in that hospital. I couldn't bear it when he talked about it. I'd have done anything to stop him.'

'Anyone would have,' said Willow carefully. 'It must

have been so hard for you to take on his sadness when you
had all your own to deal with.'

'Perhaps. But it must have been the same for him. I didn't
realise that then, but I've seen it so vividly since and felt
so guilty. At the time I blamed him for making it worse for
me and shut him out and wouldn't—couldn't—help, and
hated his not helping me. I left him with nowhere to go
except that place full of suffering, dying children. I found
out later that he used to haunt the place, trying to help them.
But he was too unhappy to be able to do anything good for
anyone. In the end the nurses told him that he was frightening the children and ordered him to stop coming. After
that he'd just sit for hours on a bench on the other side of
the road, sometimes even in the pouring rain, staring at the
door Pipp had been taken in by.'

Jemima stopped talking and just looked at Willow. Tears
welled again and spilled over on to her cheeks. She sniffed
and wiped her face with the backs of both hands. The tears
kept falling.

'It must have been torture for you both,' said Willow,
hating the inadequacy of her comment but unable to think
of anything better to say.

Jemima nodded. 'It was, which is why I didn't understand
for so long.'

'Didn't understand what?'

'That Andrew wouldn't say what he was doing on the
night of the crash because he wanted to protect me from the
knowledge that he'd been sitting outside the hospital again,
trying to find a way to bear Pipp's death because I couldn't
help him and kept accusing him of all sorts of things…'

Willow shook her head, unable to deal with the savagery
of the other woman's pain.

'I'm sure that's why the lawyers couldn't find anyone in
the office to say he'd been there all evening. I think he'd
been sitting on that bloody bench outside the hospital. And

he wouldn't tell the police because of me. It's my fault he's in prison.'

Thinking that Emma would have recognised excessive and unnecessary guilt in Jemima, Willow said directly, 'You mustn't blame yourself for what your husband did or said or didn't do.'

'There isn't anyone else to blame.'

Willow thought Jemima was in serious need of psychiatric help, perhaps not surprisingly, but she could not think how to tell her so without sounding insufferably interfering.

'Except Andrew himself,' she said at last, making Jemima start in shock at the sound of her voice. 'He chose, Jemima. He chose what to do. And if that's what he was doing that night, he must have chosen not to say anything about it. People often do feel guilty when someone they love has died. Perhaps confessing to something he hadn't done was a way of helping himself deal with that.'

By the time Willow had finished speaking, hoping that she had not sounded as patronising as she feared, Jemima's face had regained much of its self-contained expression and her tears had stopped. She shook her head and said with a resumption of the confident coolness that must have been used to defend her greatest vulnerabilities, 'Perhaps. But it was me who'd made him feel guilty. You see, I'd shrieked at him that my breakdown was his fault, that if he hadn't kept talking about Pipp's death every single day and kept us both from putting it where it ought to have been—in the past—I'd have been all right. I told him that he was tormenting me, making me feel as though he was killing Pipp over and over again.'

She stopped, looked out of the window and seemed to shudder. After a moment she collected the courage to go on.

'I said I never wanted to hear any more about his horrible memorial garden or his self-indulgent trips to the hospital and that if he ever mentioned Pipp's name to me again I'd leave him. I'd gone mad, you see,' she added almost brightly. 'Now, shall I show you the garden?'

'Yes, please.' Willow felt an urge to touch Jemima's hand or arm, but she resisted it. They were not on the sort of terms that would have allowed such intimacy.

BACK IN LONDON that evening, waiting for Tom's nightly telephone call, Willow wrote to Emma, giving a vivid account of everything she had seen and heard at the Lutterworths' house. When she was halfway through the letter, at about twenty past nine, Tom rang. They talked for an expensive but satisfying forty minutes. He still did not know when he was likely to get home and Willow tried not to let herself feel any of the wholly unfair resentment she had ascribed to Jemima Lutterworth.

Willow reminded herself that she did not resent Tom's work in the least. She admired it and she knew perfectly well that he had to be in Strasbourg. Besides, she was entirely capable of living happily on her own for a week or two with Lucinda—or much longer. She had plenty of friends if she wanted company. None of it changed her feelings, and she had become honest enough by then to admit that she wished he did not have to be away for quite so long.

SEVEN

Emma turned over the third sheet of Willow's immensely long letter to read:

And so you see I liked her. I'm not surprised she can't bear the garden her husband made in memory of the boy. She took me down to see it, and I could hardly bear it either. In a way it's very beautiful, but *so* depressing. It's just a green court, rectangular and bounded by dense, perfectly trimmed yew hedges. In the middle is a statue of a young boy—not one of those pseudo-classical marble jobs one sees in stately-home gardens, but stainless steel and very modern, almost abstract. It's brilliant—the nearest thing to the concept of misery in three dimensions that I've ever seen—but peculiar. Oh, yes: and on the plinth is a quote from Blake: 'Everything that lives / Lives not alone, nor for itself.' Which I take it means that Lutterworth just couldn't separate the fact of the boy's death from anything in the rest of his life.

The statue is in the middle of four paths that cut the lawn into sections. Each of those is guarded by a pencil-like cypress tree, quite small and very dark. You know, the sort that grows in Italian cemeteries.

You'll probably be wondering what's got into me, but I don't think I've ever been so affected by a place. I've never felt upset in graveyards, perhaps because there's something peaceful about then, as though they're an acknowledgment of lives that have been lived and are over. There's been a kind of acceptance

in all the ones I've ever visited, however sad they
seem. I think that must be it. There's no peace or sense
of reconciliation in Lutterworth's garden, just anger
and that terrible unhappiness. Perhaps I imagined it all
or have got sentimental because I sympathised with
Jemima so much.

Having met her, I'm even more interested in her husband than I was from what Jane told us. I won't go on
about her now, because this letter's getting much too
long, but if you want to ring me at some suitable moment (and I shall expect you to reverse the charges),
I'll tell you all the rest. Or, better still, drop in when
you're next in London. I'd love to see you. And I'd
love to know how you're getting on with Andrew L—
and everything else about the thesis.

By the way, Tom sends his love. We had a good
long talk this evening and things seem to be going
marginally better in Strasbourg. Hope all is well with
you, and that Jag is continuing friendly. I would love
to meet him, too. Why not bring him for a weekend
soon? Just ring and say when you'd like to come.

                                        Love,
                                        Willow.

PS This may be quite unnecessary, but I thought I
ought to pass on a warning from Jane. She said that
this man Hal Marstall she introduced you to is well
known for charming people he thinks might give him
useful information. Jane said a lot of thoroughly intelligent, sensible people have fallen for the charm and
then been dumped as soon as he'd got what he wanted.

Emma put the letter down on her desk next to Andrew
Lutterworth's polite refusal to see her and wondered why
she did not feel more grateful for what Willow had done.

After a moment she recognised that she did not feel grateful at all. Quite the opposite: what she felt was something pretty much like outrage that Willow had horned in on her work without warning or explanation.

Well aware that she was being absurd, and horribly grudging, Emma told herself that Willow could possibly have been trying to rub her nose in her comparative lack of experience—or her poverty. Willow's instruction to reverse the charges the next time Emma telephoned was a perfectly normal example of her usual generosity, not a suggestion that Emma could not afford telephone calls. And even if it had meant that, so what? It would have been almost true.

After a while she managed to laugh at herself and took the time to reread Willow's letter in a more suitably grateful spirit. As she reached the end of it she realised that, helpful though it was, it was also a kind of challenge.

When she had first discovered that Andrew Lutterworth was not prepared to talk to her, she had considered dropping his case and looking for something else on which to build her thesis. Now that Willow had taken a hand, that was no longer an option. Absurd though she might be, Emma knew that she was going to have to prove herself capable of finding out everything she needed to know about him and without asking for any more help from Willow.

The difficulty was that Willow would have been exceedingly useful. Not only could she pick her way through any tangle of fact and supposition better than anyone else, but she was also in a position to introduce Emma to all sorts of people who might have provided the information she was going to need.

'Too bad,' she said aloud, determined to get the necessary facts from other sources.

The most immediately useful would probably have been Lutterworth's colleagues at Hill, Snow, Parkes. Emma herself knew no one who worked there, but she was fairly sure that her half-brother would. A lot of his friends had become accountants; some of them must have found their way to Hill, Snow, Parkes.

Emma wondered whether she could bring herself to go to him for help. She loathed having anything to do with him and disliked the idea of adding to his conviction that she was incapable of running her own life. On the other hand it was hard to see how asking for a simple introduction could lead to any serious trouble, and she really was going to have to get over her stupidity about him soon. Shrugging, she reached for the telephone and dialled his number.

'Hello,' she said when he answered. 'It's me, Emma. How are you?'

'Fine. Fine. What about you? Sick of fossicking about in filthy prisons yet?' He laughed with a familiar—and horribly patronising—assumption of mateyness that made her ears sing.

'Certainly not. I find them fascinating,' she said, lying. 'And they're not that filthy, you know. Nowadays prisons are remarkably clean. But that's by the way. Anthony, I've been wondering whether you could give me a little help.'

'I don't see why not,' he said. 'What is it you're after?'

'Just that I want an introduction to someone at Hill, Snow, Parkes, and I wondered if you knew anyone there.'

'Oh, you don't want to go to them, Sweet Thing. They'd be far too expensive for you, especially now that you're wasting your money on this degree nonsense.'

Even though she had always detested the nickname Anthony had bestowed on her years earlier, Emma said nothing. Having failed to make him understand why it irked her so much to be addressed as 'Thing', she had never even tried to explain her distaste for the word 'sweet'. It was the least suitable description of the way she felt when she was anywhere near him.

'Look, tell me what the problem is and I'll have a word

with my own accountants. Then if they need to talk to you direct, I can put them on to you and you won't have to bother about the bill.' He chuckled. 'I don't suppose whatever it is will take them long, and I'd be delighted to underwrite any fee they might decide to charge.'

'That's very generous of you,' she said, trying to make herself feel grateful. 'But actually it's not professional advice I want. Do you in fact know anyone at Hill, Snow?'

'No, I don't think I do. What is it you're after then, if it's not accountancy?'

'I'm afraid I can't tell you that. It's to do with a case I'm looking into and I have to be discreet. I'm sure you can understand, Anthony. I'm sorry to have bothered you. I hope I didn't take you away from anything too important.'

'It's always a pleasure to talk to you, Sweet Thing. You know that. And I'm hardly ever busy on Monday mornings. I'm glad you rang. We must make a date for you to come to stay. I miss you now that you've abandoned us for the oiks in St Albans. When can you come?'

Emma thought of the days when one of Anthony's favourite tricks had been to shut her in the big cupboard in the nursery and tell her that she would stay locked in until she died of starvation. Each time he let her out he told her that he had relented 'just this once' but that she mustn't expect such mercy again. She had always nodded, promising good behaviour, swearing not to tell anyone, begging him to let her go, but nothing she could offer him would protect her from the next stage in his game. Taking her right forearm between his hands, he would twist in opposite directions. He called it a Chinese burn and told her that it was only the first stage of what he would do to her if she ever talked. And now he claimed to miss her. It was horrible.

'I'll be a bit too busy for weekends away until I've broken the back of my thesis,' she said, furious with herself for still not being able to confront him with her memories and tell him what she thought of him. 'Give Grania my love, won't you? I hope she's OK.'

'Of course, Sweet Thing. But I'll get you back here in the end. Now don't forget to let me know if you ever need anything. 'Bye for now.'

Emma put down the receiver and rubbed her hands together, noticing how badly they had been sweating. It was absurd to react as though she were still frightened of him. He had no power over her any longer, and it was nearly twenty years since he had actually done anything, but she rarely managed a conversation with him without remembering the worst times.

Siblings often fight, she told herself yet again, and lots of boys find their younger sisters exasperating and devise all sorts of torments for them.

Shuddering at the memories she could not exorcise or rationalise, however hard she tried, she told herself that she must have been mad to set them off again by ringing him up. She should have known better. Ashamed of herself, feeling thoroughly cowardly and altogether absurd, she picked up her pen and started to write:

Dearest Willow,

Thank you for your long letter. You shouldn't have bothered to do my work for me when you've got such a lot of your own. But it was kind of you to take so much trouble. Lutterworth's refused to take a polygraph test, but I'm confident that I can find out enough from other people to use the case as we planned. I hope Lucinda's better and that you're well. I'd love to come for another weekend and will talk to Jag. I'll ring asap.

Love,
Em.

Hoping that she had been properly grateful rather than revoltingly hypocritical, Emma took the card out to the nearest postbox.

When she got back to her room, she cleared her mind of everything but her determination to understand Andrew Lutterworth. As she reread Willow's account of his son's death, Emma could not help wondering why on earth his lawyers had not used it in his defence or at least in mitigation. Necrotising fasciitis was so rare and so horrifying that anyone who had had to watch his child die of it would have aroused sympathy. And most men convicted of killing, even by means of dangerous driving, would have wanted all the sympathy they could get.

When the telephone rang, she was so deeply involved that for an instant she could not think what the noise meant. She shook her head as though that could sort out her muddled thoughts and picked up the receiver.

'Hello?'

'Emma?' said a cheerful voice. 'Hi, it's Hal, here. Hal Marstall. D'you remember?'

'Of course, I do. How nice!' She felt quite breathless. 'Sorry to sound so weird. I was in the middle of something and my mind's sliding about it still. How are you?'

'Fine. I was really just ringing to see whether there was anything else I could tell you about the shit Lutterworth.'

'You are kind. Actually there is. I need to find out who his solicitors are. D'you happen to know?'

'I do, in fact. Bricton and Bromere. They don't do much crime. I suspect he went to them because he'd dealt with them on his clients' business. They're one of the big city firms used by the sort of firms he worked for, and they do have a small crime department.'

'Mainly for fraud, I suppose?'

Hal laughed. 'Spot on as usual, Ms Gnatche. Yes, but they manage to deal with other sorts of crime and misdemeanours. Careless driving is not that much rarer than fraud, even if most perpetrators are luckier than Lutterworth in hitting walls and bollards rather than people. Why d'you want to know?'

'He's declined to be interviewed for my thesis. I thought I might get hold of his lawyer and see if I couldn't persuade him or her to put on a little pressure.'

'You'll be lucky. Those sort of firms are not only utterly clamlike, but also impregnable. Even worse than auditors.'

'Thanks for the encouragement.'

'Not at all.' Hal laughed and she could not help joining in. 'Look, I've got to come up your way this week on the trail of a story. Any chance of seeing you? Taking you out to dinner, perhaps?'

'How nice!' said Emma automatically. In the days when she had been trying to live the way her mother wanted, she had always obediently accepted invitations unless they were from people she positively could not bear and when she was not thinking she reverted to the old ways.

'Great. I'll check out the local restaurants with one of my mates who does a food column and pick somewhere really good.'

'You are kind, Hal, but...' Emma remembered the post-script to Willow's letter.

'But what?' He sounded worried, which disarmed her.

'Nothing. I was just going to say that I'm not all that keen on elaborate restaurants, you know with sixteen different sorts of plates and triple tablecloths and all that. But I don't want to sound ungrateful.'

'You couldn't. And I agree with you. But I do like good food.'

She laughed and felt reasonably confident of her ability to resist any attempt to charm her into indiscretion.

'Me too,' she said firmly. 'It'll be really good to see you. Thank you, Hal.'

'I'll ring when I know for sure which day, but it's likely to be either Wednesday or Thursday.'

'Oh, help. Wednesday's out,' said Emma, remembering in time that she and Jag had arranged to go to see a film together. 'But Thursday would be great.'

'I'll see if I can swing it and let you know. 'Bye for now.'

'Goodbye,' she said. It was some time before she realised that she was still holding the receiver and that she was smiling.

THE NEXT DAY a large brown envelope was sitting slantwise in her pigeonhole when she went past it on her way out to get some breakfast. She took the packet with her and opened it as she was drinking coffee and eating a stale Danish pastry, to find a thick pile of typescript with a handwritten note on top, which read:

Dear Emma.

It struck me last week that you might find a transcript of the trial useful and it was sent up from the dead storage just after we finished speaking. I've had it copied for you.

I've sorted my diary and will be with you on Thursday, sometime around eight. Ring me if that's a problem.

Good luck and good hunting.

Hal

Grateful for his help, she castigated herself all over again for having been silly enough to have objected to Willow's. There seemed no point eating the rest of the Danish pastry, which was sticky and yet tasted dusty. She finished the coffee, wiped her fingers and stuffed the typescript back in its envelope.

Back in her room, she cleared a good space on the desk

and settled down to read the transcript of Andrew Lutterworth's trial.

An hour later she stopped reading and turned back to look again at a brief question-and-answer session between Lutterworth's counsel and the police officer who had been the first at the scene of the crash. Emma had always known that most of the evidence against Lutterworth had been circumstantial, but, having read everything that had been said in court, she was even more surprised that the jury had been persuaded to convict him. As far as she could see, the only fact connecting him to the crash was his ownership of the car.

'If a man is really innocent until he's been proved guilty,' she muttered aloud, 'then Lutterworth *is* innocent. They should never have convicted him. Never. However much they disliked him.'

Skipping ahead again to the judge's summing up, she read a fair description of what little evidence there was and a strongly worded warning that the defendant had no need to prove anything.

No grounds for an appeal there, Emma thought. It must have been the confession that did for him.

He had signed it under caution, and so it was admissible evidence even though he had later withdrawn it. The jury had not only been given the text of it in court, they had also been able to listen to the tape of his voice actually telling the police that he was guilty.

Emma could hardly bear the frustration of being unable to talk to him directly. Without knowing what levers the police had used or how they had made him feel at the moment when he decided to confess, she would not be able to get any further unless she could persuade the police officers themselves to tell her what they had done. That did not seem impossible. After all, they had got the result they wanted at the trial and might well be prepared to discuss the likely reasons for Lutterworth's change of plea with a bona fide researcher.

Having cut herself off from Willow's help, Emma realised that she could hardly ask Tom to intervene on her behalf as she might otherwise have done.

Well, she told herself, it'll probably do me good to fix it for myself; it'll certainly serve me right.

There were four police officers on her course, three men and one woman. She thought of each in turn and eventually decided to play safe and go for Janet Ranton. They loathed each other, but for some reason Janet seemed more approachable than any of the men.

There was to be a meeting in Professor Bonmotte's rooms that afternoon, at which one of the social workers was to read a paper on the psychology of serial sex offenders. Emma had not been planning to go because she had decided never to work with sex offenders, but she changed her mind.

Dressed in unmockable, unthreatening black jeans and a long beige cotton sweater, she walked through the campus towards Bonmotte's rooms just before three. It was a clear afternoon and most of the rain clouds that had been looming over the depressing concrete and brick buildings for weeks had gone. The air was almost warm and the tightly curled spears of the first daffodils were just beginning to show signs of yellow.

Emma heard a motorbike roaring to a halt and looked round in case it was Jag's, but the couple who dismounted and pulled off their helmets were strange to her.

There were only two other people with Bonmotte when she got to his rooms: Ralph Fairoak and Fran Tixall, the social worker who was to read the paper. They both nodded to Emma in a perfectly amicable way and carried on with their conversation. Bonmotte, a short stout man in his early forties, got to his feet to greet her.

'How's it going?' he asked quietly, when he had moved out of the way of the other two.

'Not so badly. I'm following your excellent advice and not giving up, even though my latest hope has just refused to talk to me.'

'That's the death-by-driving man, is it?'

'Yes. A friend of mine has talked to his wife and been given some useful background information. It doesn't get me very far, but it is a start; and I've decided that I must carry on for a while longer even though he won't talk.'

'Good. Anything I can do yet?'

'I don't think so. Unless… I think I've got to talk to the original investigating officers, and I'm not sure how best to approach them. I thought of asking Janet Ranton for help.' As she saw Bonmotte's eyebrows arch up into his forehead, Emma added, 'D'you think that's completely mad?'

'Not completely.' He laughed. 'I just wonder why you don't try an easier target. One of the men. They're much better disposed towards you, as you very well know.'

'Are they?'

'Yes.' Bonmotte's dry voice and private smile were lost on Emma, who had no very high opinion of her physical attractions. 'Ben Wrexham told me he's planning to come this afternoon. Why not have a word with him?'

'OK, I will,' said Emma. 'Thanks.'

'Pleasure. There's tea over there. Help yourself,' he said as the door opened to admit one of Emma's least favourite colleagues.

She collected a cup of tea and a small handful of biscuits and sat down, listening to the conversation between Ralph and Fran, which was beginning to sound acrimonious. Feeling a hand on her shoulder a little later, she looked up and back to see the dark, laughing face of Ben Wrexham.

'The prof said you wanted a word.'

'Oh, lovely,' said Emma, smiling up at him. 'He's absolutely right. I did actually want to ask you something.'

Seeing Wrexham's deepening amusement, she stiffened her emotional sinews and went on less fluffily, 'I need some advice about the best way of getting hold of two police officers who interviewed a man who was later convicted of causing death by dangerous driving.'

'What's your interest in the case?' Wrexham searched her face. 'D'you know the driver?'

'Certainly not. It's for my thesis on lie detection. This is a man who confessed and then withdrew his confession. Luckily the trial went ahead all right and the jury convicted him. But from everything I've heard—and read in the transcript—it's pretty clear that they wouldn't have produced a guilty verdict if there'd been no confession. I want to find out first what made him confess and then why he started lying.'

'To get the conviction quashed as unsafe?' Wrexham was still frowning, as though quite unimpressed by Emma's carefully dropped hints of sympathy for the police and prosecution. She shook her head.

'God forbid! I'm wholly disinterested. I just want to know what happened. In any case, this man hasn't got an appeal going. He's coming up for parole: this week, I think. It's academic now.'

'And if he doesn't get parole?'

Emma shrugged. 'He'll be out in a relatively short time anyway. Don't they automatically get out when they've done two-thirds of the sentence?'

'If they're in for four years or more.'

'There you are then. He was given exactly four. I really am not trying to rubbish any of your colleagues. I just want to find a case I can use for my thesis: one in which I can find out what questions the police asked him and what he said to them and what it was that made them so sure he was guilty.'

'Whatever it was, it'll have been real. They'd never have charged him otherwise,' said Wrexham firmly.

Emma raised her eyebrows. Wrexham shook his head, adding, 'It's hard enough getting a conviction for someone you yourself saw do something serious, without inviting grief by trying to push a weak case on the CPS.'

'Yes, I suppose it must be. How's your thesis going, by the way? I should have asked.'

'So-so.'

'I ought to remember what it is, but I'm afraid I can't.'

'If you ever knew,' said Wrexham, laughing at her again, but more pleasantly than usual. 'I'm working on the applications of more widespread DNA testing and the design of a much bigger multi-force database.'

'Like what? Testing the entire population at birth and establishing a national register?' suggested Emma in much the same tone he had used to suggest that she wanted to gather information for an appeal.

'I wish. Oh, how I wish. But the civil-liberties crowd would never wear that. We can't even do it with finger-prints.'

'I should hope not,' said Emma before she remembered that she wanted him on her side. 'Although I wouldn't mind giving prints and a DNA sample. Would you?'

'Nope. Looks like we're ready to start.'

Having found him more friendly than she had expected. Emma hoped that he had felt something similar enough to give her the help she needed. She smiled warmly at him. He looked rather surprised, but Fran got up just then to read her paper and neither of them had time to say anything more.

Emma tried to concentrate, but she could not help think-ing more about Andrew Lutterworth and his lies than about any of Fran's sex offenders. One particularly sickening case broke through her preoccupations for a time and she found herself more in sympathy with Wrexham's wish for a national DNA register than she had been before.

The rapist Fran was describing had committed at least five serious assaults before he had been caught, and it turned out that he had a history of lesser offences, dating back to a conviction for the theft of a woman's underclothes from a washing line when he was fourteen. If his DNA had been included in a register that could have been consulted by the police, he would have been caught, if not before any of the rapes then at least after the first. And the fifth of his victims would still be alive. As it was, he had strangled her.

Turning to see how Wrexham was taking the account, Emma caught his eye and exchanged another smile with him.

'See what I mean?' he said afterwards, while Fran was arguing hotly with one of the psychologists about the fundamental causes of violence towards women.

'I see exactly what you mean,' said Emma, 'and I agree with it as much as I always did. Look, how should I set about contacting your colleagues?'

'D'you know the names of the officers?' Emma nodded. 'OK. Give me details of them, their station, and the case, and I'll give them a bell. Is it urgent?'

'It's not exactly life and death,' she said, ripping a sheet out of her notebook and writing down the names of the Buckinghamshire officers who had taken charge of Lutterworth after his arrest by the City police. 'But the sooner I talk to them, the sooner I can sort myself out and get going on some useful work.'

'I'll see what I can do,' he said as she handed him the page. 'Be in touch.'

'Thanks, Ben.' Emma saw the time and remembered Jag. 'I'm going to be late. I must go. But you've been really kind. Thank you. 'Bye.'

As she emerged from the building at a run, she saw Jag

waiting outside. He was leaning peacefully against the bike, reading, and he seemed quite unworried that Emma was fifteen minutes later than she had said she would be. Once again the enormous contrast between him and Anthony delighted her. If anyone had kept Anthony waiting for a quarter of an hour, he would have made the rest of the day hell for them. He had completely ruined one Christmas for everyone by savaging Emma for arriving at her mother's house two hours late. The fact that there had been a blizzard that day and the roads to Gloucestershire had been clogged with traffic had seemed to her a reasonable excuse, but apparently it was not good enough for Anthony. He had laid into her verbally when she arrived and spent the rest of the time sulking. Emma, who had already apologised to her mother and been instantly forgiven, had been furious to see how everyone else in the house had spent the time coaxing Anthony out of his sulks instead of telling him to behave himself.

Jag could not have been more different. As Emma apologised profusely for her lateness, he looked at her as though she were mad. That made her feel so safe she could have kissed him.

'It's a nice day,' he said. 'I'd have been reading this wherever I was. You were doing something else. No skin off my nose, Sunshine. Let's go.'

He handed her the spare helmet. As she was buckling it on, she saw Ben Wrexham coming out of the building still arguing with Fran. He noticed Emma and she almost laughed to see the surprise in his eyes as he saw her straddling the huge bike. Jag saw it too and Emma thought he was enjoying it as much as she. He revved the engine even more noisily than usual and set off with panache.

Well, why not? she asked herself.

There was nothing she could say while the engine was filling the space between them with sound, but as soon as they reached the house where he lodged and were able to communicate again, she put a hand on Jag's arm and said, 'My friend Willow keeps urging me to go and see her again. If I went this weekend, would you come with me?'

'Sure. I'd like to see her in the flesh.'

'You won't be disappointed. At least I hope not. I'll ring her to fix it as soon as I get back. I suppose she might be busy, but she did…I'll let you know.'

'Great. Look, are you really sold on this movie?'

'Why?'

'Someone said it was overrated and I thought maybe we should just eat and talk instead. But I don't mind. Whatever you want.'

'Eat and talk sounds good to me. Where?'

'I've got plenty of food here,' he said casually. 'I thought it would be good to be on our own, but if you'd rather go out somewhere, just say.'

'No. I'd like to stay here,' she said with unusual emphasis. She slipped her hand between his elbow and his ribs.

He looked down at her quickly, seriously, and then he smiled as though his facial muscles would stretch for ever.

'Good. That makes two of us. Come on up.'

She had always liked his room, which was much bigger and better proportioned than any of the ones on campus, but she had never seen it looking so tidy. There were white narcissi in a green jug on the table, every surface looked newly dusted, and there were no piles of sports clothes by the door awaiting his next visit to the local launderette.

'It looks lovely,' she said, smiling at him and holding out her arms.

For a dreadful second he did nothing. She thought she must have misinterpreted all his signals and wondered how she was going to retrieve the situation. Then he leaned towards her and let her hug him. After a while, he began very gently to kiss her neck. At first she felt only relief that he seemed to want her as much as she wanted him, but then other sensations began to take over. As though he could feel them, he pulled back a little way to say, 'Let's go to bed, Emma.'

Neither of them said anything else for a while, but then they had no need to talk. He seemed to have an almost miraculous knowledge of her and responded to everything she did as though she, too, knew precisely what he needed.

'Jag,' she said urgently much later. 'Jag.'

'I'm here,' he said, as breathless as she.

LATER, when they had showered and dressed, he led her with rather more ceremony to the round table in the corner and invited her to sit down while he fetched their food. She noticed belatedly that as well as the narcissi, which were smelling glorious, there were sparklingly polished wine glasses, plates and cutlery neatly laid for two on the green-and-white checked cloth.

He had bought a crisp New Zealand Sauvignon for them to drink and a selection of good charcuterie with a big mixed salad. Those were followed by an apple flan that must have come from a serious French patisserie. It was very good and very simple, and Emma enjoyed it all. She realised that she felt utterly at home.

EIGHT

ON THE WAY BACK to campus the next morning, Emma found herself wishing that she was not committed to dinner with Hal Marstall. After what she and Jag had just shared, it seemed absurd to be going out with someone else and, in some way she did not quite understand, almost wrong.

When they got to her room she switched on the kettle for coffee and started to tell Jag about Hal's invitation. She need not have worried. All Jag said was that he hoped she would enjoy herself and that, if she felt like calling him when she got in after dinner, he would be dead chuffed.

Dead chuffed herself that he was such an unpossessive lover, she spent most of the day in the university library, reviewing all the published literature on false confessions in search of support for some of her own ideas. When she went back to her room to change for dinner with Hal, she was amazed to find a note from Ben Wrexham in her pigeonhole. He had already contacted Detective Inspector Joe Podley, one of the officers who had interviewed Andrew Lutterworth, and discovered that Podley had been promoted and moved to the Met. According to Ben's note, Podley was prepared to talk to Emma if she could get herself to London. The best time for him was around 5.30 in the afternoon, and the best day of the week was Friday.

Hardly able to believe that it could be so easy, Emma rang the telephone number Ben had added at the bottom of his note and was quickly put through to DI Podley himself. He told her that he could not talk for long, but would certainly meet her for a drink the following day. Sounding efficient and very busy, he gave her the address of a pub near his station and rang off.

Emma went out in a satisfactorily cheerful mood to meet Hal in the restaurant his friend had recommended. The food proved to be good, Hal was as charming as she remembered, and he did not seem to be probing her for any information about anyone except herself, and that only in a friendly way. Even so, she could not forget the warning Willow had passed on from Jane and thought carefully about everything she said, always countering Hal's questions with others of her own. He answered them so freely and amusingly that by the end of the evening she had almost acquitted him of an ulterior motive.

She politely declined his offer to escort her back to her room, thanked him for giving her such a good dinner, and vaguely agreed to see him again in London some time. He kissed her cheek and waited with her until the bus arrived. As it lurched away, she looked back and saw him standing under a streetlamp, waving, and wondered what on earth he could possibly want from her.

Back in her own room, she went straight to the telephone and rang Willow to find out whether the invitation to take Jag to stay at the Mews was still open.

'Of course it is,' said Willow. 'When d'you want to come?'

'Well, I was wondering whether there was any chance of this weekend? I know it's almost no notice, and do please say if it's inconvenient, but there's a man I've got to talk to about the Lutterworth case, and he could see me tomorrow afternoon and so it seems silly not to take advantage of it. But if—'

'Calm down,' said Willow, obviously smiling. 'It'll be lovely to see you both and this weekend's fine. I'll expect you in time for dinner. OK?'

'More than OK,' said Emma, deeply ashamed of her resentment at Willow's attempt to interfere in her work. 'It's really generous of you. Thank you. I can't wait to see you.'

'Me, too. I'm so glad you rang.'

When they had said goodbye, Emma dialled Jag's number.

'Hello, Sunshine,' he said, sounding as easily friendly as he had always done. 'Good meal?'

'Amazing actually. And quite fun, too.'

'Great. Did you get anything useful about Lutterworth?'

'Not really, no. We mostly talked about quite other things.'

'Oh, you mean you were flirting. I see.' Jag was not quite laughing, but it was clear from the sound of his voice that he was amused.

'Some of the time,' Emma said lightly. 'It's so much easier than real talk when you don't know someone very well.'

'Ah, you're a rare creature.'

'Why?'

'Much honester than most women I've known.'

'Well, that seems only fair. You're much more straightforward than any man I've ever been out with before. It's wonderful, so much easier even than flirting. Less exhausting, too.'

There was a short pause and then Jag said seriously: 'I'm not always. Don't...'

'Don't what?' she said, suddenly worried.

'Don't go thinking I'm something I'm not. I'm as mixed up as everyone else.'

'Jag, what are you talking about?'

'You said I was straightforward. I'm not, Emma, however much I try to be. No one is.'

'I'd have said you got closer to it than most,' she said, devoutly hoping that she was right. 'And you don't go in for winding people up or punishing them for things they don't know they've done or mocking them or making them feel uncomfortable—which are all the things I really hate.'

'No, I don't do any of those. At least I hope not. But I do plenty else, often things that I'm not completely aware of until a long time later. Don't make me out to be some kind of hero.'

'Without wanting to be too sentimental,' she said, trying to sound like Mrs Rusham, which was difficult, 'you do seem a bit heroic just at the moment.'

He laughed aloud then, but he did not say anything. After a moment, Emma went on, 'By the way, is this weekend too soon for our trip to Willow? I've got to go to London anyway to see one of the cops who grilled Lutterworth and so it would all fit very neatly. Willow says she can have us—if you'd like to come.'

'If you want me to be there, yes, I'd like it very much.'

'Goody good.'

'Do we get to share a room in her house?' asked Jag, laughing at her nursery expression.

'Probably,' said Emma, who was not quite sure whether she wanted Willow to know that she and Jag were lovers.

'Well that's OK then. Shall we take the bike?'

'I hadn't thought. Would you if you were going on your own?'

'Sure.'

'Then let's. Unless the times don't work for you. I've got to be near Knightsbridge by five thirty. Willow is expecting us to arrive in time for dinner, which in her house is always eight o'clock, and that leaves two and half hours for you to kill. Will you mind?'

'No. I can always find plenty to do once I've dropped you off,' said Jag. 'I'll pick you up at four. That should give us all the time we need. Dress warm: it gets cold on the motorway. 'Bye for now. Work well.'

'I will. Thanks, Jag.'

Emma put down the receiver, hoping that Willow and Jag would get on well together. The thought of his breezy open-air toughness, not to speak of his stubble, leathers and clanking boots, in the highly civilised surroundings of the Mews made her doubtful. Willow could be trusted to be much less hidebound than any of Emma's family, all of whom would be appalled by the thought that she was sleeping with a man like Jag, but there was no guarantee that she would like him. And Emma wanted them to like each other, and to understand why she should have such affection for them both.

JAG DROPPED EMMA at a pub on the borders of South Kensington and Knightsbridge a little before half past five. She pushed open the heavy, glazed doors, and almost stepped backwards as her ears were assaulted by the Friday-evening clamour. The small pub was already so full that all the chairs and stools were taken and people were standing in noisy groups, shedding the tension of their working week. She was not sure how she was going to be able to pick out Inspector Podley from the crowd. There were several men who seemed to be on their own and she felt absurdly shy about the idea of going up to one after the other to ask whether he was the right man.

Several of them were looking at her. Struggling to control her idiotic wish that she had asked Jag to come in with her, she let the door swing shut behind her and walked a few steps towards the bar. At least she could order herself a drink without looking as though she were accosting potential clients. Before she had caught the bartender's eye, a man of middle height with fading red hair and a bitterly twisted mouth slid out of one of the banquettes, leaving his coat to stop anyone else sitting in the space, and came towards her. He looked very fit indeed and rather angry.

'Emma Gnatche?' he said briskly. Even in that atmo-

sphere she could smell the whisky and cigar smoke he had
been swallowing.

'Yes. You must be Inspector Podley.'

'Joe. What can I get you to drink?'

'Let me buy them. What would you like?'

'Scotch then. Thank you.'

Emma ordered his drink and a half of lager for herself
and carried the glasses to his banquette. She noticed that
there were two cigar butts in the ashtray and realised that
he must have been in the pub for some time. The jukebox
behind her was playing some very noisy song she did not
recognise, and she had to lean forward to hear what Podley
was saying.

'Ben Wrexham told me that you're interested in Andrew
Lutterworth.'

'That's right. And he said you might be prepared to tell
me a bit about the case.'

Emma wished that she did not have to shout and was
contemplating putting some money into the jukebox herself
so that at least she could choose something that crashed and
thudded less. 'D'you remember much about it? I know it
was some time ago.'

'He wasn't a man you'd forget easily. But what exactly
is your interest?'

'Didn't Ben tell you?' she asked and, seeing that he had
not, proceeded to explain her thesis yet again. At the end
she added as tactfully as possible, 'And since one of my
principal aims is to explore the most productive ways in
which suspects can be persuaded to confess, I need to find
out how you managed to get Lutterworth to do it and what
you think it was that made him change his story later.'

'Wrexham said I could trust you,' said Joe Podley, looking at her over his glass. 'Since he was right about some of
the other things he said, perhaps I can believe this too.'

A hint of hidden laughter in his thin freckled face made Emma suddenly wary.

'What else did he tell you?' she asked, determined not to be sucked into anyone else's games.

Podley's mockery became even clearer as his lips relaxed and his eyes widened. He put down his drink and offered her an opened packet of cheese-and-onion crisps. Emma shook her head.

'He said you were the prettiest little thing I was likely to see even in these parts in a month of Sundays and not half as stupid—or as irritating—as you sound.'

Emma laughed. 'Oh, I like it. Thank you for that.'

'You're not offended?' He sounded surprised.

'No, amused,' she said. To her surprise, she realised that she meant it. Perhaps at long last she was getting over her fear of what the other criminologists said to each other about her. 'But forget about me for the moment and tell me about Lutterworth.'

'Where shall I start? What exactly do you want to know?'

'I suppose first of all, whether you were absolutely certain he was guilty.'

'Definitely,' said Podley at once. His eyes narrowed again, which made him look almost dangerous. 'Why should you doubt it?'

'Well...' said Emma, sensing power in him for the first time rather than just strength. 'Look, I'm not trying to be difficult—or criticise you or your colleagues, but there wasn't actually much hard evidence against him, was there?'

'There was enough. His alibi was off the wall, and there was no one to back it up. Besides there was no evidence of anyone else ever having driven the car.'

'Except the gloved smudges on the steering wheel, and all the hairs and fibres that didn't match his.'

'The gloved prints could just as easily have been made by him and the hairs and fibres by his passenger,' said Podley sharply enough to make Emma think that he, too, might not have been quite as certain as he would have her believe. 'He never claimed that he hadn't had other people in the car at various times and we didn't have the resources to track them all down in case there were some hairs that didn't belong to any of them. And how could you be sure he hadn't forgotten one? That's what his brief would have claimed if we'd gone down that road and it would all have been for nothing. Anyway, he was guilty. If you'd been there when we were interviewing him, you'd have seen it, too.'

'But how?' she asked, trying to show none of her instinctive distaste for such unverifiable assumptions.

'It's a gut feeling you get when you've been in the job for as long as I have. Comes from the way they look at you—or don't. Their eyes shift all over the place or else they fix on you and don't move. And then there's body language, too. And an air about them. Like I said, you can't miss it when you know what to look for.'

'What was Lutterworth like, apart from his miasma of guilt, then?'

'Typical of your usual dishonest senior City man. I haven't worked in fraud, but I've had friends who have, and their customers sound just like Lutterworth. They start off all arrogant: "How dare you insult me?" and all that. Then, when you've taken their ties, belts, braces and shoelaces and locked 'em up for a couple of hours, they disintegrate in front of your eyes and spill their guts. Particularly if you've searched them. And you always do with that sort. It breaks them down. And it's useful, too. They can have documents and credit cards stuck all over their bodies under those suits of theirs.'

'But Lutterworth wasn't arrested for fraud,' said Emma, intrigued by the insight into police work but determined to keep Podley to the point.

'True. But we did search him; and forensic took his clothes.'

'Even though they weren't the ones he'd been wearing during the day—or were they?'

Podley drank some whisky and appeared to be searching his memory.

'No. You're right. He was in jeans, by then, I think: what he'd put on when the City police picked him up for us. We got his suits later, all of them, including the one he said he'd been wearing. It was soaked through.' He laughed. 'Lutterworth pretended it was rainwater, but it can't have been. Even the lining was wet; not just damp. We thought he must've gone into the shower wearing the suit, either to get rid of some evidence—blood probably—or else to pretend it was the one he'd been wearing in the rain so that he could conceal the destruction of the real one. But we had it examined even so.'

'And was there any evidence?'

'Not as such, no. And there was too much dirt in the suit and too many chemical residues to establish whether the wet in it was rain or tapwater. But he drove that car. Don't you ever think otherwise. You should have seen him that night.'

'I wish I had,' said Emma pleasantly. 'Take me through the whole evening. That is, if you don't mind. From the moment he rang the station to report that his car had been stolen.'

'I don't know much about that. It was the local station near his office that took that call.' Podley finished his whisky but refused Emma's offer to get him some more. He lit another of the small cigars and then, belatedly, asked if she minded. Since she was a supplicant, she shook her head and smiled with all the male-soothing sweetness Anthony would have expected of her. Podley seemed to like it, too, and visibly relaxed.

'It was logged at ten forty-five, as far as I can remember,

and all the necessary details were recorded, but there's no way of knowing where he was when he made the call. He used his mobile, and you can't tell where their calls come from.'

'So when did you get him?' asked Emma, picking up her lager and trying to breathe in as little of his smoke as possible. 'If you can remember after all this time.'

'I got a mate to look up the old files when Wrexham told me what you wanted, so I should have most of the details you need. When we started interviewing Lutterworth he began by denying everything, sticking to his story about the theft of his vehicle. Oh, and we offered him a brief, of course, but he said he didn't want one.'

'Didn't that make you think he was telling the truth?'

'Why should it?'

'Come on, Inspector Podley,' said Emma with what she hoped was a friendly smile. 'I'm not that naïve. A man like Lutterworth, who must have had plenty of money and a lot of experience of lawyers? Of course he'd have got hold of one if he'd thought he was at any kind of risk.'

The smile was back in Podley's eyes. Looking at him, Emma wondered if he had ever considered having his eyelashes dyed. They would have looked a great deal better for some darkening, particularly with his pale-pink skin and washed-out blue eyes.

'It crossed my mind,' he admitted. 'But then I saw that he was so bloody arrogant he thought he'd get away with it. It wasn't until he grasped that we weren't going to fall for his grand manner that he realised he might be at risk.'

'And that was when he confessed, was it?' Podley nodded. 'Did he ask for a solicitor at that point?'

'Oddly enough, no. In fact it wasn't him at all. We were interrupted soon after that by the news that his brief had arrived, and I think he was as surprised as we were.'

Emma frowned, remembering Hal's suggestion of an influential mistress who might have been in the car with Lutterworth at the time of the crash. 'So who *had* sent for the lawyer?'

'His wife, I think.'

'He rang her, did he, in his one telephone call?'

'Yup. Or one of our men did it. I can't remember. But Lutterworth would have been asked who he wanted contacted and it was her.'

'And when exactly did he withdraw his confession? Was it as soon as he had talked to his lawyer?' asked Emma, and then answered the question herself. 'No, it wasn't, was it? You were all still expecting him to plead guilty at the trial. What happened at the committal?'

'The usual. He confirmed his name and address. That's all he was required to do. And the magistrates decided that there was a case to answer, sent him for trial at the Crown Court and set bail. All perfectly normal.' Podley looked down at his watch.

He had been cooperative and polite, but Emma realised that if she wanted to get anything useful out of him she would have to think up some more intelligent questions and ask them quickly.

'Would it be possible for me to have a copy of the interview tapes? I imagine you must have taped it.'

'Naturally we did, but we can't go handing those out. Even to researchers like you. Sorry.' He did not look particularly apologetic.

'OK,' she said at once, smiling to show that she was not going to press him or even try to make any kind of trouble. She realised that three-year-old tapes would not be easily available even if he had been prepared to let her have them. 'So what do you think it was that finally made him tell you he'd done it?'

'A mixture of exhaustion and the realisation that we couldn't be bullied and weren't going to fall for his story.'

'How did you show you were too tough to be bullied?' asked Emma, wryly amused at the suggestion that any suspect might succeed in bullying his interrogators. After what she had heard from the various men and women she had met in prison, that seemed highly unlikely.

Podley laughed. 'Suspects tend to use anger to defend themselves against the urge to confess. We cut off that route for Lutterworth early on when we showed that we weren't afraid of his temper, nor impressed by his self-importance. We pointed out the various advantages a confession would bring and the heavy disadvantages of what he was doing. Eventually he believed us.'

'But why? I mean what did you say exactly?'

'As far as I can remember we told him to stop taking the mick. We said that, whatever he thought of the police, neither of us were fools; that he might have cleaned himself up, changed his clothes, dried his hair *and* beaten the breathalyser, but that was only the beginning of the scientific evidence we'd be looking for. We told him we'd take his car and flat apart if necessary and that we knew there'd be something to find. However carefully he'd washed, there'd be traces of blood or oil in the U-bend of one of his sinks in the flat. And we'd test all his clothes and shoes, not just the ones he claimed he'd been wearing. Wherever he'd hidden them, we'd find them, and there'd be evidence on them we could use. That sort of thing.'

'Was all that perfectly legal?' asked Emma, thinking of Jane's comment about the Police and Criminal Evidence Act. 'I'm not all that well up on the rules of PACE, but didn't any of what you said constitute undue threats or inducements? Isn't that what they're called?'

'We just laid out for him what our powers are. He looked distinctly sick then.' Podley himself looked distinctly pleased at the memory. 'If we'd had any doubts before, they went at that point. He was guilty. He wasn't thinking up ways for his clients to get round their tax liabilities that night. He was out driving and killing that woman and her baby. If I could have proved he'd known her, I'd have gone after him for murder. At one point I even wondered if the kid had been his and he was trying to get rid of them both, but we couldn't find any connection at all. I think it was chance. They were there at the wrong time when a maniac who couldn't be bothered to take care tore through that village like it was Brand's Hatch.'

'You sound angry.'

'Who wouldn't be? There aren't *so* many crimes when the victim's done nothing to provoke or invite trouble, but this time they hadn't. She was a good, hardworking woman, and he was a wanker who thought his need to get home quick from whatever he'd been up to was more important than her life. He deserved everything he got and more. And if they do give him parole next week, I'll feel sorry for his wife. He's a cold, ruthless, selfish bastard, and I don't imagine prison's made him any pleasanter.'

'Right,' said Emma, for once glad of her long training in calming the anger in other people and hiding her own. 'Perhaps I should be glad that he wouldn't see me after all.'

'You certainly should,' said Podley, recovering his temper. 'Anyway that's enough of all that. What *is* a nice gi— woman like you doing mixed up with all this?'

'Getting away from nice girls,' said Emma with a slightly malicious smile. 'You can't think how deadening their lives can be. No, I don't mean deadening, but hypocritical and constricting.'

'And dealing with lying scrotes like Lutterworth is better, is it?'

Emma's smile wavered then. She drank some lager and when she looked back at Podley, she saw a surprising amount of understanding in his unattractive eyes and more gentleness than he had shown before.

'Not exactly. But somehow I thought it might be. Not him personally, I mean, but people who aren't caught up in the lying good manners and frilly garden-fêtery that I was afraid I'd be stuck in for the rest of my life. It's all been rather…disillusioning actually.' Emma could not think why she had said anything so real or so revealing to a virtual stranger, who could have had no interest in hearing it.

Podley nodded. 'Educational, though, I imagine?'

'Very,' she said drily. 'Look, I am grateful to you for seeing me.'

'I don't think I've helped much.'

'As much as anyone could, I expect. I'll tell Ben Wrexham how good you've been to me.'

'What's he like?'

'I'm not sure,' said Emma, surprised. 'I mean, I hardly know him. We're both pursuing the same course, but that's all. Haven't you ever met him?'

'No. He rang out of the blue to tell me about you. It's been a real blind date, and a lot better for me than most of those, I can tell you.' He laughed.

'In that case it was even more good of you to see me than I'd realised,' said Emma, beginning to understand quite how foolhardy she had been to talk so frankly to him. She tried to remember exactly what she had said, both about Lutterworth and herself.

'I really am Inspector Joseph Podley,' he said, fishing in his pocket for his identification. 'But it's true: you ought to have asked for this sooner. I'm glad you're not completely lacking common sense.'

Emma felt herself blushing. 'I didn't realise that what I was thinking was so obvious.'

'I've been interviewing witnesses and suspects for fifteen years or more,' he said. 'I'm trained to understand what people aren't saying.'

'You know,' she said, recovering her complexion and her

confidence, 'you almost persuade me that there could never be a miscarriage of justice with men like you in the force. But the wrong person often is suspected, isn't he?'

It was Podley's turn to look self-conscious, but in him embarrassment took the form of only the slightest extra narrowing of his eyes and lips. His colour did not fluctuate, nor his breathing change.

'Occasionally. But that wasn't the case with Andrew Lutterworth. Believe you me.'

'You really did loathe him, didn't you?'

'How perceptive of you!'

They both laughed, and Emma stood up.

'On that note, I'd better go. It has been good of you to see me, and I've enjoyed this, but I'm sure you must be aching to get home.'

He looked at his watch again, more obviously this time.

'The wife does get antsy if I'm not back in time to see the kids before lights out. Thank you for the drink.'

'That's nothing. A pleasure. Goodbye. Oh, before you do go...'

'Yes?'

'Did you know that Lutterworth had lost his son only a short while before the crash? His only child?'

'No. I didn't,' said Podley, not looking particularly interested, although Emma thought that as a father himself he ought to have had some sympathy. 'Why?'

'I just wondered whether his anger and arrogance might in fact have been attempts to control his misery.'

'Unlikely. Take it from me, he was guilty.'

'OK,' said Emma peaceably. 'Goodnight.'

''Night.'

She left him and walked along the Old Brompton Road to South Kensington tube station. Later, sitting on the Circle Line train amid the tired, angry, grey-faced commuters and overstimulated, exhausted babies who had been rescued from crèches by their equally tired mothers, she thought about everything Podley had said. It seemed important to assess how much of his apparent certainty could have come from a determination to persuade himself out of any lingering doubts about Lutterworth's guilt. Podley was a perceptive man, and sensitive to both atmosphere and unspoken comment—probably anxiety, too. But he had been angry with Lutterworth; and anger, at least in Emma's experience, could fog anyone's judgement.

When she reached Willow's Mews she saw Jag's motorcycle parked against the kerb and, conscience-stricken, checked her own watch. It was still only half past seven. Feeling the coolness of the bike's engine, she realised that he must have been in the house for some time and hoped that Willow had not minded his early invasion of her privacy. Emma rang the bell in a state of unusual nervousness.

Willow opened the door herself.

'Emma,' she said smiling easily. 'Good. Jag's here.'

'So I saw,' said Emma, gesturing at the bike. More quietly she added, 'Has it been long? D'you mind?'

Willow shook her head. 'He told Lucinda a whole string of stories that made her laugh so much I thought we'd never get her off to sleep. She loved it.'

'Good.' Emma ran her fingers through her black hair and then pinched the bridge of her nose.

'Headache?'

'No. Just too much noise and stale air. That sort of thing.'

'Drink or bath? Or both? Jag and I are quite happy chatting and there's plenty of time before dinner.'

'I must say I'd love a bath. I must stink of that pub.'

'You go on up,' said Willow, patting Emma's shoulder. 'I'll send him after you with a drink.'

'Lovely. You are kind.'

Emma, who did in fact have quite a bad headache, made her way up to the spare room, which was in its usual immaculate state with flowers in all the vases and a tray beside the bed with a bottle of mineral water and a silver box of Mrs Rusham's best biscuits on it. Suddenly hungry, Emma crammed a biscuit into her mouth and started to undress.

'What a picture!' said Jag.

Emma emerged from the bottom of her sweater, her face red and her mouth full of nuts and crumbs. When she had swallowed and brushed the evidence off her chin, she said, 'Sorry.'

'It's good to see you less than totally controlled for once. Here's your drink. Willow gave the orders and I poured it out. I hope it'll do you.'

'Why? What is it?'

'Champagne and raspberry liqueur of some kind. Sounds like one for the kitchen-whizz to me.'

'On the contrary. It's one of her Friday-night specials. Yummy. How are you getting on with her?'

'So-so. She's not sure about me and wants me to be quite clear that she's watching to see that I don't ill-treat you.'

'Is she?' said Emma, wondering whether it would be possible to tell Willow that she could look after herself without seeming hideously ungrateful. 'She is adorable, if a little overprotective.'

'Now "adorable" is not a word I would have used. I can't think why not,' said Jag.

'No? How would you describe her?'

'Formidable.'

'But didn't you see her with Lucinda?' asked Emma, frowning. It was beginning to sound as though Jag had decided to dislike Willow. 'I know she can seem tough and distant, but not when she's with the baby.'

'No. But with me she's more than frosty—and with that housekeeper, too. Poor woman.'

'Poor woman nothing. If Willow's formidable, then Mrs Rusham is Genghis Khan or Vlad the Impala.'

Jag laughed so much that Emma thought he might choke. She could not think what she had said to amuse him so much. Eventually he got himself under some sort of control again and said breathlessly, 'It's Vlad the Impaler, baboon-brain. One who impales, not some kind of deer.'

'Is it?' said Emma, completely surprised and rather amused. 'Yes, I see it must be. Funny: I've always misread it. Mad! But look here, you ought to go back down. She'll think we're having a conspiracy if we stay up here together.'

'No, she won't. She told me to see that you stayed in the bath for at least half an hour. She said it would take her that long to get dinner ready and I was on no account to let you out of the water till then.'

'You're wrong, Jag: she *is* adorable, and generous. It won't take her any time at all to get dinner ready. Mrs Rusham will have had it all laid out before she left. Willow just wants us to have time together.'

'So shall I come and scrub your back then?'

'Why not?'

WELL SCRUBBED, soothed and dressed in a long, loose skirt and the beige cotton sweater, Emma took Jag downstairs again soon after eight o'clock.

'You do look better,' said Willow. 'Thank you, Jag. I hoped I could rely on you.'

Emma immediately saw what he had meant. Willow's tone was almost headmistressly as she kindly approved of the way he had obeyed her instructions. Looking at him, Emma saw that he was irritated but managing to contain his feelings. She hoped that the two of them would find a way to relax with each other soon. Otherwise they were all in for an uncomfortable weekend.

The atmosphere eased a little as they were eating their lobster pancakes and Jag asked about Emma's meeting with Inspector Podley. She made the others laugh with her urge to advise him to have his orange eyelashes dyed and she noticed Willow looking beadily at Jag's long, curling black lashes, which made her join in their laughter.

'And apart from his cosmetically challenged appearance, what was he like?' asked Willow.

'Intelligent, angry, sincere I think, and much more perceptive than I'd have imagined.'

'And convinced of Lutterworth's guilt?' suggested Jag.

'I think so. Oh, I do wish he'd let me talk to him.'

'Perhaps he will if his parole hearing fails,' said Willow. 'Did I tell you that his wife thinks he will only get parole if he lies about his innocence?'

'Yes, you did,' said Emma, managing to feel unsullied appreciation of Willow's interest in her work again. In her fervent relief, she smiled brilliantly and hoped that Willow had never sensed any of the sullying emotions. 'I had thought of that. If he genuinely is innocent and yet forces himself to tell them that he's guilty to prove that he's accepted the seriousness of his crime, then he can hardly take a polygraph test for me that proves he believes he's innocent. Perhaps that's why he wouldn't.'

'It must be a horrible Catch-22 for any innocent person up for parole…' Willow began, but Emma interrupted her before she could finish what she was going to say.

'Awful,' agreed Emma, quickly adding, 'but a possible way into the thesis, don't you think? When lies and truth are turned on their head. When innocence is forced to lie in order to get away from unfair punishment. Oh, maybe that's the answer.' She raised her wineglass as though in a toast and drank to her two best friends.

For the first time Willow and Jag exchanged looks of pleasure untainted by any territorial ambitions. The telephone rang and Willow got to her feet with unusually clumsy haste.

'It might be Tom,' she called over her shoulder as she ran out.

It was, and she asked him to hang on while she retreated to her bedroom so that she could have some privacy while they talked.

'OH, Tom, I am missing you,' Willow said passionately after ten minutes of hearing how he was getting on in Strasbourg.

'Me, too. But you are managing, aren't you?'

'Naturally. I've got Emma here for the weekend again, and this time she's brought a boyfriend.'

'No! What's he like: a suitable aristo or a bit of rough?'

'Neither. At least not exactly. He's huge and rides a motorcycle, but he's not exactly rough trade, although I suppose he does look as though he might be. But I don't think he is. Much too gentle underneath the parade of machismo. He comes from New Zealand. I'm not sure about anything much else yet.'

'Clever?' asked Tom, knowing how much that still mattered to Willow. 'Or not?'

'I'm not sure about that either. Reasonably intelligent and he is doing a PhD, but at St Albans, so...'

'Oh, well,' said Tom with heavy, if laughing, sarcasm. 'The equivalent of an old O-level, you mean. You are a shocking intellectual snob, you know, Will, my darling.'

'And you're not?' she countered, just as amused. 'Come on, Tom. Admit it. You know you're easily as bad as me—and neither of us is as bad as all that. St Albans has a thoroughly good reputation.'

'I'm not nearly as bad as you. Oh, Will, it is good to be able to be ordinary and not guard every single word I use. I can't wait to get home.'

'Any idea of when that's likely to be?' she asked, wishing

that she could sound casual but aware that her longing to see him must be obvious.

'Sometime next week, I hope. I'd been letting myself think Tuesday might see us done, but now I've got my doubts and it may not be until Friday. If I'd had any idea it was going to drag on like this, I'd have made arrangements to come home this weekend.'

'Oh, I wish. Lucinda misses you, too. She's always asking after you, particularly last thing at night.'

'Really? I'm tickled to death.'

'Yes, really,' said Willow, remembering her old fears that Tom might lose interest in her in the excitement of his new love for Lucinda. It had not happened and he had managed to persuade Willow that it was highly unlikely to happen in the future. 'You will take care of yourself, won't you?' he said.

'Sure. And you, too.'

'I always do. How's the book going?'

'Sticky. I hate it. I can't think why I ever wanted to start it, or why I wanted to write novels. I keep asking myself why I left the civil service, where at least my work was always presented to me and I just had to do it and see that my troops did their bit properly.'

'The book must be going all right then,' he said with what she considered—and said—was a shameful lack of sympathy. He laughed again and added, 'You know perfectly well that whenever the words seem to be coming out easily you have to bin the results. It's always better when you extrude them with the greatest difficulty like toothpaste from the very bottom of an old tube.'

'I hate you when you're always right.'

'Bollocks, my dear. You always love me, almost as much as I love you, which is far too much. Blast, look at the time. I'd better go.' His voice was sobering as he went on, 'I meant it when I told you to take care. Don't let the book's stickiness lead you into any dangerous detecting or anything like that. It's usually when writing's most difficult that you start looking for something else to do.'

'No, no. I've given all that up,' she said, confident that assisting Emma with her thesis could not possibly constitute the sort of investigation Tom meant. She had reluctantly admitted to herself that he was right when he said that she owed it to Lucinda to keep away from violent criminals for a few years at least. 'Goodnight, Tom. I... Well, goodnight. I wish I were with you.'

'Me too. Goodbye, Will.'

She put down the receiver and reluctantly went back to be polite to Jag and Emma. They were just finishing the washing up and soon afterwards retired to bed.

Finding herself disturbed at the thought of what Emma might be risking as she embarked on an affair with someone of whom she knew virtually nothing, Willow told herself to stop being so possessive. It would be good for Emma to widen her circle, to be loved and to learn to allow herself some feelings that had not been laid down in the invisible rule book that had governed her life for so long.

However much she rationalised her anxiety, Willow could not altogether get rid of it. Strong emotion could do such very odd things to the sort of serenity Emma was fighting to achieve, and if Jag should turn out to be less honest than Emma assumed she might be very badly hurt.

Willow shrugged as she admitted that there was nothing she could do to prevent that. Emma would have to make mistakes and risk whatever hurts might be in store for her. Otherwise she had no hope. Willow forcibly turned her mind to other things. She knew that it was far too early for her to have any chance of sleep and so she went to see how Lucinda was. Still not reliably dry, she needed to be woken and encouraged to pee at least once every night.

She did not wake completely even when Willow sat her

on the pot, and she was deeply asleep again when Willow laid her back in her cot. Watching her, Willow wondered how she would react when it was Lucinda and not Emma who was embarking on a love affair.

'So perhaps Emma's is good practice,' she murmured.

Lucinda muttered in her sleep, and turned heavily over on to her side, thrusting her thumb into her mouth. Willow smoothed the soft hair away from the child's hot forehead and left her alone.

She had not even tried to do any work on the novel that day, but with Tom's splendidly unsentimental sympathy in mind she went down the passage to her writing room, switched on her computer and brought on to the screen the last few pages she had written. Surprised to find that they were not as dreary or nonsensical as she had expected, she managed to persuade herself to write three and half more pages during the next two hours. By then she was satisfactorily tired and went to bed confident of getting a reasonable amount of sleep.

BY THE END of the weekend Willow had come to the conclusion that Jag felt genuine affection towards Emma—and possibly something more than that—and that he was giving her something she needed. As Willow learned to smile more naturally at him, he lost some of his defensiveness and Emma began to look less worried. They zoomed off on the motorcycle after tea on Sunday, leaving a reassured Willow to deal with Lucinda's distress at the loss of her latest playmate. That sorrow was easily assuaged but it led to the much worse one of separation from her father and she began her familiar nightly demands for him.

Willow explained what he was doing and when he was likely to be home as simply and with as much patience as she could manage. Lucinda did not understand at all and continued to whine for some time. Willow hung on to her patience with difficulty and was positively relieved when it was time for her to put Lucinda to bed, knowing that Mrs Rusham would be back to take over the following morning.

NINE

ANDREW LUTTERWORTH failed to get parole. Willow heard the news from Jemima and immediately wrote to Emma, who concocted a carefully diplomatic letter telling him that she was sorry to hear what had happened and wondered whether he might reconsider his earlier refusal to see her.

She received his reply within a fortnight and was on her way to his prison four days later with all her polygraph equipment, as usual glad to be getting away from St Albans. On her way out of her building she had picked up a letter from her pigeonhole and seeing that it was from her mother, stuffed it into her pocket to read later. She opened it as soon as she had found a seat on the train.

Darling Emma,

Your last letter sounded rather depressed and I think you ought to come home next weekend for a rest. I've collected some nice people for dinner on Saturday, including Michael Bromyard.

I know you never liked him much in the old days, but time is getting on and he's one of the few young men who's still available. You'll soon be twenty-six, darling, and you can't be meeting any of the right sort in that place.

Michael is a good boy; not thrilling perhaps, but completely solid. We've known his family for ever, and he'd do you reasonably well. He's got some money, too, although that's not crucial, and a good job. You'd always know where you are with him, and that's

worth a great deal, believe me. Your father would have
been pleased. He always liked Michael.

Now, you needn't worry about clothes because I've
been through your cupboards here and taken that pretty
pink silk dress to the cleaners for you. I've made a hair
appointment for you, too, so all will be well. Tell me
which train you'll be coming on and I'll meet you. It'll
be a nice change for you and do you good.

Much love,
Mummy

Emma sighed and told herself it wasn't her mother's fault
that her ideas were so hopelessly out of date or that she
could not understand why her daughter might not want the
kind of life she had lived. But it was infuriating all the same.
Emma remembered the 'pretty pink silk dress' with a feeling
of nausea. It could have been designed at any time between
the Second World War and the end of the 1950s, and it
made her look about thirteen and quite as sweet as Anthony
would have wanted.

'Ugh!' she said aloud, startling a large man in a pinstriped
suit who was edging his way into one of the seats opposite
her.

The train was still standing at the platform ten minutes
after it ought to have left. Emma, who always hated being
rushed, had allowed herself plenty of time and peacefully
took advantage of the stillness to draft an answer to her
mother.

She wrote two versions of the same letter, while angry
commuters swore and shuffled around her, banging into her
shoulder with their briefcases and handbags as they passed.
Both versions of the letter seemed much too angry to send
and Emma crumpled them up and stuffed them in her rucksack. She did not want to hurt her mother, who meant well,

but she wanted to make it quite plain that she was going to manage her own life as she wanted and spend it with people she had chosen because she liked them for themselves and not for anything they might symbolise.

The train started to move just as she began her third attempt. A woman wearing extraordinarily high-heeled shoes tripped and fell against Emma, knocking the fountain pen from her hand. Having wiped the smeared ink away with a paper handkerchief, Emma accepted the woman's perfunctory apology in silence and bent to pick up her pen before someone trampled on it.

Dearest Mummy,

It's really kind of you to want to find someone for me to marry, and I don't want to sound horribly rejecting when I say that I wish you wouldn't. You see, I don't actually want to get married—at least not yet. I've got other things to do, especially finishing my degree so that I can get myself some work, proper work. When I was doing all those temp. secretarial and cooking jobs in the old days, I realised that I needed to do something I mind about—something that might be useful, make a difference of some kind to someone—otherwise I think I might have gone dotty.

Please don't be angry, and please, *please,* don't be hurt. I'd love to come to stay for a weekend, but I can't get away for this next one and I'd much rather be at home with just you when I come so that we can talk—instead of watching you wear yourself out entertaining a whole bunch of suitable young men for me. You see, I just don't like the suitable sort very much. Please try to understand.

Lots of love,
Emma.

Rereading the letter as the ink dried, Emma decided that it would just about do and could be rewritten more neatly after she had seen Andrew Lutterworth.

His wing governor, whom she had already met twice before, had told her that he would leave a letter authorising her entry at the visitors' door and she saw it there when she identified herself to the officer in charge. It was not long before she was through all the security checks and was being ushered into one of the small interview rooms that were set aside for inmates and their lawyers.

A few minutes after she had unpacked her polygraph equipment the door opened and she came face to face with the man whom Joe Podley and Hal Marstall had so much disliked.

Dressed in clean jeans and a well-ironed blue-and-white striped shirt, Andrew Lutterworth looked an unlikely inhabitant of that room. He came towards Emma with his right hand outstretched, saying, 'Ms Gnatche? This is such a pleasure.'

'Thank you,' she said, shaking his hand and trying to show none of her surprise at his ease of manner and attractively deep voice.

By then she was relatively familiar with prisons and knew quite well that the inmates were as different from each other as any random collection of people would be. But none of the prisoners she had met before were anything like Lutterworth. She thought that part of the difference must have lain in his air of confidence, which held none of the belligerent brashness some of her other interviewees had shown, but there was more to it than that.

All the other inmates she had met had one thing in common. They might seem angry or defeated; they might protest their innocence or make no bones about their guilt; they could be vulnerable or apparently impervious; but they looked as though they were part of the prison. Emma had often thought that it would be impossible to mistake one of them for a member of the staff, even when they were similarly dressed. The visitors, librarians, governors, assistant governors and everyone else who was free to leave looked in some way separate; the inmates did not. Of them all, only Andrew Lutterworth might have come in from outside that morning.

He was of similar height to Inspector Podley, perhaps an inch or two over the average, and much more attractive. His dark hair was thick and lightly streaked with grey at the temples. He looked fit, but his complexion was greyish and there were deep lines running between his nose and mouth as well as heavy shadows under his brown eyes as though he did not sleep well and worried a lot. To Emma's relief his handshake was firm and his skin perfectly dry.

'It is so good of you to see me,' she said as he let go her hand.

'It's a pleasure,' he answered, smiling at her with appealing warmth. 'I'm sorry I couldn't agree to it when you first wrote to me. But circumstances change.'

'Indeed they do,' said Emma, returning his smile. 'You do realise, don't you, that nothing I—'

'—discover can affect my incarceration here? Yes, Ms Gnatche, I understand that perfectly well. You put it in both your letters. But I have nothing to lose now except my undeserved reputation for wicked irresponsibility and dangerous driving. I'd like to get that cleared up if I can, even if it doesn't get me out of here any earlier. Where do we start?'

Emma set up her machines, explaining the purpose of each part, before attaching the sensors to his fingers, the heart monitor to his chest and the blood-pressure cuff around his upper arm. It felt odd to be rolling up his sleeves and touching his skin, odder than with any of her previous subjects.

'Don't worry so much,' he said.

'Worry? I'm not worrying.'

'Come, come, Ms Gnatche. You must know the signs even better than I. Your hands are sweating. It's a dead giveaway.'

Emma laughed at his gentle mockery, thinking it strange to find him so immediately likeable when both Hal Marstall and Inspector Podley had described him as unpleasantly arrogant. He did not seem at all arrogant to her.

'I'm sorry. That must be rather disgusting for you.' She pulled a paper handkerchief from her bag and wiped her hands before adjusting the blood-pressure cuff around his biceps.

'I don't mind it much. What I can't stand is people with dirty fingernails touching me, and yours are pristine. A little fresh sweat is positively wholesome in comparison with old nosepickings—or worse.'

Emma flinched. She could not help it.

'I know,' he said. 'It's disgusting when you think about the possible constituents of the filth, isn't it?'

She nodded, but it was not revulsion at the idea of dirty nails that had got to her. It had been something in his voice, something much more powerful than either the disgust or the contempt that showed so clearly in his face.

'I'm going to use what we call the Control Question Technique,' she said as formally as possible, not looking at him.

'That sounds very sinister.'

Hearing the sound of mockery again, Emma did snatch a glance at him. She was relieved to see that he was looking quite normal and went on more easily, 'All it means is that I'm going to ask you some simple questions first that have nothing to do with the case and then continue to the material points, interspersed with other control questions that also have nothing to do with it but are likely to arouse some emotion in you so that I can have a basis on which to monitor your reactions to the questions about the crash. Is that all right with you?'

'Whatever you wish.'

Emma nodded, reached for her clipboard and, in as detached a voice as possible and not looking at his face, began to ask her carefully designed questions about his meals, his house, his ideal holiday, his garden, his interests in the prison, his car, his work, what he was doing on the night when he was arrested, where he had parked his car, how far he had driven it that night, whether he had ever been to the village in Buckinghamshire where the woman and her child were killed, whether he had ever had any accidents or committed any driving offences. She knew from her study of Hal Marstall's notes that Lutterworth had twice been stopped for speeding in the past and had once, nearly ten years earlier, lost his licence for eighteen months after he had been found to be driving with too much alcohol in his blood.

She did not attempt to analyse any of the answers he gave at the time, concentrating on keeping her voice even and her own reactions absolutely steady so that nothing about her could affect the responses his body was making as she put her questions and he answered them. After nearly an hour she was done and laid down her clipboard.

'Thank you, Mr Lutterworth. That was excellent. You were most cooperative. How are you feeling?'

'Tired,' he said, pulling apart the Velcro fastening of the blood-pressure cuff. 'It takes a surprising amount of concentration, and it's been a while since I had to concentrate on anything very much, except keeping out of the way of the thugs and bullies in here.'

She took the cuff from him and unhooked all the wires. Once he was freed, he rubbed his head with both hands and she saw that his fingernails were impeccably clean. It occurred to her belatedly that his horror of people with black-

ened nails touching him might have something to do with
the thugs and bullies.

'Have I given you a headache?' she asked more sympa-
thetically.

'No.'

'I'm glad. I'd better sort all this out and then I can leave
you in peace,' she said, reaching for her cassette recorder.

Before she could touch it, he had taken hold of her wrist.
She tried to pull away, but he tightened his fingers so that
she could not get free. His strength seemed formidable.

'What's the matter, Mr Lutterworth?' Emma asked, and
then silently cursed herself as she heard the unmistakable
panic in her voice.

Trying to be sensible, she told herself that there was nothing he could do to her with a whole bunch of prison officers
just the other side of the door. She had only to call out and
she would be rescued. She forced herself to look directly at
him and then wished she had not. There was a gleam in his
eyes that she had often seen in Anthony's; it seemed to her
to carry both acknowledgment of her fear and pleasure in
it.

'Please let me go.' Her voice was better that time and
sounded much more dignified, as well as calmer. 'You're
hurting my wrist, Mr Lutterworth.'

He released her at once and sat back, watching her. When
she forced herself to look properly at him she saw that the
gloating expression in his eyes had been replaced by curiosity. She managed not to look away again or rub her arm.

'Thank you.'

'I didn't mean to alarm you. I don't know what came
over me,' he said. Apart from a suggestion of surprise, his
voice sounded so completely normal that she thought she
must have misinterpreted his reaction to her fear.

'That's fine. There's no need to apologise.'

'Actually,' he said, 'I think there might be. And if I'm

honest, I must admit that I do know exactly what came over me. I'm sorry.'

Emma did not trust herself to speak and merely raised her eyebrows.

'You see, you're the first civilised person I've seen for ages and you were about to disappear again. For a moment I couldn't bear it, but I should have said so straight away instead of scaring you like that. I can only think that my sensitivities must have been blunted while I've been in here. Will you forgive me? And stay a while and talk?'

'I could stay for a little,' Emma said stiffly. Her wish to escape seemed exaggerated and she did not want to look as though she were scuttling away like a frightened rabbit. On the other hand she did not want to stay any longer than necessary. Something about him was making her feel increasingly uncomfortable. 'But I shall have to go in ten minutes or so and I must get all this tidied up and out of the way.'

'That's fine. Just being able to look at you is enough. You see, you look just...'

Emma wished that he would not keep staring at her. She did not want to attract him or to listen to his compliments.

As though he sensed her withdrawal, Lutterworth added in the most straightforward manner possible, 'You're so unbelievably different from my brutish cellmates. You can't imagine what they're like and how much I dread the sound of the cell door being locked on us again.'

Emma went on folding up the blood-pressure cuff and then took the leads out of the machines to coil them neatly in their appointed places.

'That's that,' she said as she sat down again and looked directly at him, unsmiling. 'Now, what is it you want to talk about?'

'Anything. Anything civilised that has nothing to do with

cars, sport, women, sex, prison, rights, law, police… Anything at all, Emma. Tell me about yourself.'

'There's nothing to tell.' She spoke as lightly as she could and was surprised to see a flash of anger in his eyes.

'There must be,' he said with an assumption of jollity. 'I don't mind what it is. Tell me about your work or your boyfriend.'

'Mr Lutterworth, I don't want to sound unpleasant, but I really do not wish to talk about my life. What about you? Do you get many visitors here?'

'My wife comes as often as she's allowed, but it's only twice a month.'

'Oh, dear. That seems rather a mean allowance. I'm not sure I'd realised visits were so strictly rationed,' Emma said to keep the conversation going. She knew perfectly well how often inmates were allowed visits.

'I suspect there are a lot of things you haven't realised, Emma.'

'About life in prison?' She wished that he would not keep using her name. It seemed much too personal.

'That too. But it was life in general that I meant. You're very much younger than I'd expected, you know, and quite different. Has anyone ever told you…? No, I don't suppose they have.'

Emma was not prepared to give him the satisfaction of asking what it was he had been going to say and sat in unhelpful silence. He laughed.

'I'm not being fair, am I? You must be wondering what kind of fiend you're locked up with here.'

'Not at all. You're clearly no fiend, Mr Lutterworth. I'm just wondering what exactly it is that you want from me.'

'Only a pretence that I'm still part of the real world,' he said, suddenly sounding more vulnerable, almost likable again. 'But I've been boorish, haven't I? And rather unfair. Will you accept another apology?'

'I don't understand.' She wondered how soon she could reasonably go, and cursed herself for worrying about the etiquette of leaving a prison interview room. 'But I'll certainly accept your apology.'

'You look troubled, Emma. What are you thinking about?'

'Nothing of any importance,' she said, at last giving herself permission to escape. 'Look, I must go now or I'll miss my train. You've been very helpful and I'm grateful.'

'Good. Shall I see you again?' he asked, looking almost as anxious as an eight-year-old boy on his way back to boarding school. 'Won't you have more questions to put to me? Surely you will.'

'I suppose it's possible. It depends on what the test results show. Would you be prepared to answer more?'

'I'd be glad to. It's been almost like getting out for the afternoon, talking to you. And knowing that you've forgiven me for my bad manners is…oh, it's almost as good as knowing you believe I'm innocent of killing that woman and her child.'

'I haven't had a chance to analyse the tests yet,' Emma said, well aware that she had given no indication of believing him. She felt unsettled again and wished she could decide whether he was as manipulative as he seemed or simply all over the place because of what was happening to him in prison.

'No, I know. But you do realise that I couldn't have been guilty of killing them, don't you?' Lutterworth produced his warm, inviting smile again.

'You mustn't make me say anything like that,' said Emma, not responding to it. 'I'll need time to study the results. But for what it's worth, it seems pretty unlikely that you did it.'

'Thank you for that. I can't tell you how much it means,

Emma. Is there anything else I can do for you before you go?'

'Actually there is one thing,' she said, wondering whether she would be laying up trouble for herself if she prolonged the connection between them.

'Good,' said Lutterworth. 'I'd like to help you, Emma, in any way I can.'

'I imagine that your solicitor must have had a copy of the police interview tapes. You know, the ones they recorded at the police station the night they arrested you?'

'Presumably.'

'If he has, it would be great if you could get him to send me copies. 'D'you think you could?'

'I don't see why not. I'll ring him. I don't suppose…' For the first time Lutterworth looked embarrassed enough to give Emma the upper hand. She tried not to enjoy it.

'Would you like a Phonecard?' She had learned a certain amount about life in prison during her researches and knew that Phonecards were highly prized and often used as currency by the inmates.

'It's humiliating to have to ask, but yes, that would be very helpful. One does become rather like an incarcerated child in here. Or a performing animal. Did you know the screws don't talk about "meals", at least not for us. They call it "feeding" as though we were a bunch of sealions at the zoo.'

Emma thought it best not to comment as she scuffled in her bag and took out a twenty-unit card. 'I'm ashamed to say that I didn't think of this before I came and I have used a couple of units off this. I am so sorry. If I need to come again, I'll bring you a stock.'

'No need. This will be very helpful.' He stood up and shook hands again, looking almost as though he were terminating an interview with a favoured client of Hill, Snow,

Parkes. 'Goodbye for now. I'll find it hard to wait until next time.'

'Goodbye.'

'SMOOTH BUGGER, isn't he?' said the officer when he returned to unlock the various gates to let Emma out of the grim building.

'Perhaps,' she said, still not sure what she thought of him. 'Thank you.'

She humped her equipment to the telephone box that stood on the pavement just beyond the outer gates of the prison and called a minicab. Expensive though it was going to be, there was no other way of getting herself and all her stuff to the nearest station. The cab came within five minutes.

BACK IN HER ROOM in St Albans, with a good supply of coffee and ginger biscuits at her side, Emma spread out the test sheets and her parallel list of questions to set about proving whether or not Andrew Lutterworth could be innocent of smashing into the young mother and her child at sixty miles per hour in the middle of a filthily wet night in February just over three years earlier.

She quickly realised that she was not going to get any proof of anything. There were some extremely strong reactions recorded in the graphs, but, as she matched them against her questions, she saw that they had nothing to do with the night of the accident. Lutterworth's responses to some of the control questions were infinitely stronger than any of those caused by his talking about the crime. Emma double-checked them all.

'Oh, that bloody man!' she said aloud as she realised what he must have been doing.

One of the first things she had learned was that it was very hard indeed for someone to beat a polygraph test by controlling his reactions to questions that made him feel guilty. The only reliable way to cheat the machines was to provoke even stronger responses to control questions. Some people were known to have done that by having a drawing-pin, point upwards, in their shoes. When a question that did not worry them at all was asked, they would press down hard on the pin so that their bodies would provide misleadingly violent reactions as they answered.

The questions about Lutterworth's life in prison had provoked small reactions, but they were consistent with understandable anger. Questions about the police, his alibi, and the crashed car provoked reactions too, bigger than those about his prison life, but not nearly as big as his responses to some of her most boring questions about his interest in gardening, and about whether he routinely carried passengers in the car. She matched her questions against the peaks and troughs in the chart with increasing anger.

But when she reached the moment at which she had asked him about the death of the child, she began to wonder whether she had been doing him an injustice. The fluctuations recorded as he answered those questions were the biggest of all.

In the light of what Willow had told her about Pipp Lutterworth, Emma had tried to phrase her questions about the crash victims in such a way that they would not remind Andrew of his son. Looking at the graphs of his heart rate, blood pressure and breathing as he talked about the child who had been killed by his car, she realised she could not have been careful enough.

Angry with herself, she had to admit that the test she had been sure would be the key to her thesis had in fact told her very little. The telephone began to ring.

'Emma Gnatche.'

'Emma! It's Jane here. How did the polygraph go? And what did you think of Lutterworth?'

Emma gave Jane a carefully expurgated account of her meeting, stressing that she had reached only preliminary conclusions and still had plenty of work to do on the test results before she could write a definitive report.

'Have you had any more contact with his wife?' Emma asked when she had reached the end of the little that she was prepared to say to Jane. 'Since he was refused parole, I mean?'

'No. But Willow told me that she'd been to see her and she liked her, too.'

'I know she did.'

'You're sounding a bit defeated,' said Jane. 'Is something the matter?'

'Not exactly. It's just that I'm beginning to think I might not be able to give you any of the certainty you want.'

'Damn! Well, I don't suppose it's your fault. There may not be any to be had. I only hope I haven't sent you on a wild-goose chase.'

'I'm sure you haven't. This test may not tell us anything very much, but I'm not ready to give up yet. I'll just have to find some more about what went on in that police station. Has Hal ever told you about his theory that Lutterworth must have had a girlfriend with him in the car that night?'

'He's trailed the idea past me once or twice, yes,' said Jane. 'I can't say I'm convinced.'

'Oh? Why not?'

'It just doesn't square with the way his wife behaved or talked about him. I don't want to sound like a judge who can't imagine that a man married to an attractive and intelligent woman might stray, but I honestly cannot see Lutterworth going to such lengths to conceal an affair. Forty years ago, perhaps, but nowadays? I don't buy it, Emma.'

'Nor do I. But...'

'What?'

'There was just something about him today that led me

to think he might be fairly susceptible to women; and that made me wonder whether Hal could have been right.'

'Oh, come on, Emma.' Jane's voice was positively caustic.

'What d'you mean?'

'Lutterworth's in prison, banged up with a whole lot of men and dykey wardresses. Of course he's going to "undress you with his eyes" or whatever it was you thought he was doing. You or any other reasonably attractive woman.'

Emma laughed. 'That wasn't quite what I meant. But in a way—'

'You're sounding like the sweet naïve little blonde again. You want to watch that.'

'Yes, I probably should. Sorry, Jane. By the way, has Mrs Lutterworth got money of her own? D'you know?'

'No, I don't. That house of theirs must have cost a fortune to build, but accountancy partners, even outside the Big Six firms, were earning a fortune in the late eighties. He might not have needed any help from her. Why?'

'I just thought that if he were relying on her money, he might have had quite an incentive to keep an affair secret.'

'If he was having one at all. Yes, I suppose he might. Although plenty of blokes are getting alimony these days from rich wives. In any case, risking prison in order to keep his pocket money? Surely not.'

'I know it seems weird. But there has to be some explanation.'

'Emma, are you trying to tell me here that your polygraphs *did* suggest he was guilty?'

'No, I'm not telling you anything for sure yet. But there is a possibility, a faint possibility, that he's read one of those American books about the best ways to beat a lie-detector and manipulated the result.'

'I see. That's not a bad idea. Yes, I like it. Oh, you have encouraged me,' said Jane.

'Good,' Emma said, as always pleased to have pleased people. 'Well, if you find out anything about Mrs Lutterworth's money or Andrew's love life, will you let me know?'

'Sure. I must go. 'Bye for now.'

In need of some straightforward affection, Emma rang up Jag, who immediately asked if he could come over on the bike to see her. As soon as she had put down the telephone, she went to check that there was plenty of the strong beer he liked in the chillybin and then set about tidying up her room.

When he arrived he was carrying a large bunch of freesias.

'Jag,' she said, amazed that he should have made such a conventional gesture. 'How beautiful! They're easily my favourite flowers. They'll make the room smell gorgeous.'

'Then I wish I'd thought of buying them.'

'What d'you mean?' she asked, stepping back and not touching the offered flowers. 'You can't have stolen them.'

He laughed. 'Baboon-brain! I found them propped up outside your door. Didn't you see them when you came in?'

'No,' said Emma. 'And I haven't heard anyone knocking since I got back. How peculiar! Who could have sent them? Is there a card?'

'Sure.' He pulled it off the cellophane wrapping and handed it to her.

'Oh, right. Thanks.' She did take the flowers then and ran some water into the basin for them, before opening the small envelope. The note inside was written in an attractively firm hand in proper ink.

Emma,
   I saw these as I was passing a florist. They reminded me of you and our nice dinner together. We must do

it again some time. When are you coming back to London? Give me a ring.

> Love,
> Hal.

'They're from that journalist I told you about. The one I had dinner with weeks ago. This is the first I've heard from him since,' she said, handing Jag the note. 'He must have a big expense account. There are millions of these.'

'Or else he's a better guesser than me and knew how much you'd like them,' said Jag, scowling. Seeing her worried face, he added cheerfully, 'Perhaps I'll have to horsewhip him. Isn't that what's done to rivals in this benighted country of yours?'

'I wouldn't know,' said Emma, laughing. 'But Hal's no rival of yours, Jag, as you ought to know. You can safely ignore him and his flowers.'

'Sure?'

'Yup.'

'Great. Then come here.'

TEN

'AND SO YOU SEE, Willow, the results are so odd that I think he must have been deliberately manipulating them,' Emma said down the telephone.

Willow, who had been keeping one eye on the screen of her computer, started to concentrate on what Emma was trying to explain.

'Although,' she was saying, 'it could be possible that some of my questions upset him by reminding him of his son and that's why his responses were so erratic.'

'Hmm, I can see the problem. Odd. I'd always assumed lie-detection was more clear-cut than that.'

'Unfortunately not. That's why it's never been admissible in court. There's no one reaction that proves honesty or the opposite, just a collection of them that point towards a probability.'

'Tell me again what the irrelevant questions were that caused the most powerful reactions in Lutterworth,' said Willow, turning her screen away from her before pulling forward a piece of paper. She was amused to notice that she felt slightly uncomfortable at the thought that Emma was acquiring a skill of which she herself knew nothing.

'Whether he regularly had passengers in his car and whether he enjoyed gardening.'

'Odd,' said Willow again as she wrote them down in an effort to ensure that she did not forget the precise wording Emma had used. 'Have you talked to Jag about it? As a psychologist, I mean.'

'Yes. He's suggested that Lutterworth may still feel such guilt about his son's death that he reacted violently to any-

thing that reminded him of the boy. He must have driven
him about in the car, and he made that garden in his memory. It sounds like a possible explanation, but I can't make
it fit the man I met. He just didn't strike me as someone
who would be tormented by that sort of guilt. After all, he
hadn't done anything to his son to make him die or prevent
him being cured. I know lots of people do feel guilt when
a close relation's died, but isn't it usually when they haven't
cared enough or done enough during the person's life?'

'Probably. But that could fit Lutterworth, you know,
Emma. Everyone agrees that he worked amazingly hard.
Perhaps some part of his subconscious mind believes that if
he had spent more time with the boy he'd never have got
necrotising fasciitis. I'd have thought that could explain a
lot, including incidentally whatever aura it was that made
the police so sure he was guilty. It does add up, you know.'

'I suppose so,' said Emma, still doubtful and wishing that
she had thought up some more effective questions to ask
during the test.

'I shouldn't have thought that there could be much doubt
after what his wife told me—you know, about how pro-
foundly affected he was by the boy's death. He probably
still is. I'd have thought Jag's analysis is quite reasonable.'
Willow felt absurdly pleased that Emma had come to her
after Jag had given his views.

'But I suppose another possible answer,' she went on,
thinking as she spoke, 'is that Lutterworth did something
else that night that he's ashamed of. That would make sense
of your test results, too. Or wouldn't it?'

'Not really, but—'

'Did I tell you that Jemima believes he was haunting the
hospital where Pipp died? Could that be it, d'you think? Or
perhaps there was something nastier that he's even more
ashamed of. Maybe sexual?'

'What: a strip joint or a prostitute or something? I did

think of that myself,' said Emma, laughing at Willow's un-necessarily tactful phrasing. 'But, you see, I asked him sev-eral times and in several different ways what he was doing that night, and he went into quite a lot of detail each time he told me about the knotty tax problem he'd been working on for the difficult client. Those responses are wholly calm and quite consistent with each other; as in fact are his re-actions to questions about the reparking and going in and out of the office and finding the car stolen. Everything sug-gests that he was telling the truth at that point, even though not at some of the others. Unless he was faking the whole thing, in which case there's no point even trying to work out what any of it means.'

'Blast! Are you sure?'

'Pretty much.' Emma got rid of the last of her dog-in-the-manger feelings and added: 'Look, would you like me to send you a copy of the test sheets? To see what you think?'

'Would you?' said Willow. 'They probably won't mean much to me, but I should like to have a look at them. On a slightly different subject, one thing that's been bothering me about all this is the security men who were on duty that night.'

'Me too. As Hal Marstall said, it's easy to imagine them missing him once, but three times could be a bit much. I wouldn't let Hal persuade me at the time, but I think that was probably because I was trying so hard not to be im-pressed by him or his certainty of Lutterworth's guilt. I'm not so sure now.'

'Me neither. Although we can't be sure how closely the security men were questioned or how honestly they an-swered, can we?'

'On the other hand, why would they lie?' asked Emma, playing Devil's Advocate. Then, realising that at some level she still wanted Lutterworth to be innocent, she added, 'On yet another hand—if one can have three—I haven't seen any report of them seeing him leave at any other time that night. And if they didn't say that they'd noticed him go before, why should their not having seen him later make any difference?'

'Precisely,' said Willow with increasing interest as she contemplated the alluring possibility of being more used to Emma than Jag had been. 'But they might have been asked a *"num"* question—you know, on the lines of: "you didn't see Andrew Lutterworth coming back at half past eight, soaking wet and swearing, did you?"'—and not been asked more generally about what they saw.'

'I wonder.' Emma thought of the experiments she had conducted on the ways in which the phrasing of questions affected the answers they evoked. 'You could be right, I suppose.'

'It has been known,' said Willow with satisfaction, which made Emma laugh again. 'Well, then, why don't I go and see what I can get out of them? Wouldn't that help?'

'Oh no,' Emma said at once. 'I couldn't ask that when you've got all your own work to do. And Lucinda and everything. Honestly I'm perfectly able to do it myself.'

'Emma, what's the matter?'

'Nothing's the matter. Why?'

'You sound most unlike yourself. Stiff and very nearly cross. You're not insulted that I want to help, are you?'

'No, no, of course not. How could I be?'

'Good. I know perfectly well that you could do all of it just as well as me. I only want to save you trouble.'

'I know. And I'm grateful. Honestly,' said Emma quickly. 'And of course I'm not insulted. I mean, good heavens, it was me who rang you this morning about the polygraph results. You see, I really do want your help, Willow.'

'That's all right then. My imagination must be working overtime. Good. I'll get in touch with the security men as soon as I can. It'll be a blessing as far as the book's concerned. I'm hardly writing anything worth keeping at the moment and so it'd be great to do something useful for you instead.'

'Oh, but it might not work.'

'Why not?' asked Willow impatiently and then, when Emma did not answer, said even more sharply, 'What might not work?'

'Re-questioning the security guards. Their firm isn't working for Hill, Snow any more. Someone—Hal, I think—told me that they have electronic gates now and their new employees monitoring them. At the time of the crash they used a security firm that provided the men on duty that night. They probably don't even work for the firm any more. I don't see how you're going to get hold of them.'

'It's not exactly an insurmountable problem, I wouldn't have thought. I suppose we might have trouble if the firm's gone out of business, but only then. Look, have you got the names of the men who were on duty that night?'

'Some of them, I think. Hang on and I'll check.'

Willow waited, hearing the muted sounds of rustling paper and the occasional unladylike curse, which made her smile. At last Emma was back, saying, 'The only ones named in my files are Terry Lepe and George Tedsmore, who were on duty when Lutterworth was supposed to have gone out the first time, but not when he eventually left and discovered the car had been stolen. The shifts change over at eight thirty. But look, Willow, do you really think it's worth going to all the trouble of tracking them down? I mean, presumably his own legal team must have asked sensible—and searching—questions, even if the police asked only the sort designed to get the answer they wanted.'

'You never know. I'd have thought it was worth a shot. I'm more than happy to do it. It shouldn't take long and if I don't find anything I'll give up straight away and we won't either of us have lost anything except an hour or two in which I probably wouldn't have done anything else anyway. If I do find something I'll report.'

'Willow, I know I say this much too often, but you are amazing.'

'Nonsense. But I do like investigation.'

'Won't Tom be furious with us?' said Emma, who had worryingly clear memories of his terrified anger after Willow had been assaulted in hospital by one of her suspects in an investigation she had carried out only days after Lucinda's birth.

'Too bad if he is. I'm so bored with my beastly book. He's not here. I need something else to do. You need a spot of help. No,' Willow added quickly, 'I don't mean you *need* it, but you could *use* it. And anyway, Lutterworth is safely in prison already. He can't get at either of us. So, whatever he was doing that night, he's no threat to you or me.'

'That's true. You're right again. Well, best of luck, Willow, and many, many thanks.'

Willow was smiling as she put down her receiver. She filed the dreary chapter she had been attempting to jazz up and switched off the computer, reaching for the London Business Telephone Directory with her other hand.

It turned out to be surprisingly easy to persuade the Hill, Snow, Parkes press officer that Willow needed to know the name of the firm who had once provided security for the partnership's head office. A glance at the directory gave her their number, and a quick telephone call established that they were still in business. Willow told the young-sounding receptionist who answered her call that she was anxious to speak to Terry Lepe and wondered if she could be given the number of the place where he was working that day or perhaps leave a message asking him to contact her.

The receptionist did not seem at all surprised by Willow's request and politely asked her to wait for a moment. When she returned to the telephone it was to announce that Terry Lepe was no longer with the company.

'What a pity!' said Willow. 'He was so highly recommended to me. Then, what about George Tedsmore? Might it be possible to get in touch with him instead?'

'Just one moment,' said the receptionist, and then only a second or two later: 'Putting you through.'

Willow, who had assumed that the man would be out on duty or sleeping off a night shift at home, quickly adjusted her planned approach.

'Tedsmore,' said a growly, South London voice.

'George Tedsmore? Hello, my name is Worth, Mrs Worth. You've been recommended to me as someone who could give me some good advice about security. I wonder whether it would be possible to come and see you to discuss it?'

'What sort of problem?' he said, sounding much more careful than the receptionist had been.

'It's too complicated to discuss over the phone,' said Willow. 'It really would be easier if I could explain face to face.' She had no reason to think he would refuse to talk about the Lutterworth case, but it seemed much more likely that she would get useful information out of him if she had him sitting in front of her as she asked her questions and could watch his reactions as well as listen to his answers.

'OK. When d'you want to come?'

'When are you free?'

''Sa'ternoon? Three?'

'Fine. Where should I come?'

'Head office, Rosebery Avenue. Knock and enter, as the actress said to the bishop.'

'Thank you very much,' said Willow, curious that so unpolished a man should apparently have become part of the administration of a company that was large and successful enough to have provided security for a firm like Hill, Snow, Parkes. 'I'll see you later.'

TEDSMORE LOOKED VERY MUCH as she had expected from his voice: a big man in his late fifties, with rough grey hair and strong hands with stubby fingers. There was a broad smile on his square face and a distinct twinkle in his faded grey eyes. He half stood as Willow was shown into his small, glass-walled office, and leaned across his desk to shake hands.

'So, what d'you want from us, Mrs Worth?' he said after he had fetched her a plastic beaker of disgusting imitation tea from an automatic machine. He was not drinking anything. 'You've got some need for security? We're not bodyguards, you know. Nor yet private eyes. We supply security guards for offices mostly; or building sites and factories.'

'What makes you think I don't want that?' she asked, trying not to smile.

He gestured towards her jacket. It was some time since she had felt the need to spend her royalties on couture suits and expensive jewellery, but she still took a great deal of pleasure in buying clothes made by people who understood the luxury of understated elegance and superlative cut and fabric.

'Not many of our clients come here looking like you,' he said, 'and most of them introduce themselves with the name of their firm. If you'd wanted a bodyguard I could've understood.'

'No. I'm not nearly rich or prominent enough for anyone to want to kidnap or damage me.'

'So, why are you here then?'

'I want a bit of information.'

'Oh, yes?' he said, no longer smiling. She thought that in his younger days he might have looked quite dangerous. 'And what might that be about then?'

'About the night that a man called Andrew Lutterworth was arrested. D'you remember it? You were working at Hill, Snow, Parkes then.'

'Yeah. Not having lost me marbles, I know I was,' he said, his voice heavy with sarcasm. 'But why should I remember that night in particular?'

For a moment Willow assumed the question was meant to be taken at face value and was about to explain why the dramatic and presumably much-discussed events must have stuck in his memory. Then she realised what he meant and felt for her handbag. She had been to a cash machine on her way to his office and had just over one hundred pounds with her.

'Why not?' she said, lifting the bag on to her knee. 'What would it take to remind you?'

'A ton maybe?'

She sat in silence for a full minute, as though weighing up whether it was worth it or not.

'OK. But it had better be good for that.'

'It'll be true.'

'Well, that's the crucial point.' She opened her bag and took out the wad of money, making a mental note to keep Emma unaware of the bribe. It was not that she would have disapproved in principle, but Willow knew that she would be mortified to think of anyone spending that sort of money on her behalf.

'Not a bad bung,' he said, grinning. 'What d'you want to know?'

'Everything,' said Willow, taking out a notebook. 'Starting with whether you did or did not see Lutterworth going out to park his car that night, or coming back again to work just as your shift ended.'

'You've wasted your money, love,' he said, reaching round to tuck it away in an inner pocket of the jacket he had hung over the back of his chair. 'We already told the rozzers. He didn't go out nor come in.'

'As far as you saw?'

''Sright.'

'Would it have been possible for you not to see?'

He shrugged, showing off the fatness of his shoulders and paunch as his shirt rode up.

'Possible; not likely.'

'Did you like him?'

He shrugged again, but his face gave her all the answer she needed. Perhaps feeling that he had been short-changing her, he said, 'I didn't mind him so much as some of the lads.'

'Which lads in particular?'

'Lots of them.'

'Who specifically? Terry, perhaps?'

'You talked to Terry?'

'Not yet,' said Willow. 'They said he doesn't work for the company any more.'

'Correct. I thought you must've found him, though.'

'Found him?' Willow repeated, becoming much more interested. 'Did you think he'd disappeared?'

George Tedsmore laughed, but he did not seem amused. Willow began to feel the first tingling alertness that always accompanied a useful discovery. She raised her eyebrows in a silent question, which he did not answer.

'I see,' she said eventually, deciding to put her question more clearly later. 'So, why did Terry so particularly loathe Andrew Lutterworth?'

'They'd got across each other. Terry was a young bloke, see; not like me and some of the other lads. We've seen it all and learned to take it, but it riled him. You know, when they give us orders without looking at us, never used our names, treated us like dirt.'

'Was Lutterworth worse than the rest?'

Tedsmore scratched his neck, raising a bunch of reddish flesh above his shirt collar and then letting it flop down again. Willow wondered whether he had put on weight after he had been promoted to desk work or whether someone in the organisation had decided that he was no longer fit enough for active duty and found something for him to do in the office.

'Sort of. Ruder and more impatient-like. And as for common? I ask you.'

'I'm sorry?' said Willow, surprised that Tedsmore should mind so much about the man's class.

'A lot of them are like that, you know. Brains like razors, but thick as shit when it comes to real life; no common sense at all.'

Aha, thought Willow, amused by her own misunderstanding. Common sense, I see.

'Even Terry could've run rings around him, and he's no genius. Head in the clouds, that Lutterworth.'

'Or in his clients' affairs?' suggested Willow, interested in the first suggestion of corroboration of Lutterworth's own story that he might have forgotten the street in which he had parked his car. Ever since Emma had pointed that out to her, she had been puzzled.

'You must have seen a lot of him in the evenings when he was nipping in and out of the building to get his car out of the car park and all that.'

'So?'

'Do you remember any occasion on which he had forgotten to lock it or lost the keys or anything like that?'

Tedsmore took a moment to think, but then shook his head. ''Course I might not've heard about it. You'd do better to ask his sekertry. Nice little thing she was and always sorting out his messes for him. Dunno what happened to her, though, after he was sacked.'

Willow wrote herself a note, well aware that the Hill,

Snow, Parkes press officer would be less likely to answer questions about an ex-partner's secretary than about a security company that no longer had any connection with the partnership.

'Did she like him or was she like this Terry and full of resentment?'

'She always talked friendly enough about him,' said Tedsmore, looking surprised at the question.

'Oh. Well, I will try to see her if I can. What was her name?'

Tedsmore scratched his head in a parody of puzzlement. Willow wondered if he was about to ask for an even bigger bung and was prepared to hold out for full value for the first before she gave him any more.

'Fanny? Mandy? Candy? Can't remember, sorry. Sally? No, it's gone.' Seeing Willow's impatience he scowled. 'Look, there's hundreds of girls in places like that. I don't remember them all when they're in front of me every day and it's been years since I was there.'

'Ah, yes, I see. But look, you still haven't told me exactly how Lutterworth had riled Terry so badly.'

Tedsmore shrugged again, but after a little prodding from Willow produced a long, involved story about a mislaid parcel and unfair aspersions cast on Lutterworth's secretary by Terry, and a public bollocking by Lutterworth, followed by 'unwarrantable rudeness' from Terry and then by a formal warning from Personnel. Humiliated and spitting with fury, according to Tedsmore, Terry had gone out of his way to irritate Lutterworth whenever he could safely do so after that.

'What a pity he isn't with the company any more,' said Willow at the end of the story. 'When did he leave?'

''Bout eighteen months ago,' said Tedsmore, dashing her hopes that he might have decamped as soon as Lutterworth had been charged. 'No, more. Perhaps two years.'

'What made him go?'

Tedsmore shook his head and clamped his full lips shut. Willow told him that she did not think she had yet had enough information for her hundred pounds and was not going to leave until she had the full story of Terry Lepe's defection.

'Wanted a change of scene,' growled Tedsmore. 'Didn't he?'

'Oh, come on. You can do better than that. It doesn't sound in the least convincing.'

The door behind her opened and she looked round to see a much younger, better-dressed man standing there with a disapproving expression on his face.

'Are you very busy, George?' he asked in the voice of one who wants to say something much ruder but dare not in case he might antagonise a paying client.

'Won't be long now, Ron. Mrs Worth here was just asking whether we'd be interested in quoting for security for her brother-in-law's factory.'

'Really?' said the man called Ron, coming further into the room so that he could shake hands with her. 'Well, I hope George here is helping you. Whereabouts is the factory?'

Willow took a moment to look meaningfully at her reluctant source and then turned to say charmingly, 'Near Ashford, but it's not a very big business...'

'Ashford in Kent or Middlesex?'

'Kent, actually,' she said without any hesitation. 'But I'm coming to the conclusion that the job might be a little small for your organisation. It's just that you came so highly recommended that I thought I'd better consult you first.'

'Did we? That's great. By who?'

'An old friend of mine, Norman Addams,' she said, making up a name at random. 'He used to work at Hill, Snow,

Parkes when you did their security and he was full of your praises.'

'Oh, yes. Not sure I ever met him, but of course the name's familiar. Well, I won't keep you any longer. But I'd like a word with you later, George. Last month's duty rosters are a bit worrying.'

'Sure, Ron. I'll be with you as soon as I've sorted Mrs Worth.'

Ron removed himself. When he had had time to get right out of earshot, George said gruffly, 'Thanks.'

'It was conditional, you know,' said Willow, looking at the sweat on his forehead. 'I could still go and tell him what you were really doing this afternoon. Times are hard, I take it, even in the security business?'

Tedsmore did not answer.

'Downsizing, are they?' suggested Willow. His face gave him away. 'And most unlikely to keep on someone selling information about clients, even past clients. OK, now we know where we are. Tell me about Terry and why he left and I'll leave you in peace. Otherwise, I'll have to speak to your boss.'

It took a little more persuasion and threat, but eventually Tedsmore said, 'There was this girl, see. Terry'd been giving her one and she started creating. Up the spout prob'ly, though he said not. But she started belling him here. Just once a week at first, then every day, then on the hour every hour, hoping to catch him between shifts or getting his pay or something. She did get him one time and I heard him telling her he was leaving the country, going to America he said, where he'd got a job. He said he'd send for her when he was fixed up with a flat and all.'

'And had he? Got a job in America, I mean?'

'Nah. Gone up north more likely. Anything to get shot of her. Naggy bird, she was.'

'What was her name?'

'Can't remember.'

'Who keeps the telephone records here?' asked Willow coolly. 'Someone must in a security company. Could you get hold of them? Or should I ask Ron?'

Tedsmore lumbered to his feet. The expression on his face suggested that he was genuinely afraid for his job and bitterly resentful of the chance that had led his boss to see Willow in his office.

'Wait here. Don't move. Don't talk to anyone. And don't touch the phone.'

'All right,' said Willow, peacefully leafing through the notes she had made.

Tedsmore was back in a surprisingly short time with the information that Terry Lepe's girlfriend had been called Susie Peatsea. He also gave Willow the telephone number Susie had left. Not wishing to push her luck any further, Willow thanked him and, with the door open, said loudly that she thought she ought to look for a smaller, less well-known firm for her brother-in-law's factory. George Tedsmore did not look particularly appreciative of her efforts on his behalf and positively hustled her out of the building.

Willow returned to the Mews to type up an account of her meeting with him for Emma, adding at the end:

Clearly this goes some way to supporting Lutterworth's alibi. He was vague about practical details when concentrating on a work problem and so he could have left his car unlocked and unalarmed. And it seemed to me from the whole tenor of Tedsmore's answers that he and Lepe might easily not have noticed, let alone recorded the names of, everyone who passed their station. Tedsmore himself might easily have been out of it when Lutterworth walked out to fetch his car and Lepe disliked the man so much he could have taken the opportunity to make trouble for him. Altogether I'd

have said that this made things look better for your
man. I'll have a word with Susie Peatsea, if she's still
living at the same place, and see if I can find out anything more. Hope all's well. Love to you and Jag.

Willow

PS Tedsmore suggested that it would be worth speaking to Lutterworth's secretary. That seems a good idea,
and I have a feeling that you'd get much more out of
her than I would. You must be much nearer her age
for one thing. Will you have a crack at her or would
you like me to? W.

ELEVEN

EMMA WAS GOING THROUGH Lutterworth's polygraph results again. The charts still made no sense. He was only eight months from his automatic release date and yet he was still trying to make a stranger like her believe that he was innocent. At the same time he was displaying reactions that undoubtedly showed signs of guilt. There had to be a reason, and she was determined to find it. Her doctorate might depend on her success with Lutterworth, but there were other, perhaps even more important, things that hung on it, too.

His solicitor had written to say that in spite of his client's instructions he could not send Emma tapes of the interview with Podley and his sidekick because they had been mislaid, but he did enclose a photocopy of the transcript. With that, the records of the trial, her own notes, and everything Willow had discovered, Emma had become acquainted with a great deal of what had happened on the night of his arrest—but there were still questions she could not answer.

When Jag arrived at her room for a brainstorming session, he kissed her with ego-boosting relish, accepted a mug of tea on the grounds that it was too early for anything from the chillybin, and told her that he was at her disposal.

'Good,' said Emma, gesturing to the space she had cleared for him on the little sofa.

She herself sat with her legs tucked up under her on the neatly made bed, with the text of the interview to her left, the trial transcript to her right and her own polygraph sheets and list of questions in front of her.

'OK, shoot,' he said, looking as though he enjoyed the picture of her efficiency.

'I think I told you that when I first met Lutterworth I rather liked him,' she began.

'Yes, you did,' Jag said, nodding. 'So?'

'And then at intervals during the interview, I found him…well, creepy really and rather worrying, but then again, at the end, I felt as though I'd done him an injustice and that perhaps he was likable after all. I've been wondering which of my reactions I can trust. You see it's occurred to me that he could have been trying to suppress the creepiness in order to make me like him so that I'd accept his claims of innocence.' She paused and looked at Jag, trying to read his expression. When he did not give her any clues, she added, 'Am I off the wall here or d'you think it's possible?'

'It's possible. Likely even. But I doubt if it would have been a wholly conscious intention.' Jag waited for a moment, as though testing what he wanted to say for acceptability. When he started to speak again he showed none of his usual breezy humour: 'But you mustn't forget, Emma, that in some ways he is just your type and so you might not have needed any manipulation to make you respond favourably.'

'What on earth do you mean?' Emma looked at Jag's long legs, straggling curly black hair and general bigness. She thought of the slight, grey-faced, much older man in prison. 'He doesn't look anything like any of the men I've ever fancied or had anything to do with. Except that he's got dark hair, I suppose. Come to think of it, none of them have been fair.'

Apart from his black hair, Jag was nothing like any of the others either. Emma could not decide whether that was a good sign or not.

'I don't mean physically,' he said with a hint of impatience. 'But you do have quite a penchant for outsiders.'

'A penchant, eh? That doesn't seem a likely word for a

chillybin-kitchen-whizz-talking New Zealander,' said Emma, trying to make a joke as she usually did when she felt uncomfortable.

'Come on, Sunshine,' he said less gently still. 'You must have noticed that you go for people who don't fit in.'

Emma shook her head. Her expression was stubborn and her big blue eyes looked almost cold. 'I don't know what you mean.'

'It seems pretty clear to me, as a psychologist you understand, that because of your alienation from your own family, you are drawn to other people who are strangers within their group.' Looking at her stiffening face, he added, 'It's no criticism. It's just a point.'

Emma was surprised, both by Jag's idea and by the formality of its expression, but she was affronted, too, which shocked her. She did not approve of people who took offence. She could not think of anything to say.

Breathing evenly and still not smiling or letting her see any of his funniness or the seductive, unlikely tenderness he sometimes showed her, Jag went steadily on.

'There's me, an obvious foreigner who knows almost no one here and was more than lonely before I found you. Then there's your Willow—'

'She's no stranger,' said Emma quickly. 'She's as rooted as anything; successful and famous, too. And popular. She's not in the least lonely or any kind of outsider. She adores Tom and Lucinda and is more than adored by them. She—'

'Yeah. That's all true—now. But you told me that when you first knew her she was pretending to be someone completely different.'

'So what? She had to hide her novels and her money while she was still working in the civil service. They wouldn't have liked it at all if they'd known what she was doing and how much she was earning from it. They'd prob-

ably have stopped taking her seriously, which would have
made her job intolerable.'

'Have you never thought that she might have wanted to
disguise herself because she didn't trust anyone else to value
her real character?'

'I wonder,' said Emma, trying to be more interested than
outraged and not succeeding.

'So now perhaps there's Lutterworth, too,' said Jag, letting a little of his usual self escape around the edges of his
careful severity. 'As you said, he's a most unlikely habitant
of a dispersal prison, quite different from all the others
you've seen. He comes from a world you'd easily recognise,
he's reasonably attractive, intelligent, polite, pleasant, and
you know—or assume—that he's feeling lonely and isolated
in the new one he's trapped in, and he's probably being
bullied. You were attracted to him. It's not so surprising.'

'I do vaguely see what you're getting at,' Emma said,
trying to get rid of the sense of insult. She was not going
to be blinkered to new experiences or strange ideas if she
could possibly help it. 'But I'm not sure it's a valid point.'

'Maybe not. But it's worth thinking about. As I said, it's
nothing to be ashamed of, even if it's true.'

'And if it is true, what does that make you? I mean,
what's your interest in someone like me? A specimen for
analysis?'

Jag smiled properly then and shook his head, showing
more of the familiar character she liked so much, and said,
'Me? I've always been a sucker for lost sheep.'

'Have you now?' said Emma, not denying his assessment
of her state. 'Why?'

'That's a long story and dull. But I'm aware of it. If it
helps other people while it's helping me, why should I fight
it? It seems a relatively benign perversion, as they go.'

'And when people stop being lost, do you go off them?'
asked Emma, hoping that her face showed no sign of her

unfair irritation at being used to satisfy his dysfunctional psyche.

Jag looked at her without saying anything for so long that she began to think he was never going to answer. Eventually he put his empty mug down beside the sofa and walked towards the bed. There he knelt on the floor in front of her and took both her hands.

'It has been known,' he said. 'That's not to say it's inevitable, any more than your probable reactions to an outsider successfully integrating with the group are inevitable.'

'I still like Willow as much as I ever did,' she said, trying not to sound either angry or pathetic. 'More, really. She's more comfortable to be with now that she's so settled with Tom and everything. I think you might be wrong about *me*.'

'It's possible. A lot of psychologists often are.' After a moment he returned to the sofa and said in a different, brisker tone of voice. 'Someone once said that if we get it right fifty per cent of the time, we're doing well. So what's next on the agenda?'

Emma tried to gather her thoughts and focus on the notes she had written to remind her of the things she wanted to ask Jag.

'Come on, Sunshine. It's not that bad. It was only a suggestion. You told me there were several things you needed to sort out, and thought a trained psychologist could help. Well, I'm only a half-trained one, but, as I said, I'm at your disposal. If you want me to go away, I will.'

'Thanks,' she said, finding some of the words clearing in front of her eyes. 'I mean, I don't want you to go. But yes, here we are. OK. Yes. Um. I told you about the wild fluctuations in Lutterworth's responses to my control questions. You once suggested that might be explained by his guilt over his son's death, which seems feasible.' Emma laughed a little. 'Actually, even Willow agreed.'

'Willow agreed with me?' said Jag in a voice of pretended awe. 'My God! I must be brilliant.'

'Oh, shut up,' said Emma, feeling more like herself again. 'It's certainly true that every question that provoked a sharp change in his breathing and so on could be interpreted in the light of the boy's death, but, as you'll see if you read the questions, the connection is pretty thin in some of them. I wondered if you'd accept that there could be some doubt that it's his bereavement guilt that made him so sensitive that he saw links to Pipp's death everywhere.'

'Oh, sure. There's always doubt,' said Jag, once more sounding professional. 'It's possible that he feels more angry than guilty that his son's dead. People do.'

Emma considered that. 'In that case, there are really only two possibilities. One is that he is genuinely innocent of the crash but guilty about something else he was doing; the other, that he is guilty of the accident but knows the only reliable way to beat a polygraph is to fake violent reactions to innocuous questions. Hell! I must talk to somebody he worked with.'

'Why's that so difficult?' asked Jag, looking puzzled.

'Well, I don't know anyone at Hill, Snow, Parkes and I—' Emma broke off as Jag started to laugh. When she looked at him she saw that his dark eyes had lit up and he was looking thoroughly mischievous.

'You mean you can't talk to anyone unless you've been introduced, do you? Sunshine, you've a long way to go yet, haven't you?'

'Have I?'

'Take it from me. You want to talk to someone? You just talk. Who d'you want?'

'Well, best of all would be his secretary,' she said, remembering the postscript to Willow's latest letter. 'But I don't know her name and I can't believe any switchboard operator is going to take kindly to an enquiry for the secretary of a partner who was booted out years ago because he killed someone.'

'Don't be pathetic, Emma.' Jag strode over to the telephone, got the number of Hill, Snow, Parkes from Directory Enquiries, rang it and asked to speak to the secretary of the partner in charge of Expatriate Tax. After a moment Emma heard him say, 'Hi. I don't know if you can help me, but when I was last in England—which was a few years ago now, I must admit—I met a great girl. We've lost touch, but I'm trying to get hold of her again. She told me she worked for a man called Andrew Lutterworth in your office. When I asked to speak to her, they told me at the desk that he'd left and they wouldn't say if she's still with the company or how to get hold of her. Can you help? They were quite shirty with me, and I do want to find her. She was great.'

He put one hand over the receiver and turned to grin at Emma, saying, 'She's called Annie Frome. She left, too. They're trying to find out where she went. Yes,' he added into the receiver. 'Great. Thanks. Yes. Thanks. I will. I'll give her a call today. G'bye.'

'Well?' said Emma.

'Simple, she works for an MP now. They can't remember what his name is, but he's a backbencher and if you ring the House of Commons, you ought to get her.'

'Jag, you're a marvel. And you're right. I was being pathetic, although I could never have faked your accent or your sex. They must have helped.'

'They do sometimes, both of 'em.' He grinned. 'Well, I hope she'll be able to give you what you want.'

'So do I. At last she'll be able to say whether he'd left her anything to type that morning. If he had really spent all that time in his office, he must have produced something for her to do.'

'Isn't there anything in your files? It's so basic someone must have thought of it at the time.'

'Those are the things that usually get missed,' said Emma. 'I suspect everyone was concentrating so hard on much more important questions that they never thought to ask. Anyway, it's worth a try. I know my way around the Palace of Westminster. I did a stint there myself in my nice-girl days. Jag, I'm definitely going to go up to London again. D'you want to come? I can ask Willow if we can have her spare room for the night.'

'And risk her interrogating me about my intentions and my treatment of you again? Not likely. I'll let you go alone—unless you want protection, help, you know: anything like that?'

Emma shook her head. 'No, thanks. You've done plenty. And you've got your own work. You mustn't spend too much time on mine. You've been great, Jag, and I'm so grateful.'

'And so angry still about what I said about outsiders. Don't worry about it. It's a natural reaction to uninvited psychologising. I should have kept my mouth shut.' He smiled more self-consciously than usual. 'You'd have thought I'd know better by now. I won't do it again. Let me know how you get on. Oh, and thanks for the tea.'

He kissed her briefly, collected his helmet and clumped out of her room, boot buckles clanking as usual. Emma noticed guiltily that she felt a sense of deep relief at his absence. Deciding to ignore the feeling because there did not seem to be anything she could do about it, she pulled the telephone towards her and called the *Daily Mercury*'s number.

'Could I speak to Hal Marstall?' she said when her call was answered.

'I'll put you through.'

There was a longer pause than Emma had expected and

then an unfamiliar voice, older and rougher than Hal's, said, 'Hal Marstall's phone.'

'Oh, is he there? My name's Emma Gnatche.'

'He's not at his desk. Can I take a message?'

'Just that I called. Is that all right?'

'Sure. Has he got your number?'

Emma dictated it, feeling thoroughly silly and very unfair to Jag. There was no reason to reactivate her slight friendship with Hal simply because her dealings with Jag seemed to have been tarnished by what he had said. He was still the man he had been the previous day, when she had been almost sure that she loved him. She felt ungrateful, unsophisticated and in need of a great deal of reassurance. She pressed the buttons for Willow's number.

Mrs Rusham answered, sounding unusually flustered.

'Oh, hello, Mrs R. This is Emma. Is it possible for me to have a word with Willow?'

'She's not here, Miss Gnatche. She's already gone to Uxbridge.'

'Where?'

'I thought you'd know. As she was running out of the door, she just said that she was going there on your business. But she didn't leave a telephone number or an address or anything and I don't know how to get hold of her. And I need to.'

'Is there something the matter with Lucinda?' Emma asked urgently.

'No.' Mrs Rusham's hasty breathing began to slow a little, and she added more calmly, 'No, nothing like that. She's very well. No, it's Mr Tom. He came back unexpectedly today and he didn't seem best pleased to find Mrs Worth out.'

'That doesn't sound very likely,' said Emma at once.

'No, I know. But I think he must have expected her to be here working or something. Anyway, he's gone to his office now, but I know Mrs Worth would like to know that he's back, only I don't know how to get hold of her. She never does this, you know. She always lets me know where she's going to be and what time she'll be back. Always.'

'I shouldn't worry too much,' said Emma, realising that she could not possibly ask to be put up in the Mews if Tom had just returned, particularly not if he were angry about whatever Willow was doing on her behalf. 'I'm sure she'll be back in no time.'

'Well, I hope so. I mean, Mr Tom did sound quite annoyed. Oh, I don't know whether I'm on my head or my heels. Please forget I said that, won't you, Miss Gnatche?'

'Yes, of course,' said Emma, wondering for a mad moment whether Tom could have thrown things around or shrieked and yelled. After a moment's private amusement at the impossibility of such a thing, she had another surge of guilt at being the cause of possible conflict between him and Willow.

'Look, could you tell her when she gets in that I rang, but that it wasn't anything urgent and I'll ring her again in a few days when she's likely to be less busy?' she said. 'Will you do that?'

'Yes, of course,' said Mrs Rusham, reverting to her more familiar manner. 'She will be pleased to know that you telephoned. Goodbye, Miss Gnatche.'

As Emma replaced the receiver she suddenly remembered that she had an appointment with her professor. Having scrabbled together the papers she was likely to need, she left her room, locked it and ran down the stairs.

TWELVE

WILLOW HAD EXPECTED some difficulty in finding Susie Peatsea, in spite of the unusual surname, but when she looked in the telephone directory, there was an entry for Peatsea, P.G., at the number George Tedsmore had given her with an address in Uxbridge.

Having changed into an anonymous navy-blue suit and paler blue shirt to make herself look like a government official of some kind, and taken an old clipboard from the bottom drawer of her desk, Willow drove to Uxbridge. She found a parking space easily and knocked on the blistered black wooden door of the Peatseas' house. It was opened by a dumpy young woman in her late teens or early twenties.

She had a round, reddish face with small muddy-coloured eyes and an upturned nose, unbecomingly short, dull-brown hair and an even more unbecomingly short pink skirt worn with a tight white shirt.

'Susie Peatsea?' said Willow, trying to make her voice sound bright and official.

'Yes?' said the young woman, looking mystified and rather worried. 'What d'you want?'

Willow pulled her clipboard from under her arm, consulted an imaginary note on it and then looked up. 'I believe you have some information for us about Terry Lepe.'

'I never,' she said at once, trying to shut the door and looking as though she might cry. Willow stepped forward, saying kindly but firmly, 'Now, now, Susie, please don't be silly. I have evidence that you telephoned him at his com-

pany's head office a great many times. Now, let's get on
with it, shall we?'

'I can't.'

'Oh, dear. Why's that? Shall I come in? We do need to
talk about this, you know.'

'No,' she said, but she sounded terrified rather than stubborn.

Willow smiled reassuringly and said briskly, 'Now come
along.'

Susie walked a little further out on to the doorstep and
hissed, 'Mum'd kill me. Honest. I can't let you in.'

'Then where can we talk? It has to be today. It's imper-
ative,' said Willow, deliberately picking a pompous, offi-
cial-sounding word. It seemed to have the desired effect as
Susie's shoulders sagged in defeat.

'OK, then, if I have to. There's a café down the road.
You go and I'll join you. Joe's Café, it's called. But please
don't make a noise now.'

It had not taken Willow long to realise that Susie was
less than bright, but even so she was surprised not to have
been asked for her name or even which organisation she
represented. She was older than Susie, dressed in the sort
of clothes people in authority might wear, and she spoke
with confidence; that appeared to be enough.

'Very well. I shall await you at Joe's Café. Please be as
quick as you can.'

Hoping that Susie would not find enough courage to ignore her instructions, Willow walked down to the road to
the café. It was pleasanter than she had expected and much
cleaner. She ordered a cup of tea and a fresh-looking flapjack from a pile under a perspex dome on the counter.

Before they had been brought to her table, Susie appeared
in the doorway. Willow stood up and beckoned.

'Would you like tea?' she asked when Susie reached the
table. 'Or something else? And what about a flapjack?'

'Tea. Ta. I don't want nothing to eat.'

'Fine,' said Willow and signalled to the waitress for another cup of tea. 'Well now, sit down and tell me what you know of Terry.' She laid the clipboard on the table and sat with a felt-tipped pen poised to write.

'I don't know nothing.'

'Now, come along, Susan, and don't play games with me.' Willow was letting herself sound more severe. 'He was your boyfriend, wasn't he?'

'Well, sort of. Don't tell my mum, will you? Please, don't tell my mum. She'd kill me.'

'We have no interest in telling your family anything,' said Willow, beginning to think that Susie might have nothing more to offer than an illicit relationship with an unsatisfactory young man. 'When did you start going out with Lepe?'

Susie blushed and twiddled her fingers and then counted on them and eventually announced that it was December three years earlier, which would have made it about two months before the crash. Willow wrote the date on her clipboard and decided to get straight to the point. If Susie knew nothing about Terry Lepe's dealings with Andrew Lutterworth, there would be no point tormenting her with questions about him.

'Did he ever tell you anything about a Mr Andrew Lutterworth?'

'What?' Susie sounded as though his name meant nothing to her, but something had sparked in her eyes at the mention of his name. Willow spoke even more briskly than before.

'It's a simple enough question. Did Terry Lepe ever tell you about a man called Andrew Lutterworth, who worked for the company where he was a security guard?'

'He never.'

Willow frowned. 'But you've heard the name, haven't you? Who did talk to you about him? Come along. You'd do better to get it off your chest while I'm here. This is your one chance to straighten everything out.'

'I haven't got nothing to get off of my chest,' said Susie, crying. She did not have a handkerchief and was snivelling into her cupped hand when Willow fetched a bundle of paper napkins from the counter.

'Take these, drink some tea and try to pull yourself together,' she said. When Susie had obeyed most of the instructions, Willow added, 'Now, where have you heard his name?'

'I never heard it. I saw it, like, in the paper.' Susie's voice wavered. 'About the crash, see.'

Hardly able to believe that they had got so quickly and easily to the point of the interview, Willow said, 'When did you see his name in the paper?'

'Two years ago, it was. When the woman at the Job Centre, she said I ought to try and read them. And I do try, honest. Every day. And there was all them stories about him and the crash.'

'Was that the first you knew of the crash?' asked Willow, realising that the articles would have been published after Andrew's conviction.

She had always assumed that he had spent several months on bail before his case reached the top of the court lists, but she had never stopped to wonder how he had spent the time or what the inevitable tension must have done to his relationship with Jemima. It seemed likely that the other partners of Hill, Snow, Parkes would have asked him to take gardening leave until after the verdict. They could hardly have wanted to embarrass their clients with the presence of a man who might go to prison and yet they could not possibly have sacked him in advance of a verdict that might just as well have proved him innocent.

'Susie?'

She shook her head, more tears poured down her cheeks and made her nose run.

'Then when did you first hear about it?' asked Willow as her naturally suspicious mind latched on to the fear she could see in Susie's waterlogged eyes.

'I didn't hear. I saw it. That night. See?' Susie looked up piteously at Willow.

'Were you there? At the crash I mean?' She wondered whether Susie could be so short of excitement in her life that she had fantasised about being part of a dramatic story she had read in the tabloids. It did not seem particularly likely, and when Willow looked more carefully at Susie, she thought she could see real torment in her eyes as well as fear. 'You were there, weren't you, Susie?'

'Don't tell my mum. Please don't tell my mum.'

'I won't. But you must tell me everything now. You will feel very much better when you've done that. I shall write it all down and then you can forget about it.'

'Will I have to go to prison?' she asked through her snivels.

'I shouldn't have thought so,' said Willow, salving her conscience with the fact that it really did seem unlikely. 'Unless you were driving. You weren't, were you?'

Susie shook her head. Yet more tears sprayed out of her eyes.

'I can't drive. But he said it was my fault. He said if I hadn't been making such a caterwauling and distracting him, it wouldn't never of happened.'

'Andrew Lutterworth?' said Willow, quite unable to believe that any man responsible for commissioning the house she had seen or being married to Jemima could have had any kind of relationship with the pathetic, plain young woman in front of her. Susie looked up in dumb astonishment, shaking her head.

'It was Terry. I thought you knew. I thought that's why you come. Who are you?'

'We just need confirmation,' said Willow quickly, writing something meaningless on the clipboard. 'Was that why you were trying to get in touch with him two years ago?'

Susie nodded. 'He said no one would know it was me so long as I kept my mouth shut. Till I read the paper, I thought they must of been all right, like he said. He was going to get an ambulance, see. They weren't bad hurt, he said. They'd be all right and if I kept my mouth shut I'd be all right, too. He said I couldn't see him in case people guessed it was my fault. An' I did what he said. Honest. Till I read about it in the paper and that other man going in prison for it.'

Susie stopped, her eyes full of horror. 'He went to prison for what we done.'

'How did you know it was the same crash?'

'It must of been. It was in that village where it happened. And there was a woman with a baby in a buggy. I saw the notice of the village then. It was big letters, see. I could read it. Honest I could. And there was the picture of the car in the paper. It's what it looked like. It said in the paper they were dead, the woman and her baby, and she might've lived if anyone had got an ambulance. Terry said he'd phone for one, but in the paper they said no one had. And that man was in prison, but it was us. It was me. I had to ask Terry what to do. But he wouldn't talk to me. Then when I said I'd go round and see him, 'cos I had to, then he did. He phoned later ever so cross with me. If I tell anyone I'll go to prison, he said. And it would be for longer than that man got because it was my fault he was there just like it was my fault they got killed.'

'And you believed him?'

Susie looked so puzzled by Willow's question that it was obvious she had believed him implicitly.

'I see. Well, we'll have to speak to Terry about this, Susie. How can we find him?'

'I don't know. He said he was going to America and he'd send for me when he could, but he hasn't. Oh, miss, will I have to go to prison? Mum'll kill me.'

'I shouldn't think so, Susie. If it was Terry who was driving, then I don't think you'll have to go to prison whatever happens. But I'll find out for you. And I won't say anything to your mother.' Susie's dull, stupid honesty forced Willow to add, 'I'm not in the police force, you know.'

'Oh?' said Susie, apparently not particularly interested.

'No. Shall I telephone you, when I know more?'

'No, don't phone. My mum—'

'Could I ring you at your work, then?'

'I don't go to work.'

'But you said you'd been at the Job Centre two years ago.'

'That's right. But they never give me a job, see.'

'Oh, yes, I do see. Well, I'll come by, shall I then? At about this time in the afternoon and bring you along here to the café and tell you anything I've discovered?'

Susie nodded, still looking scared. 'And you won't tell, will you?'

'I'll have to see. I don't want to frighten you, but the truth will have to come out in the end.'

Susie nodded again without speaking, and Willow could see that she had always assumed she would be found out one day. Willow felt outraged at what Terry Lepe had done to her.

'I do need some more details of what happened that night, before I go, Susie. What happened? Did Terry come to collect you in the big car?'

'Yes. He didn't usually, see. He came in his own car. But this time he said a mate of his had lent him the car and he'd take me for a drive. It was lovely, with a music centre and

all. CDs and heating and a rug, too. And he had whisky. It
was a bad night, all wet and black and cold. He wanted me
to drink it, but I didn't like it. He had some, though.'

'Where did he take you?'

'Bucks he said it was. He drove really fast down the
motorway. I'd never been that fast before. At first I liked it;
then it was scary. So he turned off and took us to a wood.
Burning Beeches he called it or something like that. And he
went off through a gate into a sort of field thing and stopped.
He kissed me.'

She stopped talking.

'Was that the first time he'd kissed you?' asked Willow,
excited by the first real breakthrough in the case but at the
same time reluctant to force Susie to relive something that
had so clearly frightened her. Willow comforted herself with
the thought that Susie might have fewer nightmares if she
could bring the story out into the open and have it accepted
by someone else, someone she clearly believed carried some
kind of authority.

'Never like that before. It was like the motorway. At first
I liked it, but then I didn't. I'd never been with a boy before.
You know, like…sex and that. And he got…' Her voice
died again and her bright pink face grew redder.

'He got a bit rough, did he?'

'How did you know?' she asked as though amazed that
anyone should understand. Willow's heart was wrung with
pity and impatience. 'And he started pulling off my clothes
and I screamed. Then he hit me across the face and said I
was a silly bitch. I thought he was going to…'

'But he didn't?' prompted Willow hopefully.

'No. He hit me again and pushed me back in my seat and
put his seat belt on again and drove off. He went even faster
and he was swearing about silly bitches and cunts and that.
Oh, I'm sorry, miss. And I was so scared and then he was
racing through that village and I saw them and I screamed

and he drove into them. He said if I hadn't of screamed it wouldn't of happened. It was my fault, see. It was.'

'Terry drove into the woman and her baby?'

'Yes. Then he swore again 'n' stopped, and went to look. Then he came back and pulled me out of the car and said he'd have to protect me or I'd go to prison. He said I had to do everything he said and then it'd be all right. And I asked him if he was still angry. An' he stopped for a minute and touched my face where he'd bruised it. He was all nice to me again then. In a hurry but nice. And he said he was sorry about my face. But I shouldn't of done it 'cos men can't stop, like, not once they've started. He told me all about it. And he did say he was sorry even though it was my fault.'

'Susie, it was *not* your fault,' said Willow as clearly as she could. 'Neither the crash nor his anger. He shouldn't have tried to make you kiss him when you had said you didn't want to. He shouldn't have pulled off your clothes and he certainly shouldn't have hit your face.'

'It was cut too, I saw after. I had a split lip. Mum was ever so cross with me when I had to go to school looking like that.'

'So did Terry bring you home then after the accident?'

'Oh yes. He took me across the fields to somewhere he said he had friends and made me wait in a phone box. It was all wet and smelly and I was so scared. I thought p'raps he'd gone to get the police after all. But he hadn't. He came back in a car. A Metro, it was. I recognised it. I don't know many cars, but I know them ones. It was really old. He brought me back and told me what I had to say and do so I wouldn't go to prison. He was nice again then. Honest he was.'

'And that was the end of it, was it, until you saw the papers?'

'Yes. Till I left school and Mum made me go to the Job Centre.'

'So how old were you when Terry took you for that drive?' Willow tried to keep all the boiling anger out of her face and voice so as not to frighten Susie any more.

'Fifteen I was then. When it happened.'

'Oh, Susie.' Willow wanted to hug the poor stupid ugly child and take her away and educate her in the facts of life and law so that she had some chance of standing up for herself even if she never did achieve a paying job. 'I don't think you need to worry about going to prison. I'm not absolutely certain, but I think it's very unlikely. I'll find out some more and I'll let you know, shall I?'

'Yes, please, miss,' she said, looking up at Willow with a sickening dependence.

When Willow left the café, in an even more furious rage with Terry Lepe, she hoped that his erstwhile colleague was right and that he had fled to the North of England rather than to America. It would be hard enough to find him in England, but probably impossible in America. She drove home through the rush-hour traffic, looking forward to telling Emma of the extraordinary coup she had achieved, and wondering all over again why Lutterworth had lied for so long and landed himself in prison.

It was past six when she reached the Mews and she ran guiltily into the house, well aware that she was late for Lucinda's bath. Hearing sounds of splashing and squeaking, she realised that the dependable Mrs Rusham had stepped into the breach once more.

'Hello, you two,' she said, pushing open the bathroom door, and then she saw her husband bending over the bath, scooping water over Lucinda's bare back. Willow dropped her bag and notebook on the floor, hearing the keys clattering out of it. 'Tom.'

'Hello, Will,' he said, continuing to scoop water and not looking at her.

She wondered whether to ask him what he was sulking about and then decided that would probably be counterproductive. He liked correction as little as she did. Keeping as much of the excited smile as possible on her face, she asked him when he had got home.

'About three this afternoon. Mrs R said she didn't know where you'd run off to and so I dumped my stuff and went to the office. Got back a few minutes ago to discover that there was still no news of you and Lucinda needed her bath. Didn't you, Lulu?'

'Yes,' she said, kicking up vast fountains of water all over the floor and Willow's good blue suit. Lucinda giggled. Tom still did not meet Willow's gaze.

'Yes, I was held up. I'm sorry. I am so glad you're back, Tom. You two look as though you're getting on well, so I think I'd better go and change out of this wet suit. Is Mrs Rusham in the kitchen?'

'I imagine so,' said Tom.

Willow recognised the signs of a serious bout of stroppiness and thought she would probably do best to leave him to sort himself out. He rarely sulked for long and she loathed the idea of having the kind of relationship in which her part was to cajole the tough, much-burdened breadwinner into smiles and relaxation with her pretty tricks and charm. Even the silent words made her swing between nausea and deep amusement. The thought of a woman like herself indulging in pretty tricks was too ludicrous to contemplate for long.

Later, dressed in comfortable easy-fitting jeans and a loose shirt, Willow went into the kitchen to fetch a glass of cold white wine from the fridge and chat to Mrs Rusham. She apologised for not having been able to warn Willow of Tom's return and then gave her the afternoon's telephone messages, including the one from Emma. Willow thanked her and took the wine to her writing room, where she sat down at her reproachful desk and telephoned Emma.

There was no answer and so Willow turned on her word processor to begin to type up a report of Susie Peatsea's amazing revelation. After about ten minutes, just as she was completing the physical description of Susie, Willow heard Tom's footsteps in the corridor outside the room.

'I'm in here,' she called as peaceably as though they had not had their silent quarrel. 'Come on in.'

He came in and stood behind her chair, putting his big hands on her shoulders and stroking them. Willow had had to force herself not to file the document the moment she realised he was there and had left it on the screen for him to read.

'What's up?' he said mildly enough after a pause. 'That's not the book, is it?'

'No,' she said, working hard to sound neither angry nor defensive, just ordinary. 'It's a report of a meeting I had this afternoon with a woman who may know something about a false-confession case that Emma Gnatche wants to use for her thesis. She was in a panic about it and I volunteered to help.'

Willow found herself wanting to apologise to Tom for doing something she knew he would dislike, but she controlled the impulse since his dislike struck her as both exaggerated and unreasonable. She could not bear the idea that anyone she loved as much as she loved Tom might consider her position in their relationship to be subordinate to his, and so she had to make it clear that he had no right to an apology. She did what she had to do in her life, as did he. They were, or they ought to have been, equals and he had no right to set limits on what she was allowed to do. She waited for him to begin the truce negotiations.

'I'm not quite sure what to say,' he produced eventually.

'Then it's probably wisest not to say anything,' she suggested. 'I do regret that I wasn't here when you got back. I've missed you so much that it seems a pity to have missed this afternoon, too.'

'Well, that's something.'

'Tom, please don't,' said Willow, swinging round on her chair and taking his hands in hers. She looked up into his face and was glad to see that he was prepared to look back at her by then. 'You haven't been like this for ages. Just because I've been doing a minor bit of a small, unthreatening investigation for Emma, you've jumped to all sorts of conclusions, and you're acting as though I'm defying you on some life-and-death matter.'

'It could be precisely that,' he said reasonably. 'I don't mean about defying. It's not a question of defiance. But you know perfectly well that some of your previous forays into detection have been appallingly dangerous. You've taken quite unwarrantable risks with your own safety—and Lucinda's.'

'Just as you risk yourself every day,' she said mildly enough, while something in her mind was shrieking: The rules have to be the same for both of us. I know Lucinda was nearly killed in hospital just after she was born. I regret that bitterly, but are you going to throw it at me whenever I take a step outside the house? You cannot control me. You must let me take whatever risks I consider necessary. Today there was not the slightest danger to Lucinda of any kind. She was entirely safe here with Mrs Rusham, whom both of us trust absolutely.

'The investigation I'm doing isn't remotely dangerous. It's about a case of dangerous driving. There's a man in prison for it. Emma's sure he was not even in the car when it crashed and yet he's taking the punishment for it. And she wants to know why. This afternoon, I talked to a woman I thought was only peripherally involved, but it turns out

that she was in the car when it crashed and that the driver
was a friend of hers, not the man doing time.'

'I see,' said Tom, stepping back and sitting on a stool.
'Will, I know I make you angry by wishing that you
wouldn't do these things, but you must see why I don't want
you to.'

'Yes, I do. But I would really like it if you could…not
allow me my own life because it's not yours to allow, but
say that you understand why I can't be subject to your orders.'

'I do,' he said, looking unhappy. 'And they're no orders.
Look, I wish that you wouldn't treat my natural urge to
protect you as something between a psychosis and a mortal
insult.'

'I don't,' she said, saddened by his sadness, 'but I need
my freedom. It panics me when I feel as though you're
trying to confine me.'

'That's not what I'm trying to do,' he said, standing up.
'Lulu's in bed. What would you feel about switching off
that thing for the moment, bringing your drink down and
telling me all about this case of Emma's? It sounds interesting.'

She checked his brown eyes for sincerity, patronage and
anger, and thought she saw only affection and an urge to
mend their quarrel. Grateful for those, sharing both, she still
wished that his feelings for her could torment him less.

'Yes,' she said. 'Hang on a tick while I file this and I'll
come down with you.'

THIRTEEN

UNAWARE of Willow's dramatic discovery, Emma was back at Andrew Lutterworth's prison in search of more clues to his motives for lying to the police, to her, to everyone involved. He was brought into the interview room by an officer she did not know, looking as controlled and sure of himself as ever.

As soon as the officer had left them alone, Andrew held out both hands, saying, 'How wonderful of you to come back so soon! I can't tell you how pleased I am that you invented more questions to put to me. You'd better strap me into that thing quickly so that we can get shot of them and start talking about things that matter.'

Less convinced by his enthusiasm than she might once have been, Emma stayed on her side of the grey table and merely asked him how he was. He let his hands drop without showing any embarrassment and pulled out the chair on his side of the table.

'I'm well enough.' He sat down. 'But I'm not sure that you are. What's happened, Emma? You seem unhappy. Has someone been unkind to you? Surely not.'

'I'm fine,' she said, smiling. Whatever his motives might be for trying to make her like him, or hers for wanting to respond, he was being polite, and she had no reason to reject that just because of something Jag had said.

'I don't believe you. You're all edgy, and you look as though someone's hurt you.'

'No. I'm fine. If you can see anything, it's probably rage. I've been having a bit of a barney with my boyfriend actually,' she said, hoping he would leave it at that. 'I'm sorry it shows.'

'You'd better tell me all about it.' Andrew rolled up his sleeve and extended his arm so that she could fit the blood-pressure cuff around it. 'I'm sure I can help, give you a clue about the male point of view perhaps.'

'No, thank you very much,' said Emma tartly before she could stop herself. She smoothed the Velcro fastenings together. 'Sorry. I just feel as though I've had a bit too much of the male point of view recently. No, what I need from you is something to help me sort out the muddle I made over your first polygraph test. I can't think what went wrong, but, as I said in my message, I got a wildly erratic reading. The machines may be on the blink or something. I'm sorry; it must be a real pain for you.'

'Quite the reverse. I'm overjoyed the machines went on the blink. I told you, being able to talk to someone like you, who shares my language and my outlook is...oh, like I imagine food must be when one's starving.'

'Thank you,' said Emma, wishing that he could be a bit more ordinary. 'Before we start, may I just establish a ground rule or two?'

'I thought we'd already done all that. I know you can't get me out of here. Don't worry about it. I trust you implicitly and will do just as you tell me for the good of your thesis—and my peace of mind.'

'Good for you,' said Emma, a little surprised.

'And perhaps,' he said with an almost impish smile, 'your test will give me a better chance of getting a decent job when I get out of here.'

'I'm not sure...'

'I think it will, Emma. I know that I'll probably never get rid of the criminal record, but, if I can show potential employers that you've tested me and found me honest, I'm sure it'll help.'

'I hope so,' said Emma. 'Mr Lutterworth—'

'Andrew, please. Help me keep the illusion of having a friend in this friendless place for a little while longer.'

'Andrew, then. I don't want to torment you: I just want to get all this clear. And—'

'Emma, my child, you couldn't possibly torment me. You must know that by now.'

'Mr Lutterworth, please. This is both serious and important. What I have to ask you now is whether you'd be prepared to answer questions about the death of your son.'

The colour drained out of his face and the enthusiasm from his eyes. They looked like stones, hard and absolutely without light. His voice was quite as harsh as he said, 'How dare you?'

Emma looked away. Fiddling with her cassette recorder, she forced herself to say, 'Because I have to ask about it to establish the reasons for some of the responses I recorded in the last test. I couldn't bear the thought of taking advantage of you, and so I wanted to get your permission before I started. I didn't want to catch you unawares. That would have been unfair.' She looked at him again and detested the fury she saw in his face. For the first time since he had grabbed her wrist she saw the potential for violence in him and it frightened her. 'Please let me explain. I'm not trying to pry into your grief—God forbid!—simply to make sense of what looked like nonsense in the last test.'

'I can't imagine how any explanation might make me less angry about this gross intrusion into my privacy. I am sh— surprised… No, in fact I *am* shocked that a woman like you, a woman in whom I had confided and whom I had trusted and liked so much…' His voice wavered and then stiffened again as he went on: 'That a woman like you should be so crass, so intrusive, really is shocking. So cruel, too. How could you?'

He was pulling open the blood-pressure cuff as he spoke,

tearing the minute hooks of the Velcro tape out of each other with a horrible ripping sound.

'I do not think that we have anything more to say to each other, Ms Gnatche. Please do not approach me again in person or on paper. I have no wish to see you again ever.' He stood up, glaring at her, and then turned to signal to the officer who was patrolling the corridor outside the interview rooms. Emma was left feeling a fool and an insensitively cruel fool, which was worse.

'I'll be back to escort you out,' said the officer to Emma as he led Lutterworth out of the interview room.

Emma packed away her kit and decided that she ought to ask to see the wing governor before she left. It turned out that he was busy, but he sent a message to say that, if she would telephone between 5.30 and 6 that evening, he would be able to speak to her for a few minutes and would do his best to help. The assistant who brought the news added that the governor had asked her to remind Emma that he could not put any pressure on any of the prisoners to help her with her research or to take polygraph tests.

'No, I know that,' said Emma, grateful for the woman's sympathetic expression as she delivered the message. 'Will you thank him very much, assure him that I am not going to ask him to lean on anyone and say that I'll ring as near half past five as I can?'

'Yes, of course. It's been nice to see you again. Did you know that Robert Whixall has got his parole? He's ever so grateful to you for doing that test and he's sure it had an effect on his board.'

'Whixall?' said Emma, thinking back and remembering a chillingly controlling young man who had been sentenced to five years for date rape.

'He was talking about writing to thank you, and he was quite upset when the governor wouldn't give him your address.' She smiled cosily. 'Naturally.'

'I'm grateful for that,' said Emma, uncomfortably aware of how vulnerable she had been making herself.

'Don't worry about it. I must go, but I expect we'll meet again.'

'I hope so,' said Emma, knowing that she had probably blown any chance of finding out the truth about Andrew Lutterworth. 'Thank you for all your help.'

She was left to collect her keys and umbrella from security and walk out of the prison. Pausing for a moment to look back at it, she thought about the men who were locked up in the hundreds of cells it contained.

With several of the other postgraduate students she had been taken on a full tour of one of the biggest old Victorian prisons soon after she had arrived at St Albans. She had been shocked to see the smallness of the cells in which two or occasionally three men were locked up together for hours each day, men who had been complete strangers to each other until they were sent there, and might easily loathe each other.

It had appalled her, too, to discover that it was possible for a man on remand, who might well be acquitted when he eventually came to court, to be bullied, raped or beaten up by other inmates while he was in the care of the state. It would be indefensible, she thought, even if he had committed some serious crime; if he was innocent, it would be unspeakable. She had been distressed to learn that although everyone knew such things happened, no one in authority seemed worried enough to find a way to stop it.

Turning her back on the prison, with the friendly sounds of traffic and the voices of free men, women and children in her ears, she lugged her equipment over to the telephone box to call a minicab. Only when she was putting her Phonecard in the slot did it occur to her that, since she had to go via London to get back to St Albans, she might as

well take advantage of that and try to see Lutterworth's
secretary while she was there.

Within a few moments she was through to the House of
Commons switchboard and asking for Annie Frome.

'James Shrewsbury's office,' said a pleasant voice a second or two later.

'Is that Annie Frome?'

'Yes. How may I help you?'

'This may sound a bit cheeky,' said Emma, reverting to
her old drawly, carelessly snobbish accent in spite of her
dislike of the sound of it, 'but my name's Emma Gnatche,
and I'm ringing because I wanted to ask you something
about your last job.'

'About Hill, Snow, Parkes?' The voice sounded surprised
and faintly worried.

'Yes. And about your boss there. But, look, you don't
know anything about me. As I say, my name is Emma
Gnatche, and I'm doing a postgraduate degree that entails
research into cases like this. Would you be prepared to talk
to me?'

'Well, I'm not sure if—'

'It would be such a help,' said Emma, hoping to talk her
into being cooperative. 'I could give you references from
my professor and so on. Of course. Look, I know from my
own days working for a backbencher that you must be fan-
tastically busy, but could you spare me a few minutes after
work today? We could have a drink or something and I
could tell you what I'm after. Then you could decide
whether you wanted to talk or not.' She laughed. 'I'm perfectly safe, you know. But if you decided you didn't want
to say anything, then obviously that would be that.'

'Well, I suppose it'd be all right to meet,' said Annie.
'As it happens, I'm not going out this evening. Look, it's
quarter past two now. I can't really knock off much before

half past five. But I could see you then. Where shall we meet?'

'Wherever you like. It's a lovely day. Why don't we just find a bench in St James's and start getting our legs brown. Then I can buy you a drink or some food or something. Whatever you want.'

'Good idea,' said Annie. 'D'you know the bench directly opposite the Horse Guards, you know in the middle, backing on to the park?'

'Yes.'

'Let's meet at that one, then. It's the most unmistakable and we can always go somewhere else if it's too crowded.'

'Great. I'll be there from five thirty and wait for you if you're held up. Thank you.'

Emma worked out that she would have time to take all her equipment to the station before meeting Annie, which would make everything easier. She packed it all into a left-luggage locker and then took the tube along to St James's Park.

She was early at the appointed bench and sat there, watching the people emerging from their Whitehall offices. Several of them looked so like Anthony that she found herself poised on the edge of the bench, ready to get up and go if one of them accosted her. None of them did.

Noticing how hard her heart was banging against her ribs, she asked herself whether it was possible that at some level she could still feel afraid of him. It seemed absurd. As she often told herself, she was no longer in his power and in any case it had been years since he had done anything to terrorise her.

Suddenly memories of his brutality flooded into her mind. A painful spasm seized her muscles. Her jaw clamped shut. She could not have moved or spoken.

When she had got herself back under control, licking her lips to relax her jaw, she tried to be academically interested

in why she might have felt brave enough to give up her
defences against the worst memories. For once she felt not
the slightest temptation to dismiss the things he had done
to her as normal schoolboyish teasing or a younger sister.
They might have started as that, but they had turned into
something much crueller.

For the first time, she wondered how Anthony himself
remembered them and whether he would be able to give her
any rational explanation if she were ever to ask him why
he had needed to torment her so.

A young brown-haired woman was walking towards her,
dressed in a short straight black skirt and a bright-green,
gilt-buttoned jacket.

'Annie?' Emma said as she stood up. She had moved too
quickly and her head swam unpleasantly until her balance
had righted itself.'

'Yes,' answered the young woman, looking rather surprised. 'Could you possibly be Emma Gnatche?'

'Yes.' At the sight of Annie's obvious surprise, Emma
remembered her old black jeans and the torn pockets of the
jacket she had found in an Oxfam shop. They could hardly
have looked less likely for someone who had drawled as
snobbishly as she had done over the telephone or who had
once worked in the Houses of Parliament. Privately amused,
she hoped that she would be able to convince the other
woman of her respectability.

'Sorry I'm looking so tatty,' she said, drawling again.
'I've just been interviewing the sort of people who'd have
been put off by my usual clothes. Shall we sit here and talk
or would you rather walk?'

'Could we walk?' Annie said, looking reassured. 'I'm a
bit stiff actually. I went to the gym at lunchtime and overdid
it: I'd like to keep my muscles moving.' As they set off
towards the lake, she added, 'So tell me: what sort of research are you doing? You said something about cases

like Andrew Lutterworth's. D'you mean dangerous driving?'

Emma explained her interest as diplomatically as possible.

'And so,' she went on, 'wanting to know all sorts of things about what he was really like, I thought I'd come to you. After all, as his secretary, you must have known more about him than virtually anyone else. Was he a nice man?'

Annie wrinkled up her nose and bit her lower lip.

'It's hard to say. Sometimes he could be great, a really good boss to work for. You know: giving one interesting things to do, not treating one as a moron and all that. And then sometimes he could be a right bastard.'

'Had he always been like that, or did he change after his son died?'

'Oh, no. I could've put up with that. Anyone would. I mean it was awful about Pipp, and it's true Andy did go very peculiar then. Of course he did. I mean, who wouldn't? No, the bastard tendencies had always been there. I'd worked for him for a while before Pipp died and then went on with him until he was arrested.' She shivered in her good clothes.

'Do you think he was guilty?' asked Emma abruptly.

'Of that car crash? Well, yes, he must have been. It stands to reason, doesn't it?'

'Does it? Why? I don't know enough about him, you see.'

'Well, he confessed to it,' said Annie as though that were all the answer anyone could possible need. Seeing Emma's doubts she added with a humourless smile, 'Andy would never have done that in a million years if he hadn't been guilty. He loathed accepting the blame for anything and would always find someone else to pin it on if he could. I'm sure that's why he withdrew the confession when he'd had a chance to toughen up again after the shock of knowing he'd killed those people.'

'But he'd already reported his car as stolen before he was arrested,' protested Emma. 'Don't you think his story might have been true?'

Annie shook her head. There was intelligence in her eyes and the first signs of humour.

'The whole business of the car being stolen always seemed to me to be such nonsense. It was just Andy's sort of story. Someone did it. It wasn't his fault. That was the usual scenario. Whenever there was any cataclysmic trouble in the office, he'd make sure no one could blame him. Once or twice I think he even removed memos from the file to "prove" that he couldn't have known about something that went belly up and that he should've stopped.'

'Oh, surely not,' said Emma with a vivid memory of the man himself. 'At his age and with all his status at Hill, Snow, Parkes?'

'I know; you'd have thought that once he became a partner he'd have had the dignity to take whatever flak was coming, but he never could. I thought it made him look incredibly silly, but he'd go into extraordinary contortions to get out of the slightest fragment of blame, even putting it on to other partners sometimes and often on to the troops. The other partners loathed him for it, but he was always so clever—and good with clients, too—that they put up with him. Well, mostly. But quite a lot of people were quite glad to see him pulled down and humiliated by being arrested like that. I mean, he couldn't exactly get out of that one, could he?'

'I knew you'd know more about him than anyone else,' said Emma in satisfaction. 'Can you remember much about the morning he was arrested?'

'I don't think I'll ever forget it.'

'I mean in detail.'

'The same applies,' Annie said, standing on the edge of the lake, watching a group of ducks and moorhens squab-

bling over pieces of sodden bread. 'I couldn't forget anything that happened that morning. It really was awful, you
see. Much as I sometimes loathed him, I did… Well, it was
awful. But they'd taken him long before I got to the office.
There isn't anything I could tell you about that. I don't know
anything that could help you.'

'Maybe not,' said Emma, 'but on the other hand, you
might. Tell me everything you can remember about what
you heard and saw. Had he left you any work for instance?'

'Oh, God yes! Masses. There was an enormous pile of
stuff beside my screen. I could have killed him when I saw
it, to tell you the truth. I'd been late enough the night before
finishing something that he said he absolutely must get out
the door before I left. And I was due to go to the theatre
that night. It wasn't fair, but then he never was fair. I didn't
leave the building until after eight and so I missed the whole
of the first act. I was still seething next morning, and then
there was all the new stuff.'

Emma looked at Annie and realised that she had never
made the connection. Clearly none of the police officers nor
the defence team had seen it either. Rather pleased that she
had proved Jag wrong about something, Emma decided that
it was not for her to enlighten Annie. Instead she asked some
more anodyne questions and then said she probably ought
to go.

'But I haven't told you anything useful yet. Don't you
want to know more about Andy?'

'Like what?'

'Well, scandal and all that.'

'Was there any?' asked Emma, belatedly remembering
Hal's theories about a mistress, and her own sense that Lutterworth was interested in sex.

'He always had pretty roving hands. It's really frowned
on at Hill, Snow, like in most places nowadays, but it does
still go on a bit.'

'Did he try it on with you?'

'Only when I first went to work with him. It was a sort of automatic thing with him, I think. But when he saw I wasn't having any of it, he stopped at once.'

'That must have been a relief.' Emma was amused at the thought of passing on that bit of news to Jane, who had been so dismissive of her suggestion that Andrew might have been susceptible to women. 'So no sexual harassment of you. Did he have much success with other people, d'you know?'

'I'm not sure. He talked a lot about it, which suggests that perhaps he didn't actually do anything very much.' She and Emma both laughed.

'Was there ever any talk about a particular woman, a sort of long-term girlfriend, mistress, anything like that?' asked Emma.

'None at all. And he never ordered flowers or took anyone out to lunch—except clients. Too mean, probably.'

'You didn't like him much, did you?'

'No. I didn't.'

'Then why on earth did you stick it for so long?' asked Emma.

'Well, I'd been at Hill, Snow for ages and I'd only just been promoted to being a partner's secretary when they sent me to him,' said Annie. 'They pay quite well at that level, and I thought I couldn't wimp out so quickly just because he could be such a bad-tempered sod. And then, as I say, there were times when he was charm itself. You couldn't ever be sure it was real. You know, he'd appear to like you and then savage you for something that was his fault. But it always came back and while the balance was just on the side of more charm than soddery it seemed worth it. Then when Pipp died, I didn't think I could abandon him.'

'He felt it, did he?'

'Well, of course he did,' said Annie, looking astonished.

'I mean, who wouldn't? He was all over the place. I found him one morning, a few weeks after it happened, just sitting at his desk crying. He looked awful and I think he must have been banging his hands against the wall somewhere. They were bruised and his nails were filthy and all ragged. I felt so sorry for him. I haven't ever had anything like that happen to me, but I've been miserable enough to understand what somebody might feel that would make them do that: you know, crash their fists into the walls and drag their fingernails over the bricks. There wasn't anything I could do to help except put up with his temper as patiently as possible and hope that kindness would get through to him in the end. There wasn't anything else anyone could have done.'

'What about his wife?'

'What about her?' Annie asked with a hint of hostility.

'Wasn't there anything she could have done for him?'

'Heavens no! She made it far worse. She flipped completely.' Annie sounded contemptuous and then looked as though she had embarrassed herself. After a moment she added more kindly, 'I mean, obviously it was awful for her, with her son dying like that, but she did make it far worse for poor old Andy. She was in such a state that he had to get her into a nursing home at one moment, a place that specialises in crisis care for private psychiatric patients. And then she went and ran away. Imagine how ghastly that must have been! He was at his wits' end until they found her. I think honestly it was the shock of him being arrested that made her realise what she'd been doing to him. She took a pull on herself then, but it was too late for him.'

'I can imagine,' said Emma, forgetting all her ambivalent feelings about Lutterworth in a surge of sympathy. 'But what d'you mean about being too late?'

'Oh, I've always thought that the state she left him in must have been why he behaved so bizarrely about the crash—you know, that he just wasn't himself, and didn't think what he was doing. I think he must have felt all the stuff about Pipp, who was a sweet boy, you know, and Jemima washing over him again, couldn't bear the office, got the car, whizzed out on to the M40 without even planning where to go and not quite come to until he'd smashed into those people.'

'Yes, I see,' said Emma. 'I suppose I can imagine that happening. I wonder… Help, look at the time. I really honestly must go. You've been very helpful, Annie.'

'It's been a pleasure. But…' She broke off, looking uncomfortable.

'What?'

'Look, if you should write anything up about all this you won't say anywhere that I talked to you, will you?'

'No. But why?'

'It's just I wouldn't want Andy knowing that I'd gossiped about him,' said Annie. 'He'd…he'd be very pissed off.'

'No, that's all right,' said Emma, thinking that Annie looked almost frightened and remembering Lutterworth's stonelike eyes and harshly angry voice. 'I won't let on. Well, I have enjoyed talking to you. I hope the House suits you better than Hill, Snow did. 'Bye.'

IT WAS NOT until Emma was back in St Albans, aching with the effort of carrying her equipment back from the bus stop, that she found a note in her pigeonhole asking her to telephone Willow. Forgetting her stretched muscles, she hurried up the stairs to her room, almost tripping over a bunch of freesias. She unlocked the door of her room, dumped her kit, and went back for the flowers, tucking them under her arm so that she could open the note.

It was from Hal, apologising for not having been available when she rang and giving the number of his flat. Noticing that he had scribbled 'PTO' at the bottom of the small card, she turned it over to read:

'I hope your call meant that you're planning a trip to London. It would be great to see you. Do ring. Love, Hal.'

She put the flowers in a jar of water, wondering how much of her urge to see him again was connected with her dislike of the conclusions Jag had drawn about her emotions. Then, impatient with her own inability to decide what she felt about anyone, she reached for the telephone. It was a relief to know that there was at least one person she could always trust, for whom she felt unalloyed affection.

Tom answered the call, and Emma cried out with pleasure at his return, quickly asking how he had got on in Strasbourg. He answered her more shortly than usual and said he would fetch Willow.

'Em? How are you?'

'OK. Is Tom all right?' Emma did not want to betray any of Mrs Rusham's flustered confidences and she thought that Willow might expect her to comment on the fact that Tom had sounded so unlike himself.

'He will be. He's been in a bit of a sulk because he doesn't like the idea that I'm helping you out on an investigation. For some reason he thinks I should've promised never to look into any crime ever again. But he's finding his way out of the mood and we'll be all right again pretty soon.'

'Oh, I'm sorry,' said Emma. 'I never meant to cause trouble.'

'It's not you, but we'd better not talk too long or it'll look provocative.'

'Absolutely, but you rang me. What was it you wanted me for?'

'So I did,' said Willow before giving her a quick but illuminating account of what she had heard from Susie Peatsea.

Emma listened in silence and then, feeling even more confused, said, 'So, Lutterworth didn't have anything to do with the crash after all. What on earth can he be up to?'

'We'll have to find out,' said Willow. 'We can't possibly drop it now. It's got far too important. How did you get on with him today?'

'Badly. I asked... Oh hell!'

'What's the matter?'

'I've just remembered that I was supposed to be ringing his wing governor between five thirty and six and I got waylaid. Look, Willow, there's a lot to talk about, but I don't want to provoke Tom. Are you likely to be on your own tomorrow? Could I ring you then?'

'Good idea. I'll be here pretending to work on the book all morning. Mrs R and Lucinda go to the park at about ten usually.'

'I'll try then, and just hope I don't go and forget again. What a wally!'

'Not a complete wally: just busy and preoccupied. I know the feeling. Don't worry about it. I must go, but I have written you a long account of everything Susie said so that neither of us forgets anything crucial. You should get it tomorrow morning. 'Night.'

'Goodnight.'

Emma had hardly replaced the receiver before the telephone rang again. She picked it up and said her name.

'Hi, Sunshine. It's me, Jag. How are you?'

'Knackered, to tell you the truth. I've been flogging about between here and the prison and London.' She sighed. 'What about you?'

'Missing you. Can I come over? Are you too tired?'

'I am a bit. Could we take a rain check tonight? Perhaps have coffee together tomorrow morning?'

'OK. Whatever you want. Sleep well.'

'Thanks, Jag. You, too.'

She rearranged the freesias, revelling in the scent, and thought about Hal and Jag as she collected her dressing gown, towel and soap and went to find an empty bathroom.

FOURTEEN

TWO DAYS LATER Willow's lively description of her meeting with Susie Peatsea reached Emma. Having read it, she knew that there could no longer be any doubt whatsoever that Andrew Lutterworth's original story about the theft of his car had been accurate.

That left Emma even more puzzled and wanting to talk to him again as soon as possible. All her dislike of the hardness she had seen in him, and the possibility of violence, was subsumed in her need to find out the truth.

She made several efforts to reach the governor of his wing, but when she eventually got through on the telephone, she found him polite and even sympathetic over her failure to persuade Lutterworth to talk, but firm in his refusal to intervene. When she asked whether there was any information he could give her about Lutterworth's state of mind, feelings about his son's death or psychiatric reports, he sounded positively dismissive.

'You can't really have imagined that I would be able to hand over any such information, can you, Ms Gnatche?'

'No, I suppose not. I am sorry to have taken up your time. Thank you for speaking to me. Goodbye.'

Emma was left holding the dumb telephone and wishing that she had never rung the governor with such a silly request. Not only had she made herself look a fool, she had also risked losing his cooperation for the future.

It was all extraordinarily frustrating. There were plenty of people who must know Lutterworth really well—the members of his parole board, his doctor, the prison psychiatrist, even his wife—but none of them was likely to tell Emma a single thing about him.

Willow had said she thought the most important thing for either of them to do next was to track down Terry Lepe, but Emma was sure that for once Willow was definitely wrong. Susie's account of the crash had convinced them both, and Emma could not see the point of trying to get confirmation from Terry, even if they managed to find him. As far as she could see, he was most unlikely to talk about the accident and might well react to any questions about it with the sort of violence he had shown Susie. The whole idea of risking that seemed mad, but Emma knew perfectly well that she would never be able to stop Willow doing anything she wanted. Emma was afraid that her role would have to be limited to controlling the possible damage.

She pulled the telephone nearer her and pressed in Jag's number.

'Hi, it's me,' she said when he answered.

'Hi. How are you? You sound cross again.'

'Do I? It's not cross exactly. And anyway the only person I'm annoyed with is myself. I don't seem to be getting any-where and I must. Willow's doing such a lot…' Hearing overtones of resentment, Emma reminded herself that Wil-low's initiative in talking to Susie had produced infinitely more than she herself had managed to discover. 'Willow's doing such a lot for me on this Lutterworth business that I have to do my share. I just don't know what to do next.'

'Want to come over and play for a while instead?' Jag asked casually. 'You'll think better once you're relaxed.'

'I'd like that,' she said automatically and then realised it was true. She was glad that she had resisted an impulse to ring Hal again after she had read his note. 'But can I ask you for something first? I don't want—'

'Anyone could tell your mother's a lady,' he said, laugh-ing out loud. 'Too well brought up, that's your trouble. It's

OK, I'm not going to assume you're offering me your body
in return for material help. What can I do for you?'

'I just wondered,' she said, trying to stop herself sounding
like a wheedler, 'whether you might be prepared to help
Willow…'

'Me?' The word came down the line as a kind of yelp.
'What does she want my help for? You have to be joking,
Emma.'

'No. It's not she who… Oh, sod it! Look, Jag: Tom—her
husband—hates her getting involved with violent criminals,
but she won't let him stop her. And now she says she's
going to find Terry Lepe so that she can interrogate him
about the crash, and I'm afraid he could turn nasty. I can't
stop her going, but I think she ought to have some protection. I'd go with her myself, but I don't think I'd be any
good at it, even if she'd let me come.'

'Whereas a bloke like me—over six foot and strong—I
might be enough to satisfy even the great Tom Worth, eh?'
To Emma's relief, Jag sounded yet more amused. She could
not think why she had ever doubted her feelings for him
and remembered clearly why she liked him so much.

'I'll go with her if you want, but I'd have thought another
bloke might be the worst possible thing.'

'Would you? Why?'

'More men hit other men than hit women,' said Jag drily.

'Oh. But I'm not sure that would apply to Terry. Look
what he did to Susie. He sounds just the sort to pick on a
woman; you know, much less likely to hit back.'

'You could be right. It's impossible to tell without knowing more about him.'

'Exactly. Look, I know I can't stop Willow going and if
anything happened to her, Tom would never forgive me. I'd
never forgive myself either.' Emma thought for a second
and then hastily added, 'Or if you got hurt, Jag, but then I
know you can take care of yourself. If the sight of you in

your leathers doesn't scare him into doing exactly what you want, you can always thump him.'

Jag laughed. 'Tell me about it. But what does Willow think she'll get out of him?'

'God knows,' said Emma, letting out some of her exasperation. 'But she's so damn stubborn. For some reason she thinks he knows something important about Lutterworth.'

'Hm. Maybe she's right. But why don't you let me do it on my own? If it's only him and me, we can either fight it out or be blokeish together and slag off slappers like that Susie of his. Willow would only get in the way.'

'You're catching up well with your British slang, aren't you?' said Emma admiringly, diverted for the moment.

'I'm a good little researcher, you see. I like some of it now that I can join in,' said Jag, lightly. 'OK, you let me know when you've found Terry and I'll see what I can make him tell me. Now, much more important: are you coming here or am I coming to you?'

'To play?' said Emma, struggling for the right kind of cheerfulness. 'Why don't I come to you? Your room's so much nicer than mine. It'll take me about half an hour to sort myself out. Can I come after that?'

'Sure. And then we can go to Wright's lecture straight from here.'

'I can't think why I keep forgetting them. What's he doing this week?'

'Language as Threat.'

'But that's your title,' she protested. 'He can't do that.'

'He's already done it,' said Jag. 'And I need to make sure I'm not covering the same ground as him before I go any further.'

Remembering with shame that she was not the only one with hard and urgent work to do, Emma apologised and rang off. She tidied her papers, wrote herself a list of things to do, which made her feel almost as though she had done some of them, and then telephoned Willow.

'How's it going?' Willow asked at once.

'It isn't really. I'm still not sure what you think you can get out of Terry, but I'm beginning to think you might be right in saying he's the only hope we've got at the moment.'

'I'm sure he is,' said Willow cheerfully. 'But don't worry about it. I'm going to talk to him. In fact, in defiance of your orders, I've made plans to go up to Leeds tomorrow.'

'Oh, Willow, as though I'd ever give you orders. You make me sound like a dreadful bully.'

'What a thought!' she said, laughing. 'No, don't worry; it was a joke. I'll let you know if I get anything useful out of him.'

'But, Willow, what will Tom say?' said Emma. 'I mean Terry could be dangerous, perhaps even worse than that woman who half killed you in hospital two years ago. After all, she was only mad. From everything you heard from Susie, it sounds as though Terry's a real thug. If anything happened, Tom would—'

'There is that,' said Willow with a coldness that Emma did not understand. She struggled to make good whatever mistake it was she had made.

'I've been wondering if you'd…I mean, it's not that I'm trying to interfere or anything…'

'Now what's coming? You haven't gone and talked to Tom about this already, have you?'

'No, of course not. Would I? Behind your back? Willow, honestly! I just wondered whether you'd be prepared to take Jag with you,' Emma said in a great hurry, adding breathlessly, 'After all, he's a big lad, quite big enough to make anyone think twice about going for you. He's good company and intelligent, too, and aware and perceptive and all that. He could be useful.'

'But would be come?' asked Willow, sounding as though

she was controlling impatience with difficulty. 'Would he have time?'

'He says he will, if you'll have him. I know I'm being tiresome and clucky, but I couldn't bear it if something happened to you. Please, Willow?'

'He must be a remarkably generous bloke if he's prepared to waste a whole day babysitting one of your friends.'

'He is. And so are you. Not a bloke, I mean. Oh, you know what I mean.'

'Yes, I do.' The smile was back in Willow's voice. 'And I'm glad. I've been feeling awful about that night when you came here and I sent you away without any help at all. I've been wanting to make up for it ever since.'

'Oh, Willow, you mustn't,' said Emma in quick distress. 'That was ages ago, and you were so worried about Lucinda. I shouldn't have come without warning in any case. It was my fault. Anyway, it wasn't exactly help I was after; it was comfort of the sort I ought not to need nowadays. I'm far too old and tough to need my hand holding.'

'I don't think any of us are ever that. Or not all the time anyway. Try not to worry so much, Emma. I'll take Jag with me if he's really prepared to come. Do you know if he's likely to be free tomorrow?'

'I don't know, but I can ask. Why Leeds, by the way?'

'That's where Terry's working,' said Willow, clearly pleased with herself. 'Having discovered how to lean on George Tedsmore, I thought it was worth having another go at him. After some persuasion, he told me he'd occasionally heard Terry talking about mates in Leeds. I wasn't sure I'd be able to track him down because it's astonishingly easy these days to change one's name and disappear, but Terry doesn't seem to have bothered. He's working for a security firm, as I assumed he would be. I just rang them all until one lot said he was out on a job but that I could leave a message.'

'You are wonderful, Willow,' said Emma, who had not known that it was any easier to acquire a new identity than it had once been or how anyone would go about it. Deciding to ask for details at some less pressured moment, she added, 'I don't know where I'd be without you. Shall I ask Jag about tomorrow and get him to ring you to make arrangements?'

'Please. I'll have to go up and back in the day, which I hope won't bother him. The trains are very good now. Oh, and I'll pay. I'm not sure what his resources are, but don't let him worry about getting a ticket. I'll buy them.'

'I'm not sure if…I mean, couldn't I do that?'

'Don't be silly, Em. I've got much more cash than I need. You haven't at the moment. When my royalties have dried up and you're the world's living expert on polygraphs you can pay for things for me.'

'If it ever happens, of course I will,' said Emma after a struggle to contain her irrational feeling of once more having been relegated to the status of a child or an employee. 'You *are* the most generous person. Thank you. But, look, you won't go and do anything like getting first-class tickets, will you? That would seriously worry me.'

Willow laughed, but she agreed to the condition.

'Good. And will you give my love to Tom? That is if he's not so cross with me for involving you in all this that he can't bear the sound of my name?'

'He doesn't blame you for any of it, and of course I'll give him your love. I'll be in touch.'

Not at all sure that she would ever earn anything and absolutely certain that Willow's royalties would never dry up, Emma packed everything she would need for the lecture in her haversack and swung it over her shoulder. The sun was shining as she let herself out of the building and strode across the landscaped grounds towards the bus stop. Seeing several people she knew, all of whom waved at her, she began to feel almost at home in St Albans and, when Ben Wrexham stopped to speak to her, she smiled at him as though he were an old friend.

'I ran into DI Podley when I was in London last weekend and he asked after you,' he said.

'Did he? How odd! I didn't think he liked me at all.'

'I'm not sure he did,' said Ben, laughing. 'But he's curious about what you might have discovered about this con. you've been interviewing. How's it going?'

'Not well,' said Emma, salving her conscience with the excuse that until she knew why Lutterworth had falsely confessed to DI Podley there was no point in worrying him with the news that someone quite different had been driving the car when it crashed. 'I got a weird result from the first polygraph I did on him and went back for another go and got up his nose so badly that he threw me out and now he won't talk to me, and my most fruitful-looking case is dead on its feet.'

'I'm not sure that's quite the right phrase,' said Ben, laughing again. 'But I get your drift.'

'How's your thesis going?'

'Slightly better than yours sounds, but I've still got a way to go. You sometimes do Wright's lectures, don't you? Are you going this afternoon?'

'Yes. I thought I might.'

'What about a drink after?'

'Oh, that is kind. Yes, I'd like that. And I'm sure Jag would, too. We're going to the lecture together.'

'Is that the bloke with the Yamaha?'

'Yes. I think you'd like him,' said Emma. 'That reminds me, I'm late. I'll catch you later.'

'Sure.'

She found herself thinking quite affectionately of Ben as she walked on towards the bus and could hardly remember why she had once found him so daunting.

JAG WAS WAITING for her at the stop near his room and
walked her back there, with his arm heavily around her
shoulders. Having locked the door behind them, he took her
bag of books away and set about undressing her with all the
gentle, teasing skill that had always given her enough security in which to feel pleasure. By the time he was ready
to take off his own clothes, she could hardly restrain herself
from tearing at the buttons and zips and had to exercise
supreme self-control not to grab him when he eventually
laid his long, beautiful body down on the narrow bed beside
hers.

And he was beautiful. She realised that she had never
properly looked at him before, but as she stroked her fingers
up and down his smoothly muscled torso, kissing him at
intervals, talking, letting her fingers teach her about his reactions and his wants, she realised that he was glorious to
look at—and to touch. He allowed her to take the lead, and
even give him orders, which both of them found quite extraordinarily exciting, although there were moments when
they could not stop laughing so much that they had to go
back to the beginning and do it all over again more seriously.

They slept later and woke only just in time to shower and
dress respectably for the lecture.

IT WAS as Emma was sitting half asleep and failing to concentrate on Wright's intricate argument about the emotional
violence implicit in the imposition of private language and
slang on people who were unaccustomed to it that she had
what felt like her first useful thought about the Lutterworth
case. She could not wait to get back to her room to check
her memory of the interview tapes. Terrified that she would
fall properly asleep and forget, she pulled out her notebook
and scribbled a few words.

Jag, whose black eyes were alight with interest in the

lecture, half turned to smile approvingly at her industry. He glanced down at her note and then raised his eyebrows. Emma had written:

'Why was Lutterworth so worried about the forensic scientists tearing his car apart that he was prepared to confess to stop them?'

She smiled at Jag to pacify him and hoped she had not distracted him too much from what was undoubtedly an interesting lecture. When it was over she did not wait for him to ask any questions, but quickly said, 'I've got to go and check something. I told Ben Wrexham we'd have a drink with him in the Bear, but I can't stop. He must be somewhere about here, but you'll easily recognise him if you go to the pub. I'll nip back to my room and join you afterwards. OK? 'Bye.'

With her book bag slung over her shoulder and bumping against her back, Emma ran towards her building. Up in her room, she dropped the heavy load on the floor and started scuffling through the towers of paper on her desk until she found the interview transcript. Several other heaps of paper slithered on to the floor, and the vase containing Hal's freesias wobbled dangerously, but she paid no attention, simply riffling through the bound report until she came to DI Podley's threat.

As he had explained in the South Kensington pub, he had told Lutterworth that there was no point trying to pull the wool over his eyes, that he might well have washed and changed, but that the forensic scientists had hardly started their work. He warned Lutterworth that they would take his car and flat apart looking for evidence. It was, as she had thought, at precisely that point that Lutterworth had caved in.

Emma could not understand why she had not seen the significance sooner. It seemed perfectly obvious that there must have been something in either the car or the flat that he needed to keep hidden. From his reactions to her own questions, she was prepared to take quite a large bet that it was the car that worried him.

Unfortunately she could not think of anything to suggest what he thought they might find. Remembering the way Willow had used her novelist's imagination whenever she had investigated a crime, Emma set to work to invent stories of her own that might explain Lutterworth's fear of the forensic scientists. She knew that if the stories were to be at all useful, they would have to have some basis in the facts she had discovered and she set about marshalling them in her mind.

Hal had talked about a possible mistress, but he did not know anything for sure. On the other hand, Annie Frome had said that Lutterworth had wandering hands, which added weight to Hal's suggestion.

Emma herself had discovered that Lutterworth was subject to sudden bursts of temper and she knew that he was very strong. She shuddered as she remembered the tightness of his grip around her wrist and the look in his face when he told her he would not talk about Pipp's death.

She shook her head suddenly and ran both hands through her short dark hair as she told herself a tale of Andrew and his girlfriend having a ferocious row in his car. In her mind Emma could picture them so vividly that it was not at all hard to imagine Andrew braking suddenly and turning to hit the woman as well as shouting at her. He could have smashed her head against the window, perhaps, or even strangled her. He could easily have killed her.

It was only a fantasy, but for a moment it seemed wholly credible. Running through it again, Emma imagined Andrew noticing the woman's stillness, testing her pulse, holding up something hard and shiny to her lips to see whether her breath misted it. It would have been a terrible moment when he realised he had killed her and was faced with having to get rid of her body.

The best thing would have been to go straight to a hospital or police station to report what had happened, but would he have had the guts? Wouldn't most men have been much more likely to go somewhere unpopulated—a wood, a moor, even a field that was not overlooked by any houses—and dig a grave? Perhaps Andrew, not being particularly large or strong, would have taken an easier way and sunk the body in a flooded gravel pit or a river, with stones in the pockets of the clothes to weight the body down.

If he had done it at night, in some place he had never been before and was never likely to revisit, he would have felt reasonably safe. His car would have left tyre tracks, but if no one knew the body was there, who would be interested enough even to look at them, let alone measure them or try to match them up with those on any car?

'Could it possibly have happened like that?' Emma asked herself out loud as she stood in the middle of her untidy room with her hands on her head. 'No, of course it couldn't. Don't be an idiot.'

For one thing, she told herself crisply, no man with a secret like that would have agreed to take a polygraph test.

On the other hand, she thought, Lutterworth was said to be very arrogant. Perhaps he had decided that he was so clever he would be able to beat the polygraph and saw it as a chance to establish his innocence before he started looking for jobs on his release. After all, the chart had suggested that he might know how to manipulate the test results.

Suddenly Emma laughed as another point occurred to her. She let her arms fall to her sides and began to relax. The vehicle examiner who had dealt with Lutterworth's car had found no damage whatsoever to the locks or alarm system. That had always puzzled Emma whenever she had thought about it, in spite of Willow's suggestion that it could be typical of his absent-mindedness. There might be many possible explanations, but one in particular appealed to Emma.

Aware of just how difficult it would have been to remove all the forensic evidence from the car, the murderer of her fantasies could easily have decided to get rid of it altogether. He could not have sold it so soon after acquiring it without breaking the partnership's car-scheme rules. Therefore, unless he was prepared to crash it deliberately, which would have put him at serious risk, much the safest way of dealing with the problem would have been to entice some passing thief to take it. Then with luck the thief would crash it himself or, even better, torch it. That way, if any scientist were ever to examine the car, whatever damning evidence was found could be put down to the thief.

Thinking that it must have been quite extraordinarily frustrating for Lutterworth to discover that his carefully laid plans had worked beautifully up to a point and then become dangerously unstuck, Emma realised that she had begun to take her own fantasies seriously.

The telephone rang. Automatically she walked over to her desk to pick up the receiver and said her name.

'Are you coming, Emma?' said Jag's voice against a noisy background. 'We're nursing our second drinks here, making polite conversation and hating each other for not being you. If you're not going to show, we can get out of here and leave each other in peace.'

'I'm so sorry, Jag. I hadn't realised how long I'd been. I'll come now and be as quick as I can.'

Emma left the mess of papers around her desk as it was, locked her room, and ran to the pub favoured by most of the criminology and psychology graduates.

Jag and Ben Wrexham were leaning against the bar with pint tankards in their hands, looking perfectly at ease with each other when she arrived breathless in the doorway. As

Emma moved nearer to them, unnoticed, she began to distinguish the sound of their voices against the music and the rest of the crowd. To her amusement they were having a lovely male-bonding conversation about motorcycle engines, and neither showed any signs of restiveness. Even when she reached Jag's side, she had to touch his elbow to distract him.

'So where did you run off to?' said Ben, looking as though he were trying hard not to show irritation at having been interrupted in one of the things that really matter in life.

'I had a thought about one of the trickiest bits of my thesis,' said Emma as disarmingly as possible. 'And I had to get it down before I forgot it, but it all took much longer than I meant. I'm sorry to be so late. What did you think of the lecture?'

'Quite interesting,' said Ben as Jag went off to buy her a drink. 'Although I think he exaggerated the excluding effect of private language.'

'Oh, I'm not sure,' said Emma and then, when she saw some of the old derision creeping into his eyes, told him a little of how she had felt when she first arrived at St Albans.

Once Jag had returned with half a pint of lager for her, she gradually eased the discussion back to motorcycles and saw the pair of them relax again. Smiling secretly at the thought that she had followed all her mother's rules in keeping the conversation going and allowing the men to talk about what they most enjoyed, she leaned against the bar and thought in peace about Andrew Lutterworth and his car and what he had been afraid the forensic scientists might find.

As she sipped her drink, she began to think of another explanation of his confession. It was much more realistic than any of the stories she had been telling herself, and she could not think why it had not occurred to her sooner. If

Andrew had genuinely believed that the car had been stolen, he would have responded to Podley's accusations with outraged denials until he had been told about the pristine state of the car's locks and alarm. At that point he must have remembered that his wife also had keys to the car. He would have known better than anyone else in the world that she had been behaving erratically ever since their son's death. It was not stupid to assume that he must have decided that she had taken the car and crashed it.

In that case he might well have been afraid of the evidence the scientists would find and confessed in order to protect her. Later, once he had been released on bail and been able to talk to her, he would have become convinced that she had not done it. Then there would have been no reason to stick by his confession.

Emma found herself smiling at the thought that Lutterworth might, after all, be a decent and likable man. She was distracted by the smell of charring and then an almost painful sensation in the front of her left shoulder. Looking down and brushing at it, assuming that something must have bitten her, she saw that there was a small heap of glowing cigarette ash burning through her thin shirt. Moving away and shaking her shirt hard to get it all off, she looked up at the large, strange young man who had let part of his cigarette drop on her.

'Do you realise what you've just done?' she asked in a mixture of shock and anger.

'What's your problem?' he said unpleasantly.

'You've just ruined my best shirt and burned me,' she said, amazed by the aggressiveness. 'You might at least apologise.'

'Oh, fuck off!' he said, picking up his large drink with the hand that held the cigarette.

At the sound of his insult, Jag and Ben both came out of their motorcycle dreams at the same moment and moved to stand at either side of Emma. Their faces were suffused with exactly the same fury. Emma was touched by their automatic attempt to defend her, but she wished that the whole pantomime had not been necessary.

The careless smoker, seeing that the small young woman who had challenged him had two broad-shouldered male protectors, both well over six foot, pretended that he had been talking to someone else and tried to disappear into the crowd. Unfortunately it was too tight and unyielding for that and he had nowhere to go.

'I'm grateful, guys, but honestly I'd rather you didn't make a scene,' said Emma, wanting to forget the whole thing as quickly as possible.

'I'm not going to make any kind of scene,' said Jag, gritting his teeth. 'I'm just going to stop this turd doing anything like that again. Isn't that what you wanted?'

'Not enough for all this,' she said quickly. 'Ben, you're a police officer for heaven's sake. You can't go round hitting people.'

'Want to bet?' said Ben, looking as though he were enjoying himself even more than he had during the motorcycle discussion. 'I'm not on duty.'

At the mention of the word police, Emma's antagonist made an even greater effort to get away and eventually succeeded.

'There,' said Jag, brushing his hands together and returning to the bar. 'Isn't it great to be able to make people do what you want?'

'And without laying a finger on them,' agreed Ben. 'A very useful tactic, mate, believe me.'

Emma turned away, trying not to feel sanctimonious and pleased to be female since for one moment she had been quite as angry as they and had wanted quite as much to force the unpleasant stranger to grovel to her.

WHEN EMMA GOT BACK to her room, she found a third bunch of freesias left propped up against the door. Smiling at Hal's extravagance—and the delectable smell of the flowers—she opened the note.

'You still haven't rung me back. Are you angry that I wasn't here the first time, or are you avoiding me? Can I come and see you? How's your work on the shit L. going? Love Hal.'

Still not at all sure what she wanted from him—or he from her—she unlocked her door, emptied the old flowers out of the vase, washed it out and refilled it. Briefly touching on the fragile yellow petals with her left hand, she picked up the telephone receiver with her right and punched the number of his flat.

After four rings, his answering machine cut in. Emma planned her message as she listened to his recorded voice. After the beep, she said as naturally as she could, 'Hello, Hal, it's Emma Gnatche here. Thank you so much for all the gorgeous flowers. You really shouldn't, you know. I'm sorry I haven't got back to you before, but I've been chasing my tail over this Lutterworth business. I haven't any more plans to be in London for a while, but when I have I'll get in touch and hope you're around. It'd be great to see you. Thanks so much for the flowers. I love them, but you really shouldn't. Um. Well, thanks anyway. Um. 'Bye.'

FIFTEEN

WILLOW SAT OPPOSITE JAG on the train up to Leeds, hardly registering the sight of him as she thought about Tom. Ever since their quarrel on the day he had returned from Strasbourg he had been careful to ask no questions that might imply any infringement of her right to do whatever she chose. She, filled with compunction at what her outburst had—or could have—done to him, had been trying to show that she wanted to make peace without going so far as to retract anything she had said, but the message did not seem to be getting through in the way she was trying to send it. The two of them were still circling stiffly around each other and being horribly polite.

She was glad that he seemed to have absorbed the point of what she had said, but it was clear that she had hurt him and she hated that. From previous experience she knew that there was no point trying to talk the hurt away. Tom was prepared to say more about emotional matters than most men she had met, but there were limits to his tolerance of what he called 'touchy-feely chatter'. She tried to console herself with the thought that they had had plenty of difficulties in the past and had always overcome them. Hoping that they would get past the new awkwardness too, she wished that she could do something to hurry it away.

In some ways it might have seemed perverse to be pursuing a possibly violent thug, but, however much she wanted to soothe Tom's distress, she could not do it at the cost of her own independence. After all, that would have meant that the whole painful process would have been for nothing, which would have been unbearable. She told herself to stop thinking about it and to concentrate on the present.

'It's terrifically good of you to have given up your time like this, Jag. I do hope you didn't have to get up too early,' she said in an effort to do just that. 'To get to London in time for this train, I mean.'

He looked surprised at her sudden interruption of his peaceful study of the newspaper he had brought, but he shook his curly dark head and smiled at her amiably enough. In spite of the smile, she could see that his intense dark eyes were more hostile than they ever seemed when Emma was around. Willow realised that Jag must still dislike her and she was sorry for that.

'I don't mind an early start when it's necessary,' he added, presumably in an attempt to be polite. 'And this obviously was.'

'Thank you. I hope it won't be a great waste of your day.'

'Emma wanted me to come. That was enough for me. And my work's been going well. I had time.'

'Lucky Emma,' Willow said drily. 'And lucky me, too, of course.'

Jag raised his eyebrows. They slanted up in strong dark lines from the point where they met over the bridge of his nose, making him look even tougher than usual.

'I'm lucky in having your protection, I mean. I'm not sure that Emma's fears of what Terry Lepe might want to do to me are entirely justified, but it's nice not to have to worry about it.'

Jag nodded. 'It's hard to discover how justified any of her fears might be.'

'Does she have so many?' asked Willow in surprise.

'Several I think, although she won't talk about them. She's become terrified of Lutterworth, and—'

'Has she? She hasn't said anything about that to me,' said Willow, even more surprised.

'She hasn't said anything to me either,' said Jag, looking as though he was amused. 'But that doesn't mean it's not obvious.'

'But why should she be?' said Willow, suppressing the thought that she must have been peculiarly insensitive if it were that clear to someone who had known Emma for as short a time as Jag had done. 'He's in prison. There's nothing he can do to her.'

Jag shrugged. 'Well, apart from the fact that she's frightened of men in general, she—'

'What?' Willow was so surprised that she could not help interrupting him again. Jag looked irritated and more than a little contemptuous.

'You must have seen that at least.'

'Well, no. I haven't,' said Willow, allowing some contempt of her own to show. 'She's not remotely afraid of my husband or any of the men she's brought to my house or met there.' She watched Jag's face and then added slowly, 'Is she afraid of you?'

'Not most of the time, but occasionally, when she forgets she knows me, she can be.'

'But why?'

'I'm not sure.' The disdain had gone from his eyes, to be replaced by a thoughtfulness Willow would not have expected of him. 'But I have a feeling it's something to do with her brother.'

'Anthony?' said Willow in a squawk. 'You must be joking. No one as excellent as Emma could be frightened of such a pompous fool. Does she talk much about him?'

'Nope. And I don't want to crash in there and ask questions she can't answer. Or doesn't want to. Have you ever met him?'

'Briefly, but not for some years. He once took me out to dinner.'

'You? Why?' Jag's face would have served as a model
of astonishment for a traditional art class.

'I think he fancied me,' said Willow, hiding her enjoy-
ment. Then the sight of Jag's confusion was too much for
her acting skills and she burst out laughing. She thought he
looked very young in his embarrassment and she felt much
more friendly towards him. 'People have done sometimes
in the past.'

'That's not what I meant.'

'I know,' she said. 'I was teasing you. As far as I can
remember, Anthony Gnatche was hidebound, conventional,
boring and contemptuous of everything he did not know or
understand. In other words, he's as different from Emma as
you could possibly imagine. She values thought, kindness,
intelligence, openness, awareness and all the other 'nesses
you can think of.'

Jag did not comment.

'I can't imagine Emma's being afraid of him,' Willow
went on. 'I'm sure you've got that wrong, even if Lutterworth has scared her. *If* he has.'

Jag shrugged. 'There's no if about it. She's definitely
afraid. But he may not have done anything beyond showing
the kind of automatic male aggression she hates so much.'

'I don't think there's anything odd about being afraid of
that,' said Willow sharply. 'Most women are, except the
fools who find it titillating.''

'Perhaps,' he said as the amusement crept back into his
dark eyes. 'Although she minds it much more than you do,
doesn't she? You were quite prepared to go up against Terry
Lepe without any help or protection. It was Emma who
insisted that you should have a bodyguard.'

Willow nodded, intrigued to notice that, while Tom's attempts to protect her were almost always irritating, Emma's
could be merely touching. She sat in silence, working out

why. It was not particularly difficult. Nothing Emma did smacked of the exercise of superior power.

And why is that? Willow asked herself, knowing the answer perfectly well and feeling thoroughly ashamed of it.

Given the rage that Tom could make her feel whenever he showed that he thought of her as subordinate to him, she ought to have known better than to feel exactly the same about Emma. She hoped that Emma had never understood it.

'Tell me about Terry Lepe,' said Jag. 'All I know is what you wrote in your letter after you'd seen his pathetic girlfriend.'

Willow looked at him, thinking that the fates were really driving the message home. She ought not have felt either surprise or offence at the discovery that Emma showed Jag her letters, but she could not ignore the fact that she felt both and felt them sharply. Emma was not her property— or her child, even though she was the right age for that. She was an independent woman, who could do what she liked when she liked.

'I don't know any more than you, Jag. I wish I did. He sounded completely revolting from everything Susie said, but, as I told Emma, she wasn't the brightest woman in the world and she may have misunderstood or misrepresented him. Although I don't see how she could have imagined everything she told me. What do you think?'

'I've no idea. Your account of what she'd said sounded convincing. We'll know more when we've seen him and heard him talk.'

Remembering that Jag was a psycholinguist and presumably made judgements about people from the way they used words, Willow suddenly wondered what conclusions he had come to about her and wished that she had taken a vow of silence before she had got on the train.

'Does he know we're coming?' asked Jag.

Willow shook her head. 'I thought it would be better to take him by surprise. He's on an early day shift at a local factory at the moment. Head office said he was due to stop in to collect his wages on his way home at the end of the shift. If we get there around noon, we ought to be able to run into him and find a way to persuade him to talk to us.'

'It might work,' said Jag.

The doubt in his voice put Willow on her mettle and she realised that she was childishly determined to show him that she knew better than he did. Privately amused by herself, she hurried him off the train when they reached Leeds and through the ticket barrier to the taxi rank. They got to the security company's offices with five minutes to spare.

'Can I help you?' asked the receptionist. She was a very young woman with a mop of bright brown hair and a cheerful smile.

'We're hoping to talk to Terry Lepe,' said Willow, trying to smile just as warmly back at her. 'I gather he's likely to look in some time soon.'

'Yes. Probably any moment now. D'you want to take a seat? There are some magazines and you can make tea or coffee from that machine there. He shouldn't be long.'

'Thank you.' Willow took a magazine and a chair but avoided the drinks.

Jag made himself a plastic cup of black coffee and sipped it. They said very little to each other, pretending to read their chosen magazines and looking up every time the swing door opened to let in a new person. Eventually a thin man in his twenties, with a narrow, sharp-featured face and very short brown hair, came in and dumped something hard down on the reception desk.

'There's a lady and gentleman waiting for you, Terry,' said the receptionist, pointing to them.

He nodded to her, said something inaudible, which made

her smile and blush, and then swaggered over to where Willow and Jag were still sitting.

'And what c'n I do for you then?' he said, his London accent sounding harsh against the rounder, softer sounds of the northerners they had spoken to since leaving the train.

'We need your help rather badly,' said Willow, hoping that there was only the sound of pleading in her voice. 'I wondered if we could buy you a drink and tell you about the problem? Jag here... Look, is there a good pub near by?'

'Maybe. What problem?'

'I'll tell you when we get there,' said Willow, opening her well-stocked handbag with much the same gesture she had used so effectively on George Tedsmore. 'It is worth a lot to us.'

Jag stood up, topping Terry by at least four inches. Suspicion and avarice chased each other through his sharp eyes. Watching them, Willow wondered what his attraction could have been for Susie. Terry was not a particularly good-looking man, with his acne-scarred skin and thin lips. Then he smiled and she caught a hint of cleverness and even a modicum of charm. Remembering the depths of poor Susie's doughy plainness, Willow realised that Terry might have seemed sophisticated and exciting to her.

'The Lamb and Flag's OK,' he said eventually.

'Then let's go there,' said Willow, smiling over her shoulder at the receptionist, who waved as she leaned sideways to answer her ringing telephone.

The pub was barely four minutes' walk away, and there were not many customers when they walked in. Two old men were sitting peacefully nursing their drinks and pipes in silence at a small table in one corner of the room well away from the fruit machine and the jukebox, and a couple in shell suits and trainers were perched on high stools at the bar, drinking something that looked like weak fizzy orange.

Willow asked her two young men what they wanted to drink and went to the bar to order their pints and her own draught cider. She also asked for some crisps, paid and carried the trayful to a corner table where Jag had managed to persuade Terry to sit down near the fruit machine. Willow sat in the only free chair, which neatly cut off Terry's exit. She was glad to see that the publican had a clear view of their table and that there was plenty of light. It seemed unlikely that Terry would try on anything particularly violent in the circumstances.

'OK. So what d'you want?' he said, ripping open one of the crisp packets without waiting to be asked. 'And what's it worth to you?'

'This may come as a shock to you,' said Willow, reverting to her old civil service manner, 'but Susan Peatsea has given us your name as one of two possible fathers of her child, and—'

'Never heard of her,' said Terry with an unpleasantly confident smile playing about his thin mouth.

'I think you have,' said Willow. 'She told us all about you, and we got confirmation from your previous employers. There's no room for doubt.'

'Oh, the silly bitch!' Terry banged down the hand that was holding the crisp packet. The packet burst, crisps flew everywhere and the publican stared menancingly at them. 'OK, it's true I knew her. But I haven't seen her in years. If she's got herself up the spout, it can't be mine.'

'It's over two years old,' said Willow, devoutly grateful that she was not bound by any of the police rules of evidence-gathering. She had not even told Jag that she had a minute tape recorder attached to the lapel of her suit, which she had activated when she bought the drinks. Nothing she persuaded Terry to say could ever be used in evidence, but it ought to be enough for Emma's needs.

'What are you, Child Support Agency? That's a dirty

trick, that is: telling a man you've got something to say to his advantage and then trying to trap him into paying for some other man's kid. Well it won't work. You can tell that cow that I know the facts of life even if she doesn't. It can't be mine. If you don't believe me, get a DNA test done.'

Willow and Jag exchanged glances.

'It's true. I never even fucked the stupid cow.' Terry took a long swig of his beer, put down the glass, wiped his lips on the back of his hand and appeared to get some kind of control over himself. 'I'm not saying I wouldn't of, but I didn't. It's what I went for, I won't deny. But the silly bitch got scared, and I'm not one to force myself where I'm not wanted.' He preened in front of them, shooting his cuffs and slicking back his hair. 'I can get girls easy enough without that.'

'Yes, I'm sure you can,' said Willow, seeing that Jag was obediently leaving her to ask the questions. 'But let me get this straight. Are you telling us you never slept with Susan Peatsea at all? That there never was any sexual congress?'

'Are you deaf? Whatever she claims, I never fucked her, I said.'

'But her story was so full of circumstantial detail,' said Willow, pretending concern. It struck her that she might be putting Susie in some danger, but she needed confirmation of the story too much to let him go, even in the interests of Susie's safety. Hoping that his obviously well-developed sense of self-preservation would keep him miles away from the Peatseas, Willow went on, 'She told me that you collected her one wet evening nearly three years ago in a large and glamorous car she'd never seen before, and that you took her to some woods in…where was it, Jag? Berkshire?'

'Buckinghamshire, she said.'

'Oh, was it? Well, that's not particularly important. Nothing is except this question of the child's father.'

'Fine. That's it then. It's not mine. Couldn't be. I'm off.

You want to fix a DNA test? Feel free. You know where to find me.'

'Yes, we do,' said Willow, smiling and refusing to move out of his way. 'But before you leave us, there is just one other aspect to all this that we'd like to get straight before we can let you go entirely.'

'Oh, yeah?' Terry smoothed back the sides of his hair again and sat down, clearly deciding that it was more important in the circumstances to look cool than to force his way past Willow's knees, particularly when Jag was taller than he and at least a couple of stones heavier.

'Yes. It's this car you were driving. It was a large dark-green car, with a CD, wasn't it?'

'If you say so.' His eyes had turned watchful. Willow began to wonder if it might not have been better after all to have asked Jag to talk to Terry man to man and got the information out of him that way.

'Susie says so,' she said, smiling and showing no sign of her sudden self-criticism.

'You think anyone would believe anything that silly bitch claimed to remember? She can't hardly write her own name.'

'Was that why you fancied her, Terry?' asked Jag, taking a hand again. His voice carried just a suggestion of a taunt, not quite enough to provoke retaliation. 'That doesn't sound too likely. A clever bloke like you. I'd have thought you'd have gone for something a bit tastier than her. For one thing, she's fat.'

'Yeah,' said Terry with a familiar grin that made Willow want to hit him. 'But the ugly ones are much easier than the real babes. You can give them cheap tat for presents, and they're as pleased with a half of shandy as the rest are with poncy cocktails. Girls like Susie don't hardly cost a thing to take out, and you usually get your money's worth.'

'But I thought you said you didn't get anything out of

Susie,' Jag said, still taunting. 'Changing your story now, are you?'

Willow hoped that Jag knew what he was doing and how far he could go.

'No. Stupid cow wouldn't let me.'

'Whose car was it, Terry?' asked Willow, deciding that it was time for her to take a hand again. 'Did you nick it?'

'What is all this? Coming in here, criticising a man, accusing him—'

'We need to know.' Willow tried to smile ruefully. 'Look, Susie's worrying about it. That's how we got involved in the first place.'

'Silly cunt.' Terry's eyes closed as though he could barely contain his exasperation.

'You'd better tell us the whole lot,' said Jag, 'and then if you're not the father of her child, we'll go away and leave you in peace.'

'Who are you?' Terry looked from Willow to Jag and back again. 'You're not from the CSA at all, are you? If you were, you'd have been on to me long ago. And you'd not be bothered with the car. What's your game?'

'We're private detectives,' said Willow firmly, hoping that he was not going to start considering who could possibly have employed them or for what reason. 'Look, Terry, we just need confirmation of what happened that evening. You can see why we're worried after what we heard from Susie.'

'What was that then? You'd have to be barking to believe anything *she* told you.'

'Well,' said Willow, pretending to consult her notes from her bag,' she told us that there was an accident that night. She's very worried about it, worried that someone might have been hurt.'

'Well, there wasn't,' said Terry, almost shaking he was so angry. To Willow's amazement, the fury seemed to have overtaken every other emotion in him. 'She's so stupid she can't remember anything from one day to the next. I done an emergency stop, see, when an animal, fox prob'ly, ran across the road. We skidded. She banged her face on something. It wasn't nearly bad enough to spring the airbags, but she got a bang of a sort. That's what she's remembering. Silly cow's prob'ly muddled it up in her stupid pathetic brain with something she's seen on the telly since. You don't want to listen to her.'

Willow sipped her cider and smiled at him, hoping that she looked as though she believed him.

'It is true that she didn't seem exactly needle-witted,' she said, making Terry laugh.

'I believe you. Needle-witted, I like that. That's a good phrase, that is.'

'Thank you. Well, now that we've got it clear that there was no accident, all we need to find out is where you got the car. We know you couldn't have afforded to buy it, and it doesn't sound as though you'd spend that much hiring it to take Susie out in.'

'Too right.' Terry looked at her again and she showed him a blandly interested expression. 'If you must know, I borrowed it.'

'Oh, well that explains it,' said Willow. 'Why didn't you say so and save all this trouble? Tell us who you borrowed it from so that we can get confirmation and that'll settle the whole thing.'

'I borrowed it from a bloke at work. He left his keys with me.'

'Come on, Terry. You can't expect us to believe that.'

'Why not?' He glared at Willow.

'Because you were a security guard at a large firm of accountants. We've got all that already. That size of car is driven only by the most senior people. None of them is likely to lend it to a junior security man. You picked it, didn't you? Come on.'

'I borrowed it,' said Terry firmly. He was beginning to look less cool and as though he was trying to work something out in his head as he talked. After a moment, he added, 'Look here, I was going off duty. It was pissing down and I was on my way to the tube when I see this bloke get out of his car in the street. He was in such a rush he didn't even lock it, let alone set the alarm. He was sopping wet and he ran right past me; didn't even see me. I had a good laugh because he was a git, see. I thought I'd impress that little cow if I turned up in a car like his was. I knew he'd be in the office for hours or he wouldn't of bothered to repark it, and I knew I could get it back in time. It was weeks since I'd had me rocks off and I needed a screw. I thought the car might just swing it with Susie, and I'd kill two birds with one stone.'

Willow could not help wincing at the phrase, remembering the two people who had died. She wondered if Terry really could be so sure that no one would ever believe Susie's account of that crash.

'So what happened?' asked Jag, looking dangerously threatening without even trying. Suddenly distracted, Willow realised she would not have been surprised if Emma had reacted with fear if he had ever looked like that at her.

'Nothing,' said Terry quickly. 'The stupid cow liked the car, specially as we picked up speed, but she squealed like a stuck pig when I took her up to ninety and then did the stop. To be fair, she did get a bruise on her face from the window; could've been cut too. Till then I thought I was in with a chance. Get them gee'd up like that with a bit of a fright and you're home, usually. But she was too stupid even for that and once she'd hit the window it was hopeless. She was whimpering to be taken home. So I took her, di'n' I?'

'Straight home?'

'Yeah.' Terry's eyes narrowed in suspicion. 'Hey, what else has the stupid cow been saying? I told you, you don't want to believe anything she says. She can't tell what's real from what she's seen on the telly, and that's a fact.'

Jag leaned forward to pre-empt anything that Willow might say. 'She wouldn't tell us what happened, only cried when we asked. That's why we had to find you.'

They both saw Terry relax.

'What did you do with the car?' asked Willow.

Terry shot his cuffs again and looked much more pleased with himself than his situation warranted.

'Left it back near the office, at five past ten, di'n' I? Near where I found it, but not in the same place. If he'd been looking before I got it back there, he'd think he'd forgotten where he'd put it. Then I got the tube home and had a wank to make up for what that prick-tease done to me.' Terry looked as though he was trying to shock Willow, and she took a perverse pleasure in pretending she had not understood him.

'You mean you left the car unlocked? Anyone could have taken it.'

'Stands to reason. I didn't have no keys. I know how to start 'em up, but not lock and alarm them. It's not my fault if someone took it. Someone could of. But the firm wouldn't lose. They've got insurance.'

'I think that's all we need ask then for the moment,' said Willow brightly. 'If you would just give Jag the name of your GP, we can write to arrange the DNA test if it proves necessary to test the child after all.'

'Yes,' said Jag, taking out a pen and a piece of paper. 'But it does sound more likely that it's the other man, doesn't it?'

'Oh, yes,' said Willow blandly.

Terry dictated a name and address that she was almost

certain would prove to have been as imaginary as their story, and then they let him go.

'I'm sorry I stopped you,' said Jag as soon as Terry had banged the pub door shut behind him, 'but I thought if you pushed him any further or let him know what you really suspected we could be in for something nasty. He was quite near the edge at one moment.'

'I know. Presumably he's been keyed up ever since it happened, waiting for someone to come and ask him about that night.'

'Yes, I think so. And rehearsed his version over and over again.'

'It was quite fluent, wasn't it?'

'Sure. By now he's probably almost persuaded himself that it's the true one.'

'Maybe,' said Willow. 'But he's a fool all the same. If he'd denied all knowledge of the car that night, we'd be no further on. As it is, the police may have kept all the evidence from the case and be able to track down his prints in amongst all the ones they took from the car.'

Jag laughed. After a moment she nodded and reluctantly smiled with him.

'I know. We're not much further on as it is. At least as far as the police or the courts are concerned. All Terry's got to say if they do find his fingerprints among the ones they took at the time is what he told us, and he'll probably get away with the suggestion that Susie is too thick to tell the difference between what really happened and what she read in the paper. Any clever lawyer could muddle her in the witness box without any difficulty at all. She'd never convince a jury.'

'You're probably right,' said Jag. 'And he might do it. That was quite a slick story he told. It covered the bruise on her face, and it made it possible to believe that someone else could have stolen the car after he'd returned it.'

'I know,' said Willow. 'Help, look at the time. I have to get the next train back. Do you mind hurrying?'

'Not at all,' said Jag, downing the rest of his beer.

They had to run part of the way to the station, but they caught the train Willow had planned to take so that she would be back in time to give Lucinda her bath.

'What's worrying you so much?' asked Jag after they had exhaustively discussed everything Terry had said and its implications for Emma's work.

'Susie,' said Willow unhappily. 'However much Terry may have convinced himself that no one would believe her, it'd be all too easy for him to change his mind. Don't you think he might decide that it would be better if she weren't around to answer any questions?'

'Possibly.'

'And it would be horribly easy for him to dispose of her. He's only got to ring and say he's got a job and a flat and she's to take the first train or bus. She'd go like a flash, probably without leaving any word for her apparently terrifying mother. He could do whatever he wanted to her with no one any the wiser.'

'Would she go? After he frightened her so much and hit her and nearly raped her?'

'Yes,' said Willow sadly. 'I think she might. After all, he didn't quite rape her and he's the only person who's ever seemed to her to love her. She's got no job, nothing to make her feel good about herself. She's more scared of her mother than she ever was of Terry. Damn it! I can see I'm going to have to wheel in Tom.'

Jag looked at her enquiringly, but she said nothing and he was either too wise or too tactful to ask what she meant. They parted in London with much more respect for each other than Willow would have expected. She even invited Jag to go back to the Mews with her for some dinner, but he said he thought he would rather pick up the bike and get back to St Albans, and besides, he had added with a smile of great sweetness, he wanted to see Emma.

'Give her my love,' said Willow.

'Sure. G'night.'

Willow waved goodbye and went out of the station to find a taxi.

TOM HAD NOT RETURNED by the time she got back to the Mews, but Mrs Rusham and Lucinda were both there in endearingly high spirits. It turned out that they had been cooking together. The thought of Mrs Rusham's putting up with anyone else in her kitchen, particularly a messy baby, was extraordinary.

'What did you cook?' Willow asked.

'Bisdits,' said Lucinda with great satisfaction. 'Choc'late bisdits.'

'And saffron fish stew for your dinner,' added Mrs Rusham more calmly. 'It will need gentle heating for about twenty minutes when you're ready.'

'Fine. It sounds delicious. I'd better take this creature up for her bath, hadn't I? Coming, Lulu?'

They went upstairs and were still romping wetly when Tom eventually returned. He seemed to notice the difference in Willow instantly because his expression changed from guarded courtesy to his familiar warm humour, but he did not say anything. When they had finished washing and drying Lucinda, and read her story, they went downstairs. Willow took two chairs out into the minute courtyard garden, while Tom went to fetch some wine. He returned with a bottle of champagne.

'What's that for?' asked Willow. 'Are we celebrating?'

'I think so,' he said, grinning at her over the gold foil top. 'After all you've got over your rage, haven't you?'

'Not so much got over,' she said, 'as understood more about both sides of it. I—'

'Don't say it. There isn't any need and it's better left.'

Watching him, she realised that the only penance he was going to allow her to offer for her anger was the suppression of her wish for a good, long, interesting post-mortem. The fact that she would have preferred almost any other was just too bad.

'I was just going to tell you what I've been doing today,' she said, raising her glass to him, 'and ask your advice.'

'Will,' he said, peering at her with an expression of ludicrously exaggerated horror in his eyes, 'are you ill? You never want my advice.'

'Monster,' she said briefly. 'Actually, this is pretty important.'

He sobered up immediately and she realised that she had never asked for his help without being given it—and given it without stint. It was quite extraordinary, she realised, how much she loved him. She put that thought on one side and told him everything about Emma's case and Terry Lepe and her own anxieties for Susie Peatsea.

SIXTEEN

EMMA meanwhile had been spending the afternoon in the infinitely more salubrious company of Jemima Lutterworth. Inspired by Jag's example, or perhaps pricked by his amusement at her need for introductions to people she wanted to question, she had decided to try a direct approach. It worked. When she telephoned the Lutterworths' house to introduce herself as a researcher who had interviewed Andrew in prison, Jemima sounded positively glad to hear from her.

'He's told me a lot about how much he likes you,' Jemima said. 'You've done him a great deal of good, you know.'

'You are kind,' said Emma, relieved to realise that Andrew could not yet have reported on her last attempt to question him. 'Did he tell you why I went to see him in the first place?'

'He said something about some project you're doing on people who are unjustly in prison. It's wonderful to know that his case is being taken seriously at last. Although I gather you won't have finished your work in time to affect his release date.'

'I know. I'm sorry about that. But it's coming up quite soon, isn't it?'

'Fairly: the automatic release date is in just under eight months from now. But if there's anything you can do to prove that he's innocent before he gets out it will be...oh, it'll be such a help. I hate the thought of him emerging into a world that believes he's capable of doing something like that.'

'I'm doing my best,' said Emma, wishing that she could be wholly on Jemima's side. 'But I may not be able to prove anything. You see, my work is about why people make false confessions, not really about the injustice of them being in prison for things they haven't done.'

'I hadn't realised that.' Jemima Lutterworth's attractive voice held the first hint of doubt.

'I thought not, which is why I wanted to warn you before I started asking questions.'

'That was generous and very fair. No wonder he likes you so much. So what is it you want to ask me?'

'Lots of things. You and I both know that he did not kill that mother and her child, and that he was not even in the car when the crash happened,' Emma began.

'Thank you,' Jemima said simply, making her feel even worse.

'And yet he told the police he *had* done it. I still can't understand that, and I mainly wanted to ask you whether you have any idea what was going on in his head when he confessed.'

'Have you talked to him about it?' she asked, not answering Emma's question.

'Well, I did try. But something I said upset him so much that he won't talk to me any more, and I haven't been able to make sense of some of the answers he gave me when we first met. He let me do a polygraph test then, but I can't work out what the results mean and now he won't explain them. So, you see, I was wondering whether you might be prepared to let me show you the charts to see if you could understand why he said the things he did.'

There was a pause and then Jemima Lutterworth said, 'I don't know anything about polygraph testing or charts.'

'But you do know your husband.'

'Well, that's certainly true.' There was a pause, during

which Emma thought she had probably blown it completely. 'Oh, well, why not? Have you got transport to get here?'

'No. I was hoping that there might be a station within reasonable distance of you so that I could get a taxi from there.' Emma had been worrying for some time that she was going to crash her meagre budget with all the minicabs and taxis she was having to use. She was frighteningly close to her overdraft limit as it was and hated the thought of asking any of her friends or relations for help, but she was not going to lose the chance of finding out what she needed to know simply out of fear of debt. 'Is there a station?'

'Reading's not far. But I could easily fetch you. Why don't you let me know which train you'll be on and I'll pick you up?'

'Oh, you needn't do that,' said Emma automatically, but after some polite argument she accepted Jemima's offer.

THERE WERE NOT many people waiting on the platform when Emma left the train at Reading, and she had no difficulty in picking out Jemima Lutterworth. Willow's description of her pleasant face and greying-blonde hair made her easy to recognise. That afternoon she was wearing a pleated skirt in a soft pink tweed with a loose cream silk sweater over it. Her hair was pushed off her face with large tortoiseshell-framed sunglasses, and she was impeccably made up. She looked attractive, controlled, and not at all the kind of woman Annie Frome had described.

Emma introduced herself and they shook hands as though they were meeting at a party. Jemima led the way to a large grey Volvo, which she drove rather too fast for the narrow country roads, asking polite questions about Emma's work. She answered as fully as she could, but when she tried to talk about Andrew's case, Jemima asked with simple dignity whether they could leave the discussion until they were back at the house. Moving the conversation on as seamlessly as she could, Emma complimented her on the car.

'It is good, isn't it?' Jemima said, sounding pleased. 'And so safe, you know.'

'Have you had it for long?'

'Ages. I've always had Volvos ever since I was pregnant, although my husband doesn't like them. This is fairly old, but I'm not about to replace it. Andrew will just have to put up with it when he gets out. His has gone, you see.'

'Oh?' said Emma, interested but trying to sound merely as though she were keeping the conversation going. 'I hadn't realised it had been written off in the crash.'

Jemima shivered, saying, 'It wasn't. But neither of us could have borne to drive it again. And anyway, once he'd resigned from Hill, Snow, he had to turn it in—or buy it from the partnership. It was going to be very expensive and anyway, what would have been the point when he was on his way to that hellish place?'

'Yes, I suppose so. I hadn't thought. D'you know what happened to it?'

'I imagine it got sold on,' Jemima said, clamping her lips shut as though to signal that she was not prepared to talk about the car any longer.

Unable to think of any other suitable subject, Emma sat in silence until they reached the house. Even though she had been prepared for it by Willow's letter, she was amazed by the sight and managed to show convincing surprise all through the tour Jemima gave her.

Eventually they reached the kitchen, which was a disorientating mixture of the ultra-modern and the cosily traditional. Jemima invited Emma to sit down at the large zinc-topped table in the middle of the room and went to make a pot of tea.

Emma watched her moving smoothly about the big silver-and-blue room, fetching a tin of home-made flapjacks, which turned out to be almost as good as any of Mrs Rusham's biscuits, boiling water and measuring shotlike pellets of green tea into a white porcelain pot. Emma herself did not much like green tea, but she pretended enthusiasm and sipped politely.

'Andrew always loved it,' said Jemima, blinking, 'and so I nearly always have it now. I find I need to do the things he liked. I'm not sure why.'

'It must be so difficult for you, waiting for him to come home.'

'Yes, it is. But it's much worse for him. At least I'm still here in comfort with all my things, and…' She broke off and produced an unconvincing smile.

'It's none of my business,' Emma began and was not surprised to see the withdrawal in Jemima's big grey eyes, 'but I was just wondering whether…I mean with your husband unable to work. Oh, dear, this sounds horribly rude. I'm sorry.'

'You want to know how I'm getting on for money, do you?' There was an edge to Jemima's pleasant voice. Emma nodded, embarrassed, but determined to find out whether Jemima had so much money of her own that Andrew could have been lying in order to avoid giving her reason to divorce him and cut him off from full access to her riches. To Emma's surprise, the question was answered.

'Not all that well. I do some typing for a couple of local authors, which brings in a little, and of course I charge the parties of people who come round the house and garden, but that's not producing as much as it once did. In fact'— she looked across the table at Emma's attentive face and flushed—'it's one—but only one—of the many reasons why I was so anxious for Andrew to get parole. I know he won't be able to get the sort of job he had before, but I'm sure he'll get something. He's far too clever and determined not to. And it'll be such a relief. That probably sounds awful—

and I know it's selfish—but I'm nearly desperate. I've spent all my own running-away money, borrowed up to the hilt at the bank, increased the mortgage as far as I can, and I simply don't know where to turn next.' Her voice wavered and she picked up the delicate, handleless teacup and sipped.

'That's better. I'm so sorry. You didn't come to hear all about my financial woes. Visitor numbers will probably rise again when the weather improves, or I may pluck up the courage to get rid of Andrew's memorial garden, which I'm sure is what's making the place unpopular.'

'I'm sorry?' said Emma, remembering just in time that she was not supposed to know anything about the garden. Jemima looked a little surprised.

'My husband made a garden as a memorial to our son, who died some years ago. It meant a great deal to him, but I hate it, and so do most of the other people who come here. I'm afraid they may have been complaining, which could be why the organisers of these garden tours have decided to avoid us. The income they provided was never very much, of course, but it covered most of my housekeeping bills. I miss it.'

'I'm sure you do.' Emma remembered Jane Cleverholme's surprise that Jemima had not asked for money when she complained about the *Daily Mercury*'s reporting of her husband's case. If she was as badly off as she claimed, that seemed even odder than Jane had thought it, but it was not a subject Emma felt able to raise. 'But perhaps if you do change the garden they'll come back.'

'I hope so. If only I could be sure. You see, Andrew'll be so very upset if I do flatten it, but I feel it has got to be done. The whole garden will look much more attractive without that bite out of the middle, and the memorial itself is so... And it doesn't seem quite right to have it here. Inappropriate somehow. Do you see what I mean?'

Emma smiled and gently pointed out that it was not she who had to be persuaded.

'No, of course not,' said Jemima, blushing faintly. 'How silly of me! I talk too much. Where were we? Oh, yes, for some reason you wanted to know about my income.'

'I was just feeling sympathetic,' said Emma. 'And thinking how very difficult life must be for you. That's all.'

'Oh, I see. That's nice of you. Things will get better as soon as he's back and I'm sure I can last out till then. Somehow. Whatever happens about his job, at least when he's home we can put the house on the market. Then everything will be relatively simple. I've always thought we ought to have sold it straight away, but he said we couldn't make important decisions like that while he was in prison. And so I've hung on, selling bits and pieces of furniture and pictures whenever I had to.' Jemima sighed and stared at an out-of-date calendar on the wall behind Emma's head.

'If only I had some qualifications of my own, everything would have been so much easier. But I wasn't brought up even to consider a career. All I can do is type, and there aren't any secretarial jobs around here.'

'I do feel for you,' said Emma, meaning it. 'I was always told that someone else would be around to pay my bills, too. I haven't believed it for years, but I did once. Although, you know, I'm not sure it's what I'd want, even if I still thought I could rely on it. That's one reason why I set about trying to get this degree.'

'Good for you! If I had my time again, I'd... Well, I certainly wouldn't assume that being able to type was enough.'

'No. Although it's a useful skill to fall back on.' Emma laughed without much amusement. 'I may have to do that myself if I don't find out what really happened the night your husband was arrested.' Hearing that tactless statement echoing in her brain, Emma added in some confusion, 'I'm

so sorry. That came out a bit wrong. I didn't mean to sound
so selfish.'

'It doesn't matter. It's what we both want after all.' Jemima looked friendlier. 'Let's get on with it. You said something about graphs or something you wanted me to look at.'

Emma took the polygraph charts out of her haversack and
spread them on the table. Jemima listened intelligently to
the explanation of the technique Emma had used to produce
them, and herself pointed to the surprisingly jagged fluctuations in the lines that ought to have been smooth and regular if Andrew had been telling the truth.

'And the questions you asked here and here were what?'
she asked, frowning down at the long sheet of paper.

Emma consulted her list, although she knew it by heart,
and read out the questions about the car and whether Andrew had ever had passengers, adding, 'As I said, I know
as well as you do that he wasn't in the car when it crashed
and yet he's showing what in any other case I would have
interpreted as a guilty reaction to my questions about it. In
fact it's an even more guilty reaction than the ones he
showed when I asked my control questions about the times
when he actually was stopped by the police. D'you see these
ones? Here and here. That's why I'm so puzzled.'

'I'm not surprised.' Jemima traced the jagged lines with
a pink varnished fingernail. 'I don't understand it myself.
Like you, I *know* he was not driving that night. The car was
stolen, just as he always said.'

'Isn't it tricky?' Emma pulled the sheet along so that she
could point to the part of the graph that represented Andrew's reactions to questions about what he had been doing
that evening. 'This bit seems fine. He's talking here about
how he was in his office, working on the client's tax problems. He's calm as anything, not in the least alarmed by
any of my questions.'

'Have you got any theories about why he was upset by

the car questions?' Jemima asked, sounding quite unworried herself.

'For a long time I was completely stumped,' Emma said, wondering how to frame the crucial enquiry. After a moment, determined to try, she added, 'Then I did wonder—and please don't be upset—whether he could have thought that perhaps you'd taken the car that night. D'you see what I mean? *I* know you didn't, but he might have been afraid of it. After all, you had keys. And they must have told him that the car wasn't broken into. Have you ever thought that he might have told the lies because he wanted to protect you?'

Jemima shook her head so that her soft greying-blonde hair flew about her face. She did not look at all angry.

'I wondered that too at one stage and decided that it could well have crossed his mind that I'd done it. He's a highly intelligent man; and it's the obvious answer to the lock mystery. But you see I had an alibi for that night. So, even if he'd been afraid it was me while he was with the police, he couldn't still have been worried about it when he was talking to you only a week ago. Or whenever it was you saw him.'

'No, I see. Well, that's that, then. There is just one other possibility,' said Emma, impressed by Jemima's dispassionate manner and grateful for it. 'Someone I showed the sheet to at the university—he doesn't know whose test it was—suggested that Andrew might have had a guilt reaction because of some other occasion when he'd had a passenger in the car who he perhaps shouldn't have had. I mean...'

'No, no, it's all right. I understand what you're getting at,' Jemima said, still not apparently taking offence. 'You think Andrew might have had a mistress in the car with him on some other occasion. That's it, isn't it?'

'Well, yes, I suppose so,' said Emma. 'I know it sounds an awful thing to say, but—'

'But you think that he could have felt so guilty about some other woman that he confessed to a crime he did not commit, went to prison for it, and then displayed an incriminating reaction years later when you asked questions designed to prove him innocent of the crime after all. Is that what you're suggesting?'

'Put like that, it sounds unlikely, I'll admit,' said Emma, taking another sip of the peculiar tea.

'Not only unlikely: positively ridiculous.'

'I suppose it does. Sorry. Then I'm still stumped,' said Emma, smiling openly at the other woman. 'Can you help? Do you know what he might still be feeling guilty about?'

'Yes, I think I probably do, but I'm not sure it'll help your work much.'

'Any information that's true will help.'

Jemima sat up straighter, as though bracing herself for something difficult.

'I told you our son had died, didn't I?' she began.

'Yes. It was necrotising fasciitis, wasn't it? It must have been so awful for you. I—'

'Who told you that?' Jemima's voice was sharp enough to make Emma realise what she had done.

'Told me what?' she asked, playing for time and silently cursing her own stupidity.

'How my son died.'

Emma felt her jaw tighten as she tried to think whether there was any way to cover her mistake. 'Wasn't it necrotising fasciitis that killed him?'

'Yes, it was,' said Jemima coldly. 'But I didn't tell you that. And Andrew can't have because he doesn't talk about it. In any case, if it had been him, you'd have said so straight out. Who have you been talking to?' She stared at Emma. 'Why are so many people suddenly coming here to ask me questions about Andrew and Pipp?'

'I don't know what you mean.' Emma wished she had

sounded more convincing, but she could hardly go back and try again.

'I think you probably do. Have you got some connection with the *Daily Mercury*?'

Emma did not think she had moved or shown any sign of discomfort, but Jemima laughed contemptuously.

'That's it, isn't it? You'd better learn not to blush if you want to make a career of this sort of thing. Or is that why she sent you here, because you look so naïve and she thought I might be distracted by that and let you get under my guard?'

Emma bowed her head and then, valuing the truth as she did, forced herself to look up and say, 'It's not actually as bad as it sounds.'

'No?' The monosyllable was almost expressionless, but Emma thought she could imagine the outrage that Jemima must be feeling. 'D'you work for her?'

'Who?' said Emma, in a pathetic attempt to deflect the wrath she was sure was coming.

'Jane Cleverholme, editor of that filthy rag.' As Emma still hesitated, Jemima added so coldly that Emma almost shivered, 'Please don't humiliate yourself or bore me by lying. Just do me the courtesy of explaining precisely what's going on here and exactly what you have been trying to trick me into saying.'

'No one's been trying to trick you into anything, Mrs Lutterworth. And please don't blame Jane for any of it. I went to her, not the other way round.'

'Are you some relation of the woman who was killed?'

'Good heavens no! It's nothing like that. Honestly, everything I told you about my thesis and the polygraph tests is entirely true. Listen, Mrs Lutterworth, please don't look at me like that. I'll tell you the whole thing, if you'll just listen. Please?'

'I'll listen,' Jemima said after another uncomfortable
pause. 'I don't promise anything more than that.'

Emma described her pathetic attempts to find enough material for her thesis, her collapse on to Jane and Jane's suggestion that she should look into the Lutterworth case.

'She was worried, you see,' Emma said pleadingly. She
was not at all sure that Jane would forgive her for talking
so frankly, but she did not think she had any option. 'She
found you so convincing—and so likable—that she was
worried about what you said to her. She thought that if I
could find out more about the truth of what happened the
night your husband's car was crashed and even discover
who was driving it, then she'd be able to publish a huge
vindication of him. That would have been good for you and
him as well as helping both her and me. You must see that
it would.'

There was silence. Jemima Lutterworth's lined and pretty
face looked more obstructive than at any time that afternoon.

'And Cressida Woodruffe? Where does she come in?'
She laughed with unmistakable contempt. 'You know, you
really must do something about that blush.'

'She's a friend, too. She introduced me to Jane. That's
all.'

'Then why couldn't you—or she—have come to me honestly in the first place? That's what I don't understand. I
would have answered anything any of you had wanted to
ask in such a good cause.'

'I thought I had to talk to your husband first. For all I
knew, he might have…well, you know, the police might
have been right. It wasn't until after I'd seen him and read
up some of the stuff about the crash that I realised how
wrong they'd been.'

Emma stopped talking and sat staring at the shiny table,

feeling as though she were about six and in dire trouble. Jemima Lutterworth did not move.

'Well, now you've come this far,' she said eventually, sounding completely implacable, 'you'd better tell me whatever it is that you really believe about my husband.' Emma shook her head, feeling sick. 'You've insulted us both. You've abused my hospitality and my trust. You might as well go the whole hog. Who knows? You might even find out something you could use to your advantage.'

'I still don't know what I believe,' said Emma doggedly, wondering how she was ever going to get back to the station if Jemima was too angry to telephone for a taxi for her. She had brought no map and had no idea of how to reach a main road, let alone Reading itself.

With visions of herself walking round and round the lanes of Berkshire until she fell apart, Emma added, 'Only that something the police said that night must have made him think it safer to confess to something he hadn't done than go on telling the truth. I still want to know why. But perhaps I never will.'

Jemima was smoothing the pleats of her well-made pinkish shirt.

'I think you'd better leave now, don't you?' she said.

'Probably. Would it be too much of an abuse of your hospitality to ask you to telephone for a taxi to take me back to the station?' Emma spoke with all the humility that she found useful in defusing anger in the past. Either that or her genuine embarrassment seemed to soften Jemima's fury a little as she shrugged.

'I suppose I might as well drive you.'

'Oh, I couldn't let you do that,' said Emma. 'Not after all this.'

'Don't worry. It will at least assure me that you're well and truly off the premises and not poking around the house or digging up the garden. Come along.'

Feeling her cheeks pulsating with the treacherous blush, wishing that she had power over space and time and could magic herself away, Emma followed Jemima down the long passage from the kitchen to the back door and the car.

They drove back to Reading in excruciating silence. Emma fumbled with the door lock as she tried to get out as quickly as possible. Once her feet were on neutral ground, she bent down so that she could look back into the car, and attempted to apologise once more and even thank Jemima Lutterworth for the tea.

She merely looked witheringly at Emma and put the car in gear again. As she drove out of the station forecourt much too fast, she only just missed another large car that was manoeuvring out of its parking space. Emma thought that Andrew could have been forgiven for being afraid that his wife had caused the crash. She wondered whether he had really been convinced by Jemima's alibi and wished that she had been forceful enough to ask what it was. She also wished that she had ignored her embarrassment and made Jemima tell her what she had been going to say about why Andrew might still be displaying signs of guilt.

The journey back to London proved to be a suitable punishment for someone who had betrayed a friend, mucked up a potentially useful interview, and seriously upset a woman who had already suffered a great deal. There was a bomb scare only ten minutes after the train had left Reading and everyone was herded off it at the next station. The replacement train, packed tight with at least twice its proper complement of passengers, left half an hour later and then broke down fifteen miles short of London. Several of the passengers were determined to get out and walk to the nearest station, but the conductor would not open the doors on the grounds that it would be far too dangerous for them to risk being hit by other trains. One imaginative if dangerous man loudly suggested setting fire to the seats since, after all the awful railway fires of the recent past, the conductor would be bound to open the doors at the first sight of flames.

Eventually a third train was shunted back along the line and the hot, furious, exhausted travellers were at last allowed out of their prison. The relief train got them in to Paddington only an hour after the first should have arrived. Emma pushed her way on to the tube to Blackfriars, was propelled out of it by yet more furious commuters and fought her way to the right platform. Amazingly, a train for St Albans appeared five minutes later and she was soon sitting in relative comfort.

Lying back against the seat with her eyes closed and her head aching, she tried to make her mind blank. She felt someone else sitting down in the seat beside her, heard a polite 'excuse me' and muttered something reasonably friendly but not encouraging in return.

'You have a nice sleep,' said the voice. 'You look worn out, you poor dear.'

Emma opened her eyes, saw an elderly woman's broad, lined face, and managed a smile.

'That's right, dear. You go to sleep. Which is your stop?'

'St Albans.'

'You don't need to worry, then. I'll wake you. I don't get off till after that. Sleep well, dear.'

'Thank you,' murmured Emma, knowing full well that it was humiliation rather than exhaustion that was making her look peculiar.

WHEN EMMA had dragged herself up to her room she found that some friendly person had pushed her post under the door. On top of the small pile was a letter with her name in Andrew Lutterworth's small, neat, auditor's handwriting. The address underneath it had been added by someone else, presumably by the governor's secretary. Emma was not sure that she wanted to have anything more to do with Lutterworth, but, remembering how much work everyone else had already put in on her behalf, she knew she could not ignore the letter. She opened it.

Dear Emma,

    I have an irritating feeling that an apology is due to you. You caught me on the raw by talking about my son. I cannot bear to talk about his death. On the other hand, now that I have got over my shock, I can see that you can't have meant to hurt me and that your intentions were good. If, therefore, you are still in search of material for your thesis, I am prepared to see you one more time. I must stress that the subject of my son is not for discussion, but if you wish to ask me anything else, you may.

Yours sincerely,
Andrew Lutterworth

The telephone began to ring. Emma moved across her small room, reading the note as she went, and picked up the receiver.

'Hello?' she said, hoping that it would be Jag, or even Hal, to give her back her sense of herself as someone worthwhile.

'Sweet Thing. Hello. How are you?'

'Oh, hello, Anthony. What can I do for you?'

'Nothing at all.' He laughed. 'Luckily, because you don't sound very helpful. What's the matter?'

'Nothing. I've had a heavy day, that's all. I'm tired.'

'Ah, you poor little thing. You'd better have an early night and don't go drinking too much coffee. It's not good for you. If you would only—'

'What is it you want, Anthony?' asked Emma, not bothering to tell him that she would drink whatever she wanted and stay up all night if she chose, and work herself into terminal exhaustion come to that. There seemed no point.

'Only to sort things out between you and your mother. She came for lunch the other day, and she's unhappy and very worried about you. I promised I'd have a word and find out why you're being so unlike your sweet self. What has got into you, Emma? You've changed.'

'Yes, thank goodness. I don't pretend any more. I'm fine and there is nothing for you to do,' Emma said, holding on to her temper with difficulty.

'Well, if you are fine, then I don't think there's any excuse for the way you've been upsetting your mother.' Anthony sounded not only as pompous and patronising as usual but also as though he was enjoying the opportunity of giving her a reprimand. 'You've been thoughtless, Sweet Thing. It's quite uncalled for and very hurtful. She's your mother. Has it never occurred to you that the most important thing to remember in life is that you should do everything you possibly can to avoid hurting your family?'

Emma was counting to ten to get some kind of control over herself before giving voice to her protest when Anthony said loudly, 'Are you there? Emma? Have we been cut off? Hello? Hello?'

'No, Anthony, we have not been cut off. I was simply trying to understand how you of all people could dare to say something like that to me,' she said, surprising herself.

'What *do* you mean?' All the pomposity and pleasure in his voice had been overtaken by astonishment.

'Oh, come on. You must know what I'm talking about.'

'I haven't a clue. What is the matter with you, Emma?'

Tempted as usual to say 'oh, nothing' and smooth him down, Emma thought that she would never be able to respect herself again if she did not tackle him once and for all. She breathed deeply and loosened her grip on the telephone, which had been so tight it was making her whole arm ache.

'Anthony, do you remember when we were children?' She was glad to hear how calm she sounded.

'Naturally. But what has that got to do with it? You got on very well with your mother then.'

'Yes, I know,' said Emma, remembering the simplicity of the early days, when her mother had seemed unquestioningly wise and benevolent. 'But I'm not talking about her. I'm talking about you and what you did to me then.'

'Oh, for heaven's sake! You never could take a joke and you always used to make the most ridiculous fuss about a little brotherly ragging, but I can't believe you're still going on about it now. Really, Emma. How childish can you get?'

'Don't you remember,' she said, feeling a welcome surge of anger banish the last scrap of her impulse to retreat, 'how you used to threaten to hide me from the grown-ups, lock me up and starve me to death?'

'Nonsense.'

'Or drown me by squeezing water from your flannel into my nose and mouth while I was asleep? Or burn my eyelashes off with the cigarette lighter you stole from Uncle Angus? Or put poisonous mushrooms in that foul porridge Sarah and I were made to eat every morning in winter? Don't you remember how you told me you'd done it one day when Sarah was ill and so there weren't any witnesses?'

'Certainly not.'

'When I wouldn't eat it,' Emma went on, still amazed that anyone could have behaved as Anthony had, 'you held my nose so that I had to open my mouth to breathe and you forced that stuff into me until I gagged and threw up. And when my mother asked why I'd been sick, you persuaded her that I'd stuck my fingers down my own throat so that I could get off school. And she took a slipper to me. Don't you remember that?'

'Emma, you're exaggerating. You're blowing a few practical jokes right out of proportion. All children do those sort of things.'

'No, they don't, Anthony. That's what I have at last come to accept. Normal children do not behave like that. And you were hardly a child anyway. I was five, but you were fifteen then, huge and unbelievably powerful in comparison to me. You were a sadist.'

'You're mad.'

'You enjoyed my terror, didn't you?'

'Don't be ridiculous.'

'I don't know how you can go on pretending. I certainly can't. I just wish I'd told you so years ago and not tried to contain what you made me feel.'

'I can't think what's got into you, Emma. Have you been talking to one of these trick cyclists? Or is it a bunch of feminist loonies who've been winding you up?'

'Neither, Anthony. I've just got far enough away from you to see it all in perspective. I used to blame myself, but now I can see you for the revolting, cruel thug you were. It's odd: for years I've been too scared to admit even to myself how much I hated what you did to me. But it doesn't seem to matter any more. I don't care any longer and I don't have to have anything to do with you. Thank God.'

'You're hysterical. I can't think what's been giving you these stupid fantasies. Father would have been appalled. You ought to see a doctor and get yourself sorted out, Emma. And if I hear that you've been repeating any of this nonsense to Sarah or your mother or anyone else, I'll—'

Emma put a finger on the cradle of the telephone, stopping his voice in mid-flow, and realised that she was free.

The explosive mixture of exhilaration and anger that her long-delayed rebellion had generated made it impossible for her to stay in her tiny room. She went out, not even bothering to lock the door behind her, and plunged into the dark-

ness of the campus. As she walked, breathing deeply in the
cold damp air, she realised that she was muttering aloud to
herself, saying all the things she wished she had said to
Anthony. It was deeply satisfying to hear the words spoken,
even though he would never know what they were.

Eventually she walked and thought herself into a kind of
calm. She had said everything that had to be said, and her
brain had done its work of sorting her feelings and allowing
her new confidence to banish the old fears.

Those seemed more acceptable to her than they had ever
done. She had at last come to accept that the terror Anthony
had induced in her throughout her childhood might have
been reasonable. Even though he had never carried out any
of his threats, at the time she had always believed they were
real.

Later, once she had grown up, she had criticised herself
for being so gullible, for taking what was probably no more
than teasing in such a tragic way, and she had blamed herself for the effect it had had on her life. At last she could
allow herself to believe that it might not have been her fault
that she had been so afraid.

She also came to understand as she walked up and down
the hard paths, talking to herself, why she had felt such a
strong need to learn how to distinguish truth from lies. The
roots of that must have lain not so much in her high-flown
assumptions that she might one day save an innocent from
going to prison or prevent a criminal being freed, as in the
muddle of feelings in which she had found herself whenever
she had attempted to complain of what Anthony had been
doing to her.

'Boys do that sort of thing,' her father had told her over
and over again. 'Show you're not afraid of him. Stand up
to him and then he'll stop. Don't give him the satisfaction
of seeing that you mind.' Her mother's line had been rather
different. 'Poor Anthony,' she had always said. 'He lost his

mother. We must all do what we can for him. Be nice to him, Emma, and then he'll be nicer to you.'

Both lines of advice had put all the fault on to her, she realised. Her father had implied that she was failing in courage; her mother, that she was not kind enough. Both of them had obviously believed that Anthony had not been doing anything very odd. On the few occasions when he had hit her in public, he had been soundly punished for it, but Emma had not minded the occasional punches or slaps nearly as much as the private mental tortures in which he had excelled.

She asked herself what exactly he could have been trying to achieve. Had it been the sight of her frightened eyes and trembling lips begging him to stop, or the feel of her sweaty hands as she had tried to keep him away? Or had he actually wanted her dead as she had believed at the time?

Perhaps not with his conscious mind, she decided after a while, but at some level he probably had wanted precisely that.

At last she turned to go back to her room. As she reached the archway that led to her building, her mind produced an extraordinarily vivid picture of Jemima Lutterworth standing between the climbing plants in the atrium of her amazing house. She was saying that she wanted to see Emma off the premises to make sure 'that you're not poking around the house or digging up the garden'.

Emma repeated the phrase to herself several times, wondering whether it could be only the strange calm that had followed her own emotional storm that made it seem both so peculiar and so significant.

As she hurried up the stairs to her room, she remembered Annie Frome's description of Andrew Lutterworth sitting at his desk one morning some weeks after Pipp's death. Andrew had been crying, Annie had said, and trying to hide his swollen eyes behind his hands, hands that were bruised and scraped, with nails torn as though he had been ripping them against a brick wall.

Emma could not understand why it had taken her such an unconscionable time to see the significance of that. The whole idea of Andrew wrecking his hands against a wall seemed ludicrous once she applied her imagination to the scene. Likelier by far was the picture she was beginning to create for herself, a picture in which Andrew was on his knees in the dark, digging.

SEVENTEEN

BACK IN HER ROOM Emma stripped off her clothes and went to stand under one of the showers for fifteen minutes. Later, as she lay in the dark and tried to stop thinking of Andrew Lutterworth's damaged hands, she realised that she was going to have to see him again.

She turned heavily over in bed and buried her face in the hard polyester pillow. The prospect of being alone with him appalled her in itself and the idea of asking him whether he had killed his mistress and carried her body in the car back to Berkshire so that he could bury it in the memorial garden seemed impossible. But she knew she would have to do it. Her need to prove that she had grit was one thing; her gratitude for the enormous amount of help she had had from her friends, another. But much more important than either was the possibility that her cowardice might allow a murder to go undiscovered and a murderer unpunished. That would be unbearable.

Having slept only intermittently, and dreamed of prisons and flooded quarries, graves and knives and stranglings, she got out of bed at half past seven for another restorative, stinging shower and two cups of very strong coffee. She could not ring the wing governor to set up her interview with Andrew Lutterworth until after nine, which gave her another hour to decide what she was going to say.

When her own telephone started to ring, she flinched as though the sound had triggered an electric shock against her skin. Wondering whether the caller was going to be Anthony, perhaps apologising or else trying to blackmail or bully her into keeping silent about what he had done to her in the past, she picked up the receiver and coldly said her name.

'Is this too early?' came Willow's voice, invigoratingly alive and thoroughly welcome. 'I wanted to find out how you are.'

'No, it's not too early at all. I've been wanting to talk to you, too, but I thought I'd have to wait until much later. Was everything OK yesterday? Did you meet Terry?'

'Yes, we did. And I must admit that I was glad of Jag's company. I might have found out just as much—or even more—on my own, but I might also have ended up beaten to a bloody pulp.'

'Oh, don't, Willow. Even as a joke.'

'You sound a bit wobbly, Em. What's up?'

'Nothing. I'm fine. You did find Terry, then. Good. What did he say?'

'Hasn't Jag told you?'

'No. I didn't get back myself until quite late and then I had to go out again. I was going to ring him a bit later this morning. He doesn't usually surface until about ten. So what did you discover?'

Willow described everything they had heard from Terry Lepe, and Emma began to feel better. There was still, she realised, a possibility that her melodramatic ideas were nonsense and that Andrew had never had a mistress at all and certainly never killed her. After all, the whole idea of the mistress had come from Hal and there had been no evidence to support it.

'Do you think he could have been telling the truth?' Emma asked with a new enthusiasm in her voice. 'About having no more than a skid and then taking the car back to Holborn? Do you suppose all this time we could have been barking up the wrong tree altogether and it was Andrew who crashed? Or even Jemima?'

'No. I believe Susie implicitly. I'm perfectly sure it was

Terry who crashed. Anyway, it certainly couldn't have been Jemima,' said Willow. 'She told me when she was walking me round that creepy garden that she had the Lord Lieutenant and his wife and sister-in-law round for supper and bridge that night. I haven't bothered to check it, but it would be so easy to verify that I can't imagine she'd lie about it.'

'Oh. Right,' said Emma, feeling deflated. If Jemima's alibi was really watertight, and if Terry had said nothing to disprove Susie's story, then the reasons for Andrew's fear of what the forensic scientists might find in his car would have to be investigated, however much she hated the idea.

'You really do sound depressed, Emma. What's the matter?'

'Nothing. Not really. I had a slightly bruising encounter with Jemima myself yesterday and I'm eating at myself for having been so stupid with her. Can I tell you about it? I have sort of dropped Jane in it a bit, you see, and that may redound on you. Is that the word? Redound, I mean. Or is it rebound?'

'The second,' said Willow, adding with a mock threat in her voice, 'What have you done? You'd better confess before it's too late.'

Emma described everything she had said and heard, adding with a sigh, 'And now Andrew has said he *will* see me after all and I'm going to have to go as soon as the governor can arrange it in the hope that I get there before Jemima's managed to warn him off me.'

'And you don't want to go?'

'No. To be honest, I hate the idea.'

'But why? You went quite happily before.'

'Because,' said Emma reluctantly, 'I have a sort of idea of what it might have all been about, and so now I can't not tackle it, but...'

'Would you like me to come with you? Moral support and all that.'

'Would you, Willow? Really? Oh, that would be fantastic. But wouldn't Tom be furious?'

'No. We made peace last night; real lasting peace,' said Willow, laughing. 'In any case nothing's going to happen to either you or me under the eye of a warder in a well-regulated prison.'

'We don't have an officer with us all the time. They just look in at intervals to ask if everything's all right. If we could have one all the time, I wouldn't mind so much. Although I don't suppose we'd get anything useful out of Andrew if there were a warder.'

'Emma,' said Willow much more seriously, 'you don't have to go at all. I could perfectly well go on my own. We could ask Jag to go instead. Or we can drop the whole thing.'

'No, I must go myself. Having got this far, I can't give in now. But I don't think any of the standard lie-detection tests is going to help much. If I knew for certain what had been done and just wanted to find out whether he had done it, then I could use a Guilty Knowledge Technique test. But since I want to make him tell me what it was he once did that makes him show signs of guilt, I'm stuck. You see, without having the knowledge myself I can't design the questions I'd need for a Guilty Knowledge test. And I don't think it's worth even trying another Control Question Technique one. Perhaps I ought to abandon tests altogether in the hope that they'll bounce him into telling us the truth. If I can. And if it doesn't turn him violent on us.'

'You'll have to explain the difference in the tests sometime,' said Willow soothingly, 'but don't worry about it now. I'm sure that between us we can manage Lutterworth, whatever he may try to do. After all, he won't have access to any kind of weapon and, with two of us there, even if he goes berserk with rage we'll be able to overpower him and yell for an officer. Jane said that he's a bit of a shrimp, and only about five-foot-eleven. I think I'm just as tall and you're young and fit. Come on, Emma, where's your bottle?'

'I'm not sure,' she said, realising that the excited feeling of liberation she had felt the previous evening had gone completely. Her standing up to Anthony had not, after all, given her the complete confidence for which she had longed. There were some things that still scared her, and male anger was one of the worst.

'What is it, Em?' asked Willow seriously.

'Nothing important.' One day Emma thought she might be able to tell Willow about Anthony, but for the moment she had to deal with it herself. She might tell Jag, too, but on the other hand she might not. 'But, look, if you really are prepared to come to the prison with me, I'll fix it with the governor for as soon as possible. Are there any times and dates you can't do in the near future?'

Willow had a look in her diary and said that she was already booked for something else in two days' time, but that she could go with Emma to the prison on any other day. Mrs Rusham would be available to look after Lucinda, and Tom was busy at Scotland Yard, and so she would be free. Emma promised to ring her as soon as the governor had suggested an appointment.

Putting down the receiver, Emma felt better and sat down to sort out what she had to say to Andrew. When she had got all her ideas into order and had written herself a list of questions, she rang the prison. To her amazement the wing governor said that if she were in a serious hurry the interview could be arranged for the following morning at half past ten. Seizing the opportunity, she said that would suit her and that she would like to bring an associate with her.

'Ah, I'm afraid that won't be possible,' said the governor, sounding genuinely regretful.

'But why not?' asked Emma. 'She's entirely respectable,

and will be there only to help me gather data. What possible objection could you have?'

'Our security procedures mean that we could never admit someone so quickly. It normally takes at least three or four days to vet possible visitors.'

'Oh, I see,' said Emma, rushing to explain. 'But look, she's Willow Worth, the wife of Superintendent Worth of the Met. Wouldn't that make it easier for you to speed up your vetting? I imagine she must already have been checked out through all sorts of Scotland Yard routines.'

'That might make a difference. If it's really so urgent I suppose I could phone... Very well. Let me know where I can get in touch with you this afternoon, and I'll see what I can do.'

'Oh, thank you,' said Emma, wishing that she could ask him to see that Tom was not involved in Willow's vetting. Even if she had made peace with him, it would be silly to rub his nose in her detecting if it was not necessary. 'If you say when you're likely to ring, I'll make sure I'm here.'

'It'll probably be between five and five thirty this afternoon, then.'

'Great. That's marvellous. Thank you.'

'Hold on to your gratitude until I've got Mrs Worth admitted,' said the governor with a faint laugh in his voice. 'I won't see you tomorrow, I'm afraid, but no doubt we will meet again in due course. Don't forget to bring your documents and ask her to come with her passport. I'll leave a letter for you both at the security desk.'

'I won't forget. Thank you.'

HE WAS AS GOOD as his word and rang Emma at twenty past five to say that Willow had been cleared to enter the prison, on the same research basis as Emma. Like Emma, she would have to provide identification and submit to a search at the gate, as well as to observe the various rules and restrictions

Emma had learned. On Willow's behalf, Emma accepted them all.

The following morning she was standing outside Willow's neat cream-painted house at half past eight. Mrs Rusham admitted her and begged her to have some breakfast while Willow finished dressing. Superintendent Worth had already left for Scotland Yard, she said, but there was plenty of breakfast left and she had only recently made a fresh pot of coffee.

Emma declined the offer, far too impatient to sit down to eat. Instead she stood waiting in the hall until Willow appeared in a surprisingly dull-looking suit of smooth navy-blue cloth. She had Lucinda in her arms and the child shrieked with pleasure at the sight of Emma.

In spite of her fear of being late at the prison, Emma held out her arms and took the child for a moment's bonding romp before handing her over to Mrs Rusham.

'We'd better go, Em. The traffic may be pretty awful, although we will be going against it most of the way.'

'OK.' Emma kissed Lucinda and said goodbye to Mrs Rusham.

'Be good, Lucinda,' said Willow, blowing her a kiss. 'Mrs Rusham, I won't see you again until this evening, but I should be back easily in time for her bath. Come on, Emma, let's go.'

As they drove out through south London, Willow pointed out the street that led to the flat where she had once lived, and Emma smiled at the incongruity between it and the Mews.

'Isn't it odd how one has no idea how life is going to turn out?' said Willow vaguely, apparently looking at Clapham Common. 'Or what one wants of it.'

'I thought that was only me,' said Emma, feeling encouraged.

'Far from it. By the way, I meant to say that I'm coming

to like Jag more and more,' Willow went on, still in that unpushy voice, 'but I'm not sure that he likes me much.'

'I don't think he understands you,' said Emma, smiling fully at last. 'He's noticed your strength of character and your establishment-ness, but none of your anarchic tendencies. If he had, he'd think differently.'

Willow laughed. 'Anarchic tendencies. What a splendid notion! I'm not sure I'd have admitted to those, but now you come to mention them, I suppose they are one of the things you and I share.'

'Me?' said Emma, suddenly remembering Jag's analysis of her predilection for outsiders and his suggestion that once Willow had been one. Before she could stop herself, she suddenly asked, 'Were you ever lonely, Willow, while you lived round here?'

'Most of the time,' said Willow with an eagerness that surprised Emma. 'Only I didn't know that was what it was. I knew I was quite out of tune with everyone I had anything to do with and sometimes seemed not only to be speaking in a different language but actually breathing a different kind of air. I used to get furiously impatient with people who couldn't see what I saw and didn't agree with me about what was important. They used to mock me for that, and resent it.' She laughed. 'I didn't mind the resentment, but I sure as hell hated the mockery.'

'I think we turn left here, don't we?' said Emma, relieved to have something she could say easily.

She did not know what to do with Willow's confidence or with what was clearly supposed to be an invitation for other confidences to be returned. There was a lot Emma wanted to tell her, and to ask, but she did not know how to start.

'D'you want to talk about how we ought to tackle Lutterworth?' asked Willow as she braked for a red traffic light.

'I mean, if you're not in fact going to do a polygraph test, should we plan an old-style good-cop-bad-cop routine?'

'I'm not sure. Oh, hell! That sounds incredibly pathetic but it's not as bad as that. Honestly. Look, I've decided that we ought to pretend I'm carrying out a polygraph test. You know, at least have the thing switched on and operating even if I don't try to use the data afterwards. I think that if he's attached to the monitors, he'll be less likely to react violently. I've written a whole list of dullish questions that I hope will get him so used to talking without thinking much about the answers that when I get to the one that really matters he'll answer that, too. D'you see what I mean?'

'Of course. I think it's a sound idea. What exactly are you planning to ask once you've softened him up?'

Emma was silent for a while. Willow put the car in gear as the light changed and drove slowly across the junction to avoid a clutch of bicyclists who were labouring up the shallow incline.

'This may be going to sound even sillier,' Emma said eventually.

'If there's one thing I've learned above all others, it's that there's nothing more stupid than refusing to ask a question because it might make one look a fool. Emperor's new clothes and all that. Go for it, Em.'

'OK. Here goes. I want to ask Lutterworth whether he used to drive his mistress about in his car and murdered her one night before burying her body in the garden in Berkshire.' Emma had screwed up her face, assuming that Willow would either laugh or explode with contemptuous irritation. Instead she said, 'The memorial garden? That could explain why it's so vile. Is this just a leap of intuition, Em, or have you got some evidence for it?'

'Not much. Jemima gave me a sort of hint yesterday and something his secretary said makes it seem feasible.' Emma explained in detail all the reasons she had for her suspicions,

adding at the end, 'So you see, if I'm right, then he's capable of the sort of violence I find terrifying even to contemplate. And if I'm wrong he'll be devastatingly hurt and
probably furious. Justifiably so. If he's fundamentally a
good man, which he may be, the last thing I want to do is
hurt him like that—you know, with the suggestion that I
think he's capable of killing someone. I just wish I had
something real to go on so that I could be sure.'

'Hmm. I can see that. But don't forget you have got his
wildly erratic polygraph charts. There was something going
on in that first test that he's been careful to conceal. He's
clearly guilty of something. Hang on to that. I think it's a
reasonable basis for suspicion. And, as you say, his secretary's evidence about his hands is interesting.' Willow
thought for a little longer. 'No wonder you were scared of
confronting him on your own. I think a spot of good-cop-
bad-cop might be no bad thing. He likes you, doesn't he?'

'I'm not sure. At the beginning I thought he did, but you
see, Willow, I'm so very bad at working out whether that
sort of liking is real. It's one reason why I...' Emma had a
sudden vivid memory of Hal looking yearningly at her in
the winebar, almost as though he had adored her for years.
She remembered his flowers and the attractive notes that
had come with them, and her own longing to talk to him
when Jag had been difficult. And she remembered the warning that Willow herself had passed on from Jane.

'What are you thinking about?' asked Willow, who had
glanced sideways when Emma's silence had begun to worry
her.

'Oh, nothing much. I was just remembering Jane's journalist.'

'Which one? Oh, you mean the wicked seducer who
dumped her when she'd given him what he wanted? It's a
very unlikely picture, isn't it?'

'I think so. But Jane must know the truth about him.

That's what I mean. I liked him, and I thought he liked me, but it sounds as though I was just being naïve. I can't work out who's real…' She bit her lip and tried to get a grip on her emotions. In a cooler voice, she added, 'But this is different. At least it ought to be. Lutterworth is a subject. Between us I'm sure you and I can get him to reveal who he really is and what he's done.'

'Good for you, Em. I'd better let you take the lead and be nice to him, asking gentle questions and showing trust and affection for him, and then I'll crash in at some pivotal moment and try to force him into telling you the truth. How's that?'

Emma took a deep breath. 'Sounds good to me. And—'

'And if he's angry,' said Willow, who thought she knew considerably more about Emma than Jag had allowed, 'I'll take the flak. Don't worry about it. This way I'll be the villain.'

There was another long silence until Emma said quietly, staring out of the window at her side, 'You make me feel very ashamed of my cowardice.'

Willow lifted her left hand from the steering wheel in order to brush Emma's thin shoulder. It felt rigid with tension.

'There's no need for that. I'm more than twenty years older than you and more experienced and secure. The things that could hurt you are not likely to damage me. I've nothing invested in Andrew Lutterworth—nothing he can say will bother me too much. But I think he probably could hurt you. It's no shame to want to avoid that.'

Emma did not answer.

JUST OVER AN HOUR LATER they reached the grim-looking prison. Willow parked the car and helped Emma carry her polygraph equipment into the visitors' entrance, standing in a queue of impatient-looking women and children who where also waiting to be admitted.

When it was her turn to be checked at last, Emma produced their documents and explained that there should be a letter authorising Willow's entry. It was found after a few minutes' search and they were given plastic-coated passes to hang around their necks and told to wear them all the time they were within the prison.

Their bags and all Emma's equipment had to be sent through the X-ray machines, as usual, and their keys were taken away from them.

'Do you have any maps or umbrellas?' asked the officer who gave them back their bags. They both answered 'no' and were passed on to another officer, who showed them to the room that had been booked for the interview and said that Lutterworth would be with them shortly.

'Maps?' said Willow when he had left them and Emma was arranging her equipment on the table.

'Presumably in case any of them are planning an escape. It's always the same. In the London prisons they ask if you've got an A to Z on you.'

'And umbrellas?'

'I don't know. Unless the spokes could be used to make weapons. I know people have been stabbed with daggers made from the spokes of bicycle wheels, so...'

'Probably. Oh, this must be him.'

Emma straightened up and faced the door as Lutterworth was ushered into the room.

'All OK?' said the officer and when Emma had smiled and thanked him he shut the door and left the three of them alone.

As usual Andrew was looking impeccably clean and well shaved. His striped shirt looked as though it had just been laundered, and his jeans had such a sharp crease down the front of each leg that Emma thought he must have slept with them under his mattress. His hair was newly cut and he smiled graciously at Willow.

'They told me Emma was bringing a friend,' he said, walking forwards to shake hands with her. 'Andrew Lutterworth. How do you do?'

'Willow Worth. It's good of you to see us.'

'Willow? That's an interesting name.'

'It's short for Wilhelmina,' she said, making a face. 'One of my teachers decided that no five-year-old should labour under a mouthful like that and renamed me.'

'How sensible. I quite agree. Children ought to be given straightforward, unmockable names, preferably ones that cannot be shortened at all.'

Emma was busying herself with her machines, glad that Willow was there to absorb some of Andrew's attention, and did not feel that it was incumbent on her to make any comment. Willow, who had no way of knowing whether Jemima had told Andrew anything about her visit to their house, merely smiled as though he was an ordinary acquaintance and started to talk casually about Lucinda and whether she would come to curse her parents for her name when she grew older.

'All set,' said Emma at last. 'Mr Lutterworth?'

'I thought we'd settled on Andrew, Emma,' he said, smiling up at her as he stripped his sleeve and offered her his arm.

'Very well, Andrew. Thank you.' She strapped on the blood-pressure cuff, attached the heart monitor to his chest and the pads to the ends of his fingers. Then, having checked that all the printer arms were able to move freely, she switched on both the machine and the tape recorder and began by thanking him for letting them come to talk to him again.

Then she asked his name, the name of his cellmate and what he had had for breakfast, before asking him again about the night of his interrogation by the police. The arms moved more wildly on the spool of paper, but that was hardly surprising. He was still likely to be both angry and upset by what had happened.

'And when the police officers told you that they would have your car searched, what did you say?'

'I don't remember,' he said as the arms moved sharply up and down the paper. They made a curious scratching noise, which Emma had never noticed before. She hoped that they were not going to break on her before she had persuaded him to produce the information for which she had come.

'It was after that, according to the notes, that you made your confession,' she reminded him calmly. 'Was that confession true?'

'No,' he said and the lines scrolled out steadily.

'Was it a lie?'

'Yes.' The lines were still steady. Emma stopped looking at them. 'Did you want them to search your car?'

'No.'

'Why not?'

'Damned impertinence,' he said, sounding angry enough to justify the sudden change in the sharpness of the graph.

'Who had been your last passenger in the car?'

'Can't remember.'

'Who had been the last passenger you had driven to your house in Berkshire?'

As the arms leaped about again, scratching the paper, Willow nodded slightly. Emma glanced at her and saw that she was getting ready to intervene.

'I can't remember,' Andrew said again and the lines had settled down. Then he added more irritably, with the lines shooting about again, 'It's years now. You can't expect me to have irrelevant details like that to hand.'

'Where is the car now?'

'It was returned to the partnership. I imagine they sold it.'

'Does that please you?' asked Emma, hoping that Andrew never had read any of the books about how to beat a polygraph test. If he had, he would have known just how far she had deviated from the proper format of such a test. She was leading him towards the crucial question and that was all that mattered to her.

'What's the matter, Emma?' he asked, sounding concerned. 'Aren't you feeling well?'

'I'm sorry,' she said, putting a hand over her eyes to grab a moment's privacy in which to deal with her doubts. 'I think I must have a migraine coming on. Andrew, I must ask...' The words would not come.

Willow leaned forward, as though to speak, and that pushed Emma into saying, 'Andrew, did you know that your wife was planning to have the memorial garden dug up?'

The thin, wirelike arms of the polygraph machine all moved convulsively over the paper as Lutterworth's breathing changed, his heart rate speeded up and the electrical impulses in the skin of his hands flashed faster.

Oh God! thought Emma. It's really true. She found herself staring at his bare arm, noticing the coarse black hairs that sprouted out of his skin all the way down to below his wrist. His hand was lying relaxed on the table and looking quite harmless, but she remembered the strength of his grip. As before, his fingernails were perfectly clean. She wondered whether his loathing of dirty fingernails might be in some way connected with the night when his own had been torn and filthy, the night when he had killed someone and scrabbled the earth over her mutilated body.

'Emma?' His voice was seductively gentle, almost as gentle as Jag's when he was making love to her. Emma shuddered. She could not help it. Then she forced herself to look away from Lutterworth's hand. For a moment she could not remember what she was supposed to be asking him.

'The memorial garden,' she said, trying not to sound too vague and peculiar. 'It seems to worry you that it might be dug up. Why?'

He took a moment before he answered and then, sounding only mildly annoyed, he said, 'I told you, I didn't want you to speak about my son. I also told you that I would not answer any questions that related to him. I am not going to talk about the garden that is his only memorial.'

'I'm afraid you must,' said Willow sharply. 'Why are you so worried about it? What are they going to find when they dig it up, when they peel back the turf and start shovelling the soil away from under those trees?'

'Roots and concrete foundations for the statue,' he said, fighting to imply a calmness that was completely belied by the machines to which he was attached. As though he had suddenly realised how much they might be giving away, he wrenched the pads off his fingers and then began pulling at the cuff from his arm.

'Will you take these things off me? At once.'

Emma sat unable to move. She ought to have been feeling triumphant, or at least relieved. But she was not. All she could feel was a coldness that seemed to reach right into the depths of her body, a sensation she had only felt once before, during an appalling bout of seasickness. Then came a familiar lurching in her brain and a nausea in her gut that made her think she might actually vomit.

'Take them off! Get these things off me.' Andrew Lutterworth was almost screaming.

'Emma?' said Willow quietly. 'Would you like me to help?'

She shook her head, coughing to get rid of the vile sensation in her throat, and then leaned across the table to remove the various monitors. As she struggled with the Velcro fastening of the blood-pressure cuff, fumbling far more than usual, her fingers met his and she almost screamed herself.

Calm down, she ordered in silent savagery. There's nothing he can do to you. Get a hold of yourself or you'll lose everything. You'll never get another chance. He's given himself away now. With the right spur, he'll tell you the whole lot. There's a body in the memorial garden. It'll be found anyway as soon as Jemima gets the workmen in. It's not your responsibility. Yes, it damn well is. Talk. Talk to him. Don't let him escape.

'There,' she said, panting a little but once more in control. 'That's the last. I'm sorry they upset you so much, Andrew.'

'I want to go back to my cell,' he said, looking over his shoulder as though in the hope of seeing one of the officers. 'Get the screw in here. Now.'

'In a minute,' said Willow, apparently unmoved. 'There's something I have to say to you first. Sit down, Emma. This does not concern you.'

Emma stared at her, having forgotten their plans.

'Mr Lutterworth, you may pull the wool over Emma's eyes, but you can't deceive me. We know that you were not involved in the crash; we have found the man who stole your car that night and killed those two people. We also know perfectly well that the only reason you confessed was to stop the police searching the car for the evidence that would convict you of a different killing. Murder. But you don't have to worry about the blood in the car or the hairs and fibres. Even if the car could be traced, nothing anyone could find in it is going to incriminate you now. It's all too long ago.'

Emma thought she saw a very slight slackening in his muscles as he listened. She could not think why Willow thought such reassurance would help to make him confess.

'But the body in the garden is a different matter,' Willow went on with perfect calm as Andrew's left hand moved.

He managed to keep his face quite still and put both hands in his lap, gripping them together.

'I want to go back to my cell. Fetch the screw.'

'It's no wonder you haven't let Jemima sell the house,' said Willow. 'She was saying to me only the other day that—'

'What the hell have you been saying to her about me?' he shouted, leaning across the table until his face was only a foot or so from Willow's.

Swallowing, Emma started to take part again.

'Nothing yet,' she said. 'But we've both interviewed her, Andrew, and she's told us a good deal herself. She's not as ignorant as you think. And I've talked to Annie Frome, too. We don't need much more than her description of your hands that morning when she surprised you at your desk. There were tears pouring down your face and scratches all over your hands and soil under your nails. You see, Andrew, we know it all. We know exactly what you did to your girlfriend.'

Emma realised as she reached the end of her little speech that she was losing him. He moved back, almost smiling, and crossed his legs. 'You know nothing. Nothing at all. You've made a fool of yourself, Emma, but it's worse than that, you know. You've been tormenting my wife about some fantasy you've invented, and you've been harassing me. I can sue you for that, and I will. I shall be out of here in little more than six months, and then you just wait. You can kiss goodbye to your degree, madam.'

Emma shook her head, but before she could speak, Willow said, 'Do you really think, Mr Lutterworth, that Jemima is going to put off her garden labourers for six months until you get out, particularly with both of us encouraging her to start digging? And we will, believe me. Six months is a very long time to sit in your cell wondering which day is going to bring the news that the body's been found. It's

only a question of time. You're going to be exposed for
what you really are: a bully, a liar—and a killer. There's
nothing you can do to prevent that, stuck in here as you are.
You'll emerge through that gate on the day of your release,
and a polite man in civvies will ask your name and walk
you gently over to an unmarked car. It'll all happen all over
again, Andrew, and this time it'll be worse. Murder means
you go down for life.'

'Don't be absurd,' he said, turning to laugh in Emma's
face. 'You poor silly child. Have you been trying to impress
this friend of yours and make yourself interesting to her?
Tut, tut. All you've done is make yourself look a complete
fool.'

Emma decided that she was not going to take any more.
She started to tidy up her equipment, saying, 'Fine. We'll
be off now. There's nothing more for us to do, here, Willow.
Let's go. It's not our problem to see that Jemima gets some
warning of what her husband's left in her garden. What it's
going to do to her I can't imagine. Think of it: losing Pipp
like that, being chucked into a mental hospital because Andrew was too selfish to give her the support she needed; and
now discovering that he—the man she married, the man she
slept with, whose child she bore—is a murderer. I'm not
sure she'll want to go on living. But it's not our problem.
We can go and leave them to their own damnation. Poor
Jemima.'

'Shut up.' Andrew's shout cut across Emma's gentle
voice.

'If I were her, I think I'd be seriously tempted to kill
myself,' she went on, no longer at all sorry for him or in
any way troubled about her assessment of him.

'Shut the fuck up.'

Emma looked at him and saw that his distorted face was
plum-coloured. He was shaking. She could feel the fury that

was charging his body like a surge of electricity. She thought she could also feel an agony of frustration in him.

'Won't you help us warn her?' Willow asked, taking over the good cop's part. She sounded as gentle as she would have been with Lucinda after a nightmare. 'If you tell us, Andrew, we can at least get Jemima away from the house before anything's found and make sure she's looked after, not left alone to kill herself.'

'Bitch!' said Lutterworth. 'Bitches, the pair of you.'

'It's going to come out. You might as well tell us,' said Willow, putting a hand on Emma's wrist to reassure her.

'And take your filthy hands off Emma,' Lutterworth shouted with supreme inconsistency. 'Leave her alone. It's your fault. She'd never have done anything like this without you. You sick bitch. Filthy dyke. Get out of here, the pair of you.'

'We can't go until you tell us who it is who's buried in the garden,' said Willow.

Emma was not sure how much more she was going to be able to take and hoped he would break soon.

'Oh, for Christ's sake. It's no one who matters. And it's none of your fucking business. Just bugger off and leave me alone.'

'Everyone matters,' said Emma. 'Who is she, Andrew?'

'It's not a woman, for Christ's sake.' He sounded tired suddenly, as though, like Emma, he would not be able to take much more.

'Not a woman?'

'No. A boy.'

Emma looked quickly at Willow and saw her own terrible doubt reflected in Willow's eyes.

'Pipp?' she whispered.

'No,' Andrew howled, burying his face in his hands. 'Christ! You're sick.' Tufts of greying black hair protruded above his clasped hands. The muscles in his back were working as he fought to get his lungs under control. Eventually, his breathing grew calmer and he looked up again. His eyes were wet and his skin was even greyer, as though all the blood had left his head. He looked as though he might faint.

'What boy?' asked Willow.

'I told you. No one who matters.'

'How did you know him?'

'I didn't. He came up to me when I was at King's Cross one afternoon.'

'What were you doing there?' asked Willow when he did not continue. She thought he looked as though he had given up and hoped that meant he would at last tell them everything they needed to know.

'I'd been to see clients in Peterborough. I'd got off the train and suddenly it hit me all over again. Philip was dead and Jemima mad. My life was hell. There seemed no point in going on any longer. And then this boy came up to me. This child.'

He stopped talking again. Emma saw that he had no idea that the tape recorder was still running. Until that moment she had not noticed it either. She was not sure whether to ask him anything or to wait for him to carry on of his own accord. She looked at Willow, who very slightly shook her head.

Andrew shuddered. 'He came up to me and said something. I didn't hear it the first time so I bent down to find out what he wanted and I saw how like Philip he was. And like you, Emma. With that short black hair and the big blue eyes and that smile of yours, perky sometimes, but a bit afraid, too, you do look like Philip.'

Emma turned away.

'For a second I thought I was going as mad as Jemima. I thought it was Philip on the station. He even had on the same jeans and trainers.'

'What did he say to you?' asked Willow, thinking that Lutterworth was beginning to find some kind of relief in talking about what had really happened. If he had enough energy left to worry about the consequences, he must have been well aware that nothing he said to them would be admissible in court.

'He asked me to go with him. And then I understood. He was a rent boy, trawling for clients. He'd come up to me to offer me filthy perverted sex for money. I wanted to shake him, rap his head against the station wall to shock him into reality. But I couldn't move. I can still hear his voice, you know, whiny but knowing: "Come on, mister. No need to be shy. You've done it before, ain'cha? Ten quid and you can do what you want."'

Emma watched him in horror.

'I was so revolted that all I could do was stand there. "Got a car?" he said. "Yes," I said, "I've got a car." And then he led me out of that station, asked where the car was, made me take him there, and hopped cheerfully into the front seat. "I know where we can go," he said. "Just get us out of here. I'll duck down when you go through the gate. You won't be stopped. Go south straight over the river and I'll tell you where to turn."'

'And did you?' asked Willow.

'No of course not,' said Andrew, still looking at Emma. 'I drove out of the car park and on to my usual route home. I think I had some notion of handing the child over to a policeman. He was a child, you see, a shockingly young child and vulnerable for all his disgusting knowingness.' He gagged suddenly as though he was about to be sick. Emma looked wildly around for a wastepaper basket or anything that might do. There was nothing. Andrew put both hands over his mouth and gazed at her as though he expected her to help him.

'So why didn't you?' At the sound of Willow's voice,

Lutterworth dragged his gaze away from Emma. She felt an intense relief at being released from his attention. He took his hands away from his mouth. 'He was crouching down on the floor and I felt his hands on my flies,' said Andrew with almost no expression in his voice at all. 'I looked down and tried to push him off. I told him to stop it. He laughed at me and told me not to pretend. We both knew what I wanted, he said. If I wanted to make believe I wasn't involved that was OK. Lots of his punters liked that, he said. He knew how to give me a good time. All I had to do was pull over and park. No one else need see what he was doing either. Then if I wanted the full whack when we got to the quiet place he knew, I could have it. I was trying to push him off. I was revolted. I had one hand on the steering wheel and the other at his neck. And he looked up and said something so unspeakable that the obscenity that he was alive and my son, my clean, decent, honourable son, was dead, was too much.'

He sat, saying no more, still staring at Willow.

'And so you strangled him,' she said in her most matter-of-fact voice. 'Just him or are there more of them buried in Philip's garden?'

As tears spurted out of Andrew's eyes, he collapsed forwards against the grey formica table. Emma pushed her chair back so that there was no risk of his touching her.

'Are there more than one, Mr Lutterworth?' asked Willow.

'Four,' he said, choking. He banged his fists on the table beyond his head. 'It's not my fault. I didn't go looking for them. They were all the same. They offered themselves to me. I didn't mean to do it. I love children. Decent children. But they weren't. They were filth.'

He sat up again, wiping his eyes and his nose on the back of his hand. When that was not enough to contain the fluids, he used his sleeve. Once more Emma, horrified though she was, recognised something Podley had said about the way arrogant men like Andrew Lutterworth can be made to collapse and give up all the information they have.

'They were children,' she said in disgust at what he had done. 'Whatever they did, whatever they said, they were still only children, just like Philip. It wasn't their fault someone had corrupted them. But you killed them.'

Andrew shrugged. His tears were drying and he was beginning to look like himself again. Even his voice had regained a little of its old confidence as he said coldly, 'They had no hope of a decent life. If I hadn't done what I did, they'd probably have been sodomised and tortured by now. They'd be dead anyway and have felt both terrible pain and terror. I couldn't let that happen to them. As it was, they didn't suffer. They didn't even know what was happening.'

'Except that you were murdering them,' said Willow tartly. She had had enough of Andrew Lutterworth, his manipulation of his own conscience and his attempted manipulation of their sympathies. 'And then you buried them under the four trees, I take it, around the statue in the memorial garden?'

As Willow allowed a certain satisfaction into her voice, the door of the interview room opened and a uniformed officer popped his head in to say brightly, 'Everything all right, ladies?'

'No. I think this interview should be terminated,' said Willow, aware that Emma was on the point of collapse and longing to be shot of Lutterworth herself.

He made no protest. When the officer had taken him away, Emma let herself sit down again, slipping back into the plastic chair as though her legs would not hold her up any longer.

'I'm sorry, Willow,' she said at last. 'I didn't know it was going to be as bad as that. I'm sorry I brought you here.'

'Don't be. I'm glad I was with you. I'd have hated you

to have to face all that on your own.' She breathed deeply
and then said with a passion Emma had not seen in her
before, 'Let's get out of here and into some decent air.
Come on. Can you stand?'

'Of course I can,' Emma snapped. 'I'm not as fragile as
you think. Oh, I'm sorry, Willow. I didn't mean it like that.
I'm all over the place.'

'I know. But you look very white. And you need air as
much as I do. Come on. Let's get all this packed up.'

'I'd rather leave it.'

'No, you wouldn't. You need it and it's important. How
does this fit?' Willow asked, trying to cram the blood-
pressure cuff into its box.

Emma took it from her and realised that she was not the
only one with clammy hands. For all her sensible instructions and calm voice, Willow was just as much affected as
she had been. That seemed comforting. Together they got
everything packed away eventually and stumbled out of the
prison.

EPILOGUE

'AND SO, Ladies and Gentlemen,' said Emma, gripping her cue cards to stop her hands shaking, 'I embarked on my researches, hoping to find some common factor or factors in the police interviews that had led to false confessions.'

She glanced around the audience, collecting the attention of even the sleepiest, smiled at Tom Worth, who smiled warmly back, and then looked towards the left of the hall, where her mother was sitting in the front row.

Emma had telephoned, begging her not to come to the lecture, explaining that she would very much dislike what she would hear.

'But Emma, you've done so wonderfully well,' her mother had said, by then aware that her daughter was an entirely different person from the one she thought she had known. 'And to have been invited, out of your entire group, to give the Silver Memorial Lecture? You can't really imagine that I'd stay away from that, can you?'

'But you'll hate it,' Emma had wailed down the telephone, feeling about twelve again, instead of secure, almost twenty-seven, and the proud possessor of a doctorate and several job offers.

'So what? The least I can do is listen to what you've been doing these last few years. Even if I don't enjoy it much, I shall be interested, and I shall want to be there to support you.'

'Oh, Mother, you are brave,' Emma had said in genuine admiration. 'But how will you get here?'

'I'll ask Anthony to drive me. I know he'll do it even if *you* are determined to keep up this silly quarrel.'

'I'd rather you didn't do that.' Emma had stuck by her agreement not to tell any of the rest of the family why she no longer had anything to do with her half-brother, which meant that both her mother and Sarah kept trying to bring them together again. 'He and I have agreed that we will both be happier if we don't see any more of each other. Please don't try to change that. I mean it, Mother. It's important to me not to have to worry about seeing or talking to him just now.'

'Very well, Emma.' She had sighed but added, 'If that's what you feel, I won't try to interfere.'

At that declaration, Emma had almost cheered, and she felt like cheering again as she saw her mother doing her best to look as though she was enjoying herself. There she was, dressed impeccably if far more formally than was necessary, sitting between two complete strangers of about her own age. Her back was perfectly straight and did not touch the chair. Her feet were planted squarely on the floor and her hands were crossed over her gloves, which lay neatly on her good leather handbag. She had her late husband's regimental brooch in diamonds on her left shoulder and a little discreet make-up on her fine face.

Proud of her, able to love her once again, Emma regretted the shock she was likely to feel before the end of the lecture, but there was nothing to be done about it. Emma could not fudge what she had discovered to protect anyone's sensibilities.

'At first I found nothing,' she went on, turning again to address the less vulnerable people who were sitting on the opposite side of the room.

Jag was sitting with Tom and Willow, dressed in a dark-blue cable sweater Emma had given him the previous Christmas. She could not see what trousers he was wearing, but she assumed he had left off his leathers for once. Every so often he allowed himself to catch her eye and smile encouragingly, but there was enough tension in his body to remind her of the conviction that had been growing in her for the past few months. Jag was restless. They still got on well together, and liked each other, but something had gone from their relationship.

With her heart still pounding from nervousness, her hands and feet sweating profusely and the top of her head feeling as though it was being pushed off by the force of her anxiety about her lecture, Emma made herself concentrate on what she had to say. Jag and their feelings for each other had to wait. This was work. Her future might depend on it.

Her voice sounded bizarre in her own ears, but her audience appeared to be listening and no one was rolling with laughter at her mistakes or quite comatose with boredom.

'In all those interviews,' she went on, 'with men and women who had made confessions they later retracted, I felt that I was finding nothing that would enable me to reach my conclusions at all. It was not until I had the good fortune to be introduced to the case of A, as I shall call him during this lecture, that I began to understand I might have been looking for something else.

'What interested me, as I later realised, was not so much why people wrongly accused of crimes sometimes confess, but how often the truth of what has happened is missed, both because of our tendency to hear what we expect to hear and because of the way our legal system is organised. As you know, Ladies and Gentlemen, it is not the truth that our courts are set up to establish, but the guilt or innocence *in law* of people who are brought before a jury. I do not know whether the Continental system—that is the inquisitorial rather than the adversarial—results in more people being justly convicted or released. But I do know that with our way of operating justice, which pits clever barrister against clever barrister, truth is often of less importance than the legal game.'

Emma caught sight of a sharp movement out of the corner of her left eye and could not stop herself looking sideways. An angry-looking man had bent down to pull a flat legal pad out of his black leather pilot case and was scribbling notes on it.

'In the case of A, as you shall hear, he was arrested for a crime, interviewed quite properly, and quite properly offered legal advice and every other safeguard the law has set up for the protection of the innocent. One of the officers who questioned him has told me that he and his colleague "knew" the man to be guilty, and that their tactics were therefore directed to the end of persuading him to confirm it.

'What they did not know was that, although he was indeed guilty, he had not committed the crime for which they had arrested him. He had done something much more serious. But that did not emerge until long after he had been tried, convicted and imprisoned for the crime someone else had committed.

'I shall explain how the case appeared to the officers whose job it was to interview A, and I shall then describe to you what exactly had happened on the night of the crime they were investigating, and what had happened on four separate occasions during the previous month.'

Emma stopped, took a deep breath, smiling at no one in particular, and, taking the first cue card from the top of the pile, pushed it to the back. Then, for most of the time remembering not to gabble, she relayed everything she, Jag and Willow had learned about the three different strands of the case. As she spoke, she was encouraged by the growing interest she could see on many of the faces in her audience. It was not just her friends who were alert and listening, but most of the other criminologists and several of the many strangers there.

Professor Bonmotte looked benevolently approving

throughout, if not exactly surprised by anything Emma said. He hardly could be, since she had discussed her thesis with him exhaustively before she had completed it. Continuing her explanation, speaking more fluently as she got further into her story, losing the high, formal edge to her voice and sounding much more natural, she began to recognise other faces in the audience. When she saw, sitting right at the back, the unmistakable figure of Jemima Lutterworth, Emma hesitated and almost dried completely. Only the knowledge that Jemima had sat through her husband's second trial and had heard every scrap of evidence about the four young boys he had strangled kept Emma on her feet and talking.

That trial had been a surprise to her because she had been afraid that even if the car could be traced there would be no evidence left in it, and there might be nothing else with which to convict Lutterworth of the murders. But to her extreme admiration, the police had set up a full-scale investigation of her allegations. Once the four pathetic corpses had been exhumed from the memorial garden, the investigators had moved smoothly forwards, not giving up until they had identified them all and accumulated enough evidence to persuade Lutterworth's second jury of his guilt.

Emma's tapes of his outburst in the prison were not, of course, admissible, and he took full advantage of his right to silence. His counsel did not allow him to give evidence at all, and managed with great skill to suggest that he was not guilty and he was merely refusing to speak in order to avoid laying the blame where it would more properly lie. He did not go so far as to state that it must have been Jemima who had killed the four boys, but he made it quite clear to the jury that she could have done it and that in the frenzy of her bereavement she might not have known exactly what she was doing.

The jury were not having any of it, and not only because the prosecution made it abundantly clear that two of the four boys were known to have disappeared during the time that Jemima was being closely supervised in the nursing home to which her husband had taken her.

There had been no such neat ending to the case of Terry Lepe. Tom had encouraged Willow to report everything she had learned to the proper authorities, who had expressed polite interest but eventually decided not to pursue the case. There was no evidence beyond Susie's confession, and the Crown Prosecution Service decided that it would not be in the public interest to pursue the matter. Willow had been to see Susie twice more, partly to reassure herself that Susie was not in danger from Terry, and partly to urge her to do something to make herself employable. She had even met Susie's mother, who turned out to be a wholly sensible woman, driven to distraction by her anxieties about what was going to happen to her clueless daughter when she herself was no longer alive to protect her.

Emma watched Jemima at intervals through her long recitation of the case and the conclusions she had drawn from all the bits and pieces of evidence she had collected. It was impossible to know what she was thinking; her face showed nothing but mild interest. Emma had not been able to banish the feeling that Jemima had known—must have known—something of the truth, but she had had to face the fact that she was unlikely ever to be told exactly how much.

At the end of the long lecture, the audience had clapped for what sounded like at least five minutes, but was probably only seconds, Emma clambered shakily down from the dais and, seeing that her mother was politely talking to the people with whom she had been sitting, went to speak to her own friends first.

Jag put his hand on her right arm at the same moment as Tom hugged her from the other side. As Jag headed off to the other side of the hall to talk to Bonmotte, Willow smiled with such open and approving warmth that Emma felt she had truly earned her place in Willow's world at last. Jane, who had appeared unexpectedly with Hal Marstall, pushed forwards to hug Emma, too.

'You did brilliantly, Emma. It was absolutely stunning. I want to talk to you quite seriously and soon. What are you doing after this?'

'I'll have to have a word with my mother, make sure she's not too appalled by what I've just said, and then—'

'Then, my dear Jane,' said Willow, 'as you very well know she's coming back to London with us for the celebration dinner Mrs Rusham has spent days cooking.'

'So she is. Can Hal and I come too?'

Emma had a moment's embarrassed anxiety that Willow was going to say 'no', but she laughed.

'You know perfectly well that you agreed to come weeks ago.'

'Yes, but Hal?'

'Didn't he tell you that he's accepted an invitation, too?'

Emma stared at Willow and then looked quickly at Jane, who seemed as puzzled as she was.

'I didn't know you knew him,' Jane said, saving Emma the trouble.

'Oh, Hal and I have become great friends,' said Willow.

Emma thought in some irritation of the amount of time she had spent resisting what she had taken to be Hal's attempt to pump her for information about Willow and Tom.

'Since when?' she said, noticing that Hal was looking remarkably pleased with himself.

'Six or seven months now, isn't it, Hal?' said Tom, who was standing with his arm around Willow's waist.

'About that,' agreed Willow. 'He just came to the Mews and rang the bell one evening.'

'And he's standing here, listening to you all,' said Hal as he handed Emma the freesias he had been holding and leaned forwards to plant a kiss on her pale pink cheek. She moved a little away from the others so that he had to move too.

'What's been going on, Hal? Why did you go and see Willow?'

'Well, when I couldn't fathom what you were up to, I thought I'd ask for help,' he said, smiling down at her with all the easy affection she had come to like so much and tried so hard to resist.

'I don't know what you mean.'

'I'm sure you do, Em. There you are, happy to chat for hours on the phone, happy to eat with me, apparently happy in my company, and yet blind to every possible signal I put out. I couldn't exactly fall on you like a stallion, now could I? Or should I have?'

'No,' she said, laughing. 'And what did Willow advise?'

'Bide my time,' he said airily. 'I thought you were stunning today.'

'Thank you.'

'But then I always think that, as you know. Emma—'

'Not now, Hal. There's rather a lot going on just now. Can we leave it all on hold for a bit?'

He looked carefully at her and after a while he nodded.

'Spot more biding of my time, you mean?'

'Just a spot,' she agreed.

'OK.'

She felt Jag's hand on her shoulder as he returned to her side and she looked up to smile at him.

'You two know each other, don't you? Hal Marstall, Jag Turrant.'

They shook hands and Jag said, 'I gather from Willow that we're all dining together. I'm afraid there's only room for the two of us on the bike, Hal, and we ought to get going soon if we're to see Lucinda before she goes to sleep. So, are you ready, Emma?'

'Nearly. I'll follow you in a minute. I must go and have

a word with my poor mother, make sure she's all right after all that.'

Lady Gnatche's face was betraying all the shock Emma had wanted to spare her, but her courage kept her smiling as she kissed her daughter and congratulated her.

'Thank you,' said Emma, kissing her back. 'It was lovely of you to come, and I am sorry you had to listen to all that.'

Lady Gnatche took a shaky step backwards. For a moment Emma thought that she was so horrified she could hardly bear to touch her, but it turned out that she simply wanted to see her better.

'You warned me. You know, your father would have been very proud of you,' she said at last. 'He would have minded your being involved with people like that, but he would have admired the way you stuck with it until you had found out everything that mattered. I wish he could have been here.'

Emma had to blink hurriedly and breathe deeply to keep from showing too much emotion, but she managed it and so did her mother. They nodded to each other formally.

'Henry and Serena will take me back now, and I'll be home again tomorrow. I hope that when you have some time to spare you will think of coming to stay for a weekend.'

'Yes,' Emma said, grateful for the immense difference between the invitation and the kind of blustering order Anthony used to deliver whenever he thought she should go back to Gloucestershire. 'I'd love to, and I'll ring as soon as I know what I'm going to be doing and where I'm going to be based.'

'Excellent. I shall look forward to it. Now, Henry.'

A tall, elderly man who had been waiting patiently some distance away came forward to take her arm. Emma thought she saw in his face all the naked disgust and shock her mother had tried to hide.

'The car's outside, Honor,' he said. 'Shall we go?'

'Thank you, Henry. Goodbye, Emma.'

'Goodbye, Mother,' said Emma, feeling as though she had been given the keys to her own life just at the moment when she understood that the doors had never been locked and had merely needed a light push. She waited while her mother made her slow way out of the hall beside her friend and then went back to Willow, Tom, Jag and Jane. Hal seemed to have gone ahead.

'I couldn't have done it without all of you,' she said, reaching them. 'I am so very grateful.'

'You made full—almost fulsome—acknowledgment in your talk,' said Jane, 'but if you really are feeling grateful I'd like you to consider a proposition.'

'She can do anything she wants now,' said Willow forcefully. 'And she's had lots of good job offers.'

'Yes, I know, but she's her own woman, too. She can choose without your advice.'

Willow scowled at Jane and then, as though remembering her moment of revelation on the train to Leeds when she and Jag had been on their way to interview Terry Lepe, she smiled. 'Yes, of course she can.'

'Good. Emma, I want you to think about becoming an investigative reporter for us. We'd pay you a lot more than any of the other jobs you've been looking at. Will you think about it?'

'Don't do it, Emma,' said Tom, laughing. 'You and I'll end up on opposite sides if you do.'

'But we are on opposite sides anyway,' she said, laughing back at him. 'You were nearly ready to have me arrested for kidnapping Willow at one moment.'

'True enough.'

'Jane?'

'Yes, Emma?'

'I'm not sure, but I am flattered. I will think about it. But there's something else. Look, I've been wanting to ask you for ages about Jemima. Do you think she really came to you to stop you printing anything more about drivers who kill, or was she making some kind of cry for help before Andrew got out again?'

Jane shrugged. Her face had lost all its usual brilliance and excitement.

'I've been thinking about that too. Could she have known? I kept looking at her while you were talking, and at one moment I caught her eye. Neither of us had meant to do it, but we couldn't look away. Then I did think she'd known something and hoped I'd find it.'

'Yes, I thought so, too,' said Emma. 'Poor woman.'

'Nonsense,' said Jane. 'She should have gone straight to the police. What I don't understand is why Andrew ever agreed to a polygraph test in the first place. It seems quite mad.'

'Oh, I think I know,' Emma said. 'He must have been afraid that he wasn't going to get any kind of decently paying job once he got out of prison—partly because of the criminal record; partly because of his age. I think he assumed that a polygraph would have proved him innocent of the crash so that he would come out a vindicated man. He must have assumed that he could stop me asking any questions that would have revealed his killings.'

'Maybe. But he was pretty foolhardy, wasn't he?' said Willow.

'Arrogant,' said Jane. 'Just like they all said. Look, Emma, are you going to London with Tom and Willow, or would you like a lift with me? I'm taking Hal, but there's plenty of room for one more.'

'No thanks,' said Emma, smiling at her. She looked around for Jag, who was coming back into the hall in his leathers with the two huge, globular yellow helmets dangling from his right hand. In his left, he had another set of leathers and a pair of boots with quite as many jangling buckles as his own.

'You are breaking out, aren't you?' said Jane, half in amazement and half in admiration.

'Yes,' said Emma, 'and I suspect that if I do come to work for you, it'll be so that I can afford a Harley.'

They all laughed. Jag handed her the leathers and she took them to the nearest cloakroom to change. Then, almost unrecognisable, she clanked out to find him. About to slide the helmet over her head, he said, 'You're home now, aren't you, Sunshine?'

'Yes. And you've got your doctorate, and the sheep and the green valleys are calling, aren't they?'

'How did you know?'

'I might make you an offer for the bike, pending my Harley,' she said, not answering because it did not seem to matter at precisely which point she had begun to understand that it was kindness and not love or even lust that was keeping him with her.

He swept her into a huge embrace, quite unbothered by all the people milling around them, and then kissed her.

'You might not have to. I thought if you wanted it I'd give it to you when I go. There's nothing like a bike for real freedom, Emma.'

Laughing, she took the helmet from him, and led the way out to where the gleaming black and silver machine awaited them both, and thought of herself roaring up to the quiet Cotswold manor with the bees and the lavender and the linen sheets and realised that she did not need any internal combustion engine to make her feel free.

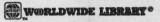

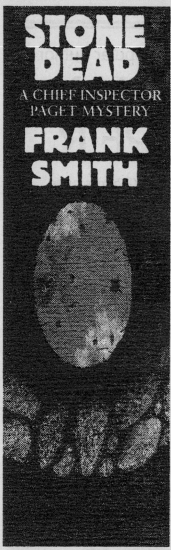

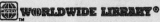